The Glass Trumpet

D1160845

Mark Cairns

First Edition
First published in 2008 in the United Kingdom
Scorpio Eye Press, 23a Highbury New Park, London,
N5 2EN

© Mark Cairns 2008

For my mother, who waited so long.

Contents

1 - Battle of The Thing

December 1957

The boy clung to the thick black drainpipe in the freezing darkness as the winter wind whipped at his jacket and his teeth chattered. He looked up and wondered if he should try and return to the safety of his room, and then down at the three remaining storeys of the building and the gardens below. It seemed an awfully long way, especially if one were to fall. He longed to cup his hands and blow some warmth and feeling back into the fingers but dared not release his grip on the icy pipe for fear of falling off.

Eventually, after carefully clambering down its various branches, he edged from the pipe onto the relative safety of the study windowsill. He had just breathed some life into the tips of his fingers again, when his whole body suddenly froze with fear as the light snapped on and the angry voice of his father rose, bellowing out through the glass.

***

May 1958

Jim opened one eye. He peered down the table at the hunched figure of his father and strained to hear the old man's prayer, a sustained mumble, rising and falling at regular intervals, accompanied by the even tick of the grandfather clock that stood behind him. The prayer, quiet though it was, seemed to reverberate in the spartan dining room. Jim looked around in the soft grey light filtering through the net curtains.

To his right, his mother was curled over her plate, her fingers and eyes bound tight shut, a supplicant at her own table. She murmured the occasional response, prompted by almost inaudible changes in the rhythm and cadences of her husband's prayer.

The slightly dank smell of the food led Jim to examine his plate of boiled cabbage and brawn, as it cooled under his nose. He looked at the meagre portion and wondered if she knew that rationing had ended four years ago.

He began to drift, his mind tiptoeing over the opening phrases of Haydn's Trumpet Concerto from this afternoon's music lesson. As the room lost focus, his father's voice retreated, leaving him alone with the looming string arrangements which preceded the first call of the trumpet. This was Jim's retreat; at will he could disappear from the world around and exist only in the centre of a soundscape so real that he could have been sat among the orchestra itself. Other people had record collections; Jim had recall, perfect recall.

He almost missed the rising intonation in his father's prayer that signalled its end, only just closing his eyes and lowering his head in time for the Amen. His heart beat at the near miss but his father had a blow ready prepared for him anyway.

'You'll not be travelling away with the Outsiders,' he said, snapping his napkin open and tucking it into his collar.

There was no more, no explanation, no reasoning or apology. Any pain Jim felt he knew he would be expected to relish, as a chance to draw nearer to God, and so no more need be said. He squirmed with disappointment but remained silent. His face flushed and he felt his skin tighten on him like a drum. He looked across at his mother but she did not look back at him and seemed lost in prayer still, although her husband had already finished thanking God for their dinner. When he did manage to catch her eye, his most desperate and imploring look just made her twitch, as if the thought of interceding for him would be enough to bring on one of her fits.

Jim finished his dinner and seethed in silence, waiting for his father to conclude the meal with another round of thanks to Our Lord; that the food had made its way safely inside them.

Only later, when he had climbed the stepladder to his attic room and listened to it being removed, did he feel the drum skin gradually slacken; releasing the tension across his chest and with the relief came tears. With the tears came anger. Not so much anger at his father, who was at least reliably obstinate, or at his mother for her flinching subservience, but at himself. Against his better judgement he had launched this slender raft of hope and now, as it sank under him, he tasted his own salty tears and railed against the pity he felt for himself. He took a deep breath and held it a few seconds before releasing it, letting all the air run out of his lungs and squeezing the last of the tears from his eyes.

He rose from the bed, crossed the floor and opened the small dormer window, which looked west across London. Jim rested his chin down on his hands and watched the sun sink towards the tall poplars at the bottom of the garden.

'Outsiders,' he repeated to himself bitterly. The word was given a twist in the Church by stressing the 'out', in the same way other people said 'outlaws'.

Everyone, apart from the three members of his immediate family, were Outsiders to his father. A few years ago there had at least been the Church, but since the Great Schism his parents saw virtually no one, apart from each other and himself. Even the big lawns of the house had been converted to lines of vegetables, mainly so that contact with Outsiders could be kept to a minimum, but also from puritan thrift and to ease the shortages caused by rationing, although this had finally ended in 1954, fully nine years after the end of the war. If he leaned slightly forward he could see over the broad sill of the dormer window and just make out the lines of cabbages in the gloom beneath.

The irony was that the Schism was caused by one of the church marrying an Outsider, but now that he could no longer attend the Church School he had to go to an ordinary school, at which he himself was the Outsider. Although, at first, he was happy and excited to go to the local school, the differences between his life and that of his new classmates set an unbridgeable gap. He wasn't allowed in their houses and nor were they welcome to visit his. Jim wouldn't have dared to bring them home anyway as his father seemed built by God to intimidate ordinary folk. Although much older than most parents (Jim wasn't even sure how old he was) his father was still well over six feet tall and his long grey beard, matching bushy eyebrows and his way of staring, as if there were something not quite right about you, put most people off. Jim wasn't even meant to talk to the other kids at school but this, at least, was one rule that could not be enforced.

Being forbidden to attend the concert in Leeds was a bitter blow. He had been chosen to play the solo from Haydn's Trumpet Concerto and hoped that maybe, just maybe, this special honour would touch his father's heart and he would be allowed to attend.

Jim whistled up Corky and tempted him across the roof with a piece of brawn saved from dinner. The big black and white cat finished the titbit gratefully, then jumped down into the attic room and settled on Jim's bed, turning round and round and clawing at the old bedspread until ready to curl up. Jim lay there with him as the light faded across the beams of the old house, his fingers gently stroking the cat under the ears as he played his favourite trumpet tunes in his head. The notes ran freely through his mind and, as he so often did, he found himself adding little changes and embellishments to them. He imagined them floating out across the big auditorium in Leeds, touching people and making them feel the same feelings that he had, as he played the notes. He imagined the feeling growing over everyone there and all of them becoming like one big person, all knitted together by the rising swelling music, as if all their hearts were holding hands. A robin sang from the garden and Corky purred beside him on the bed. Despite the tears drying on his face Jim drifted off to sleep with a small smile playing on his lips.

***

School was a strange mixture of pleasure and terror for Jim. After the close knit world of the Church, where all the children were taught together in a room behind the Temple, Garside Secondary Modern seemed the size of a city.

The sun glinted off hundreds of windows in the new main building. As well as dozens of classrooms there were staircases, labs and storerooms, an enormous gymnasium, a hall, a huge canteen, changing rooms and a football and rugby field. Outside, a modern sculpture known throughout the school as 'The Thing' rusted peacefully on the grass by the front gate. His earlier school days, with the emphasis on the quiet contemplation of God's wonders, left him unprepared for the rough-house that was Garside. The unending chatter and banter of the pupils, the ringing bell and constant shifting from one classroom to another had unnerved Jim after the quietness of the Temple School.

One aspect of his earlier education, however, was to prove its worth. The Church was a believer in what was once termed 'Muscular Christianity' and the only sport taught the boys was boxing. Brother Campbell had been a boxing instructor in the army during the war and took the boys to a local gym once a week. Although not particularly tall or burly for fourteen, Jim had the wiry frame of a bantamweight and, said Brother Campbell, was the best pupil he ever had.

The first day at Garside had been frightening enough. The boy set to look after him as he settled in seemed to drop Jim totally by lunchtime. Nobody had wanted to make friends and he felt largely ignored. Whenever he sat in the playground shelter there always seemed to be an invisible island around him and he began to think that other people were whispering behind his back.

It was the very size of the place that enabled him to disappear for the first few months but when the local bullies eventually got bored with their regular victims, something happened that pointed them firmly in Jim's direction.

On that Friday, a large unpleasant looking boy with a small band of followers walked up to Jim as he ate his sandwich in the shelter.

'Tell you what you got there...'
He leaned forward so that his face was close to Jim's.

'That's your last supper, Creeping Jesus.'
The boy's gang all laughed and Jim began to get that tightening in his chest, the pace of the drum rising in his ears.

Jim already knew about Cracker. His real name was Simon Cracknell but this had been rendered into Cracker, since it was said that that he liked to hear the sound of your bones crack when he got you in one of his 'death grips'. How to avoid him was one of the few things Jim had actually learned at school in his first weeks. He was an ugly child, big for his age with a jutting chin and a lip that seemed to have set permanently in a nasty sneer. His nose was of the squashed up type and seemed to be pressed against an invisible window. Piggy eyes permanently scanned the horizon for something smaller and weaker than himself.

Somehow, Cracker had got to hear about Jim and where he came from. A new girl, in the year below Jim, lived in the same street as the Temple and had seen him as he passed her house every morning to spend his days with the 'Holy Moleys' as the members of the church were known locally. There were worse names.

'We don't like brainwashers round here,' growled Cracker

'That's what my mum says you are,' piped up one of his assistants.

'After school, Creeping, by The Thing.' With that Cracker took the remains of Jim's sandwich and ground it into the tarmac beneath his heel, before striding off, his band of hangers-on trailing behind him.

***

A long history lesson on the Paris mob during the Revolution did nothing to ease Jim's wait for the last bell of the day. At half past four he stood uncertainly by the doors out of the main building, wondering anxiously what would await him down at The Thing, out of sight behind the thick fir trees planted all round the school.

'Ah, Davis.'

Jim turned to see Mr Eldridge, his music teacher struggling through the door of the staff room, gripping a gaping briefcase as well as two violin cases and trying hard not to spill his tea from an over large mug. He thrust this at Jim.

'Bring that and follow me, Davis.'

Mr Eldridge led him out through the double doors and down the broad path towards the main entrance. As they rounded the bend in view of the gates, a grumbling cheer came from the crowd gathered round The Thing. They were to be disappointed, for now at least, as Mr Eldridge stopped at the last of three mobile classrooms, produced a key and ushered Jim inside. There was a muffled groan from the Garside mob.

'Only place I can get any peace and quiet.' He opened the bag and removed a huge mass of papers, which he banged down on the desk. 'Once they bog off,' he said quietly to himself, sitting down and looking out of the window at the noisy crowd.

'Marking,' he said a little sadly, indicating to Jim to put his tea down.

Mr Eldridge reached again into the bag and produced a letter in a heavy grey envelope with familiar copperplate writing. Jim felt his stomach tighten.

'I have been passed a letter your father has written to the Headmaster.' He nodded towards a chair and unfolded the single sheet of paper.

'In it he expresses his surprise that you have been selected to play in the school orchestra as you do not attend the twice weekly practices.'

Jim said nothing

He thought desperately for an explanation but none came. Then:

'He's, he's … forgotten that I come.'

'Well that's alright then Jim, because I've written to your father assuring him that you do come *religiously* to practices.' Jim imagined his father reading the word in that context and the fury that would overcome him.

'And I have asked him to consider again his decision to stop you attending the Leeds Concert.

14

We need you with us, Jim, you're easily the best boy the school has ever had on trumpet, or anything else come to that.'

Someone outside shouted something unintelligible and the crowd jeered a little. Jim felt his heart contract with a double dose of fear. Even if he got past Cracker and the Mob he would still have his father to face when he got home.

One last hope flared.

'Did you…'

He stumbled, Mr Eldridge made his question mark face, with one raised eyebrow and the pursed mouth.

'Did you…post the letter yet, sir?'

'Yes, Jim, it went late yesterday so it should have arrived second post today.'

He looked across his pile of papers at Jim's worried features before reaching over to pat his arm reassuringly.

'Don't look so worried, young Jim, I'm sure we can change his mind!'

All Jim could think of was the strap hung on a nail where his ladder came down from the attic. It was kept there so as to remind Jim every morning of his duty of obedience to both his father and to Our Father Who Art in Heaven. Jim shuddered as he stood up to leave.

When he emerged from the hut a cheer went up and he could hear people summoning back their friends who had started to drift off down the road to the bus stop.

***

As Jim walked towards them, The Thing seemed to rear up higher and higher over the crowd. Its angular jutting of cast-off scrap, spray painted white but with the rust showing, threw a jagged shadow across the path. Children clung to its various pipes and rods in order to get a grandstand view.

Cracker stepped forward into the crescent formed by his audience. He sneered at Jim but let him walk past, only for the crowd to close and push him back into the arena they had created. The ends of the crescent came together as those who had not gained a place on The Thing ran round for a better view.

Jim faced Cracker across the circle. He froze with fear. Cracker took a step forward and shoved Jim hard in the chest making him stagger back into the crowd and drop his bag. The mob ejected him back into the ring like a pinball, where he bounced off his adversary and fell over.

'Get up, you brainwashing little creep!' he snarled. There was laughter and one of his henchmen rang a rock against The Thing and shouted, 'Round One!'

As Jim got back to his feet Cracker charged and took a swing at him with one mighty clenched fist. Big as he was, Jim felt, he was clumsy and, as it turned out, quite predictable. Cracker had never really had to learn to fight. His size and his ugliness alone were usually enough to put paid to his much smaller opponents. Jim sidestepped easily and raised his fists into their fighting position. A wry cheer went up for his pluckiness. Cracker came again, same three steps, same wide wild swing with the right. Jim could hear Father Campbell shouting in his head. 'Inside Jim, get inside, lad!' Jim let him come once more, just to check Cracker's action and then, on the next charge, instead of stepping back he took a half step forward, inside the flailing right and straightening up brought his fist, bunched as tight as could be, up under Cracker's unguarded chin. It was an uppercut; the most powerful punch in boxing. Delivered with perfect timing and sufficient force to the chin, the most vulnerable part of a boxer, it was capable of ending a fight on its own.

For the first time in Garside's history it was Cracker who emitted the sound for which he was named. Everyone heard it and then a gasp followed as Simon Cracknell fell to the ground, like some great ugly sack of potatoes. His body rolled and his eyes lolled and then he just lay there on the muddy grass in the silence.

Jim looked down at him for a moment before picking up his bag and heading for the gate. This time the crowd parted like water before him.

2 - Escape

*J*im sat stiffly on the bus, his eyes open but unseeing, his fists clenched on his knees and his heart still playing a loud double Tom-Tom beat in his ears after the fight. The trees in the park and the shops in the high street, the busy voices of the children; all receded to a distant blur and babble as he thought of what waited for him at home.

His mind ran back to his many escapes down the heavy Victorian drainpipe that began just below his dormer window. He had begun sneaking out after lock up time to attend the school orchestra practices last December. Having learned to play the trumpet in the Temple band, Jim already had a head start on many of the other pupils and soon began to shine in music lessons with Mr Eldridge. The school orchestra was a relatively new idea and had given several successful concerts in the school hall, but the big concert in Leeds was the first time it had been asked to play beyond the school gates.

The climb was perilous that first freezing night, but being an agile boy he soon made the old black iron pipe as familiar as the school's best trumpet. The only tricky bit was where he had to step off the pipe and onto the windowsill of his father's study, so as to be able to reach down a leg to the roof of the garden tool house, from where it was an easy jump onto the bit of lawn still bordering the vegetable patch. The room was on the first floor and, as his parents were people with a fairly rigid timetable, Jim knew that he could usually count on it being unoccupied. One freezing night however, a little before Christmas, he had just clambered from the pipe to the windowsill and was blowing into his cupped hands, trying to get the feeling back into his fingers, chilled as they were by the cold black metal, when the door of the study suddenly flew open and the light snapped on. Jim teetered with shock but managed not to fall off the ledge. He could see his parents in the room just feet away through the thin curtain. His father was ranting, marching up and down the old study carpet brandishing a folded letter.

'No, Emily, never. He must never know. Never, never, never!' he was shouting.

'But, Abraham, it's a legal document, look it says here…'

She took the letter from his hand and as she did so, Jim's father looked straight up at him.

Jim was paralysed with fear but realised almost immediately that his father could not see him through the curtain. He was hidden by the black of the moonless sky behind him and the thin but brightly lit curtain covering the window.

'There is only one law, His law.'

'But he's left him everything,' said his mother tearfully. 'Can't we at least tell him when he's twenty-one?'

'After what that man did to her, are you mad woman, are these the Devil's words?'

He held out his hand to the quivering woman before him.

'Give…Give!' he shouted.

'Oh, Abraham…' As he snatched the letter from her Jim noticed a business card, which had been paper-clipped to the corner of it, fly off and flutter down out of sight beneath the window. His father strode across the room to the fire.

'No!' she cried, but it was too late. His father threw the letter into the fire where it was quickly wrapped in flames.

And then Jim saw something he had never seen his father do in his entire life. He knelt down and comforted his crying wife as she sobbed, hunched in the big chesterfield armchair. The faint murmur of a familiar prayer could be heard as the fire in the grate died back to the embers. Jim had edged his way quietly from the ledge, dropped into the darkness and was gone.

***

Any faint hope that Mr Eldridge's letter may not have arrived evaporated the second Jim's father opened the front door. The very fact that Father opened the door himself was a bad sign for, humble as he was, he left most of the menial tasks to his wife. The face confirmed the bad news but Jim was, for the second time that day, left to await his fate. Nothing was said before or during dinner. At bedtime Jim was almost ready to believe that he had somehow got away with it, but it was not to be.

As he got to the top landing he saw that the loft ladder was in place. His father's voice came up the stairs from the floor below.

'You are to change into your night things and bring the strap down to me in my study.'

Jim felt his legs shake as he ascended the ladder. His room, he discovered, had been thoroughly gone through. Clothes from the small chestnut wardrobe were stacked on the bed, the contents of his drawers spread out over the top of the desk. His eye lifted to the loose brick set high among the roof eaves; it seemed untouched.

'Immediately please,' came the booming voice from below.

Jim slipped into his pyjamas and stepped gingerly down the ladder. He lifted the leather strap from its nail and went down the stairs to his father's study. He found him sat behind the desk, the family Bible open before him. A fire was burning in the grate and two large candles stood either side of the gigantic old book. His father looked up and his eyes seemed to glitter in the near darkness.

He picked up a small pile of music manuscript from his desk and came round to Jim's side. He held out the first one.

'And what is this?'

Jim looked at the title.

'It's Fantaisie and Variations by Jean Baptiste Arban.'

'And what is it doing in your possession?'

'We…we,'

Jim's tongue felt dry and stuck to the roof of his mouth.

'You practise it with the school band, is that what you're trying to say, James?'

'They call it the orchestra, Father,' said Jim, fixing his gaze on the embers.

'And this music, is it in Praise of Our Lord?'

'Well…not directly…but…'

'Is it, James, or is it not, in Praise of Our Lord?'

'No, Father.'

The old man threw the manuscript dismissively onto the fire. Jim stole a look up at his face in the flaring light. The eyes glittered all the more in the rising flames.

'And this one?'

'That's Aida by Verdi.'

'And this, James, is this music in Praise of Our Lord?'

Jim gave the smallest shake of his head.

'No, Father.'

The fire rose up again, and then again and again as each manuscript was given to the flames.

Eventually there were no pages left. The old man went and sat back down behind his mighty Bible.

'Take the polish, James, from the tallboy drawer.'

Jim went over to the old stack of shallow drawers and pulled open the top one. He took the tin of tan cherry boot polish and the shoe brushes over to the small armchair. He would get to use the chesterfield by the window in a while but had never once sat in it.

His father nodded at him.

'You may begin.'

Jim turned the little lever that popped open the polish tin and dipped the end of the small shoe brush into the greasy wax.

He began to polish the strap.

'Do you remember your Psalms, James?'

'Yes, Father.'

'And do you remember Psalm fifteen, verse two?'

Jim thought for a moment.

'"He *whose walk is blameless and who does what is righteous, who speaks the truth from his heart"*, Father.'

'Exactly, James, and are you blameless?'

'No, Father.'

'Righteous?'

'No, Father.'

'And did you speak the truth James?'

'I didn't lie, Father.'

'But James,' the old man said sadly. 'Nor did you tell the truth.'

He stood again and came round the desk to take the strap from Jim.

'Do you love this strap, James?'

'No, Father.'

'Oh but you must, James, for it is this little fellow who will help me steer you back to the Path of Righteousness and save your immortal soul...' He paused, as if for effect and leaned down, his face close in the dark study.

'From the Eternal Flames of Hell!' he rasped.

He gestured Jim over to the deeply studded chesterfield armchair by the window. Jim stood slowly; he could feel his legs shaking beneath him.

His father followed him over and in his best prophesying voice said:

'Kings, twenty-two sixteen: *The king said to him, 'How many times must I make you swear to tell me nothing but the truth in the name of the Lord?'*'

Jim's mind raced back to Bible class at the Temple school. Bible study was more important, they were told, than all the other subjects put together. He had always done well, having a good memory for anything that he had heard. It was as if he had a tape recorder in his head and could play back anything at will. He could hear Brother Thomas intoning the words of Kings as the soft rain fell against the window one afternoon. The chapter played through his mind as he leaned down, his chest over the fat arm of the chair, the old man's hand pushing him gently down into position.

Jim started up suddenly.

'But, Father.'

The old man raised his big eyebrows.

'Yes, James?'

'Well one of the spirits steps forward and says: *"I will go out and be a lying spirit in the mouths of all his prophets."'*

The old man looked down at Jim and a shudder seemed to run through his body.

Jim continued, trying to keep his voice level: 'And then the Lord says: *"You will succeed in enticing him. Go and do it."* Father…it says after that, verse twenty-three I think: *"So now the Lord has put a lying spirit in the mouths of all these prophets of yours. The Lord has decreed disaster for you."'*

The old man looked at Jim with horror.

'Are you calling…are you calling…our Lord…a…a…liar?' he asked hoarsely.

'No, Father, but…'

It was too late, the strap sang through the air and Jim felt as if a hot poker had been laid across his skin.

He tried to twist round. 'But, Father, that's what it says.'

The blows began to come faster and closer together. The hand pushed Jim down against the chair. He heard the old man shouting, almost chanting, 'Liar, liar, liar!' with each swing of the strap. The pain began to take over Jim's mind as he tensed over the chair, his fingers reaching down, grasping the edge of the rug. He felt them close around something just under it and then the nails began to dig into the palms of his hands.

***

Afterwards in the loft, he finally unclenched his hands to find the palms bleeding. 'Just like Jesus,' he thought. Bloodied and slightly torn by his nails was a small card that his fingers had found under the edge of the rug.

He knelt down by his bedside table and spread it out under the lamp. It was a business card with beautifully scrolled printing.

Mr G. Armstrong

The House of Glass

No.1, The Pier, Walsham-on-Sea

Jim stared at it. He remembered the argument all those months ago when his father had thrown that letter on the fire and a card had come fluttering off to settle under the window where Jim had accidentally spied. He heard his mother imploring, 'Can't we at least tell him when he's twenty-one?' and his father shouting, 'Never', over and over again. Maybe he had been blind then, for it had seemed that the letter could have been about anyone, or anything. One of the long running battles over Temple property that had gone on ever since the Great Schism had seemed likely but now, the more Jim stared at the card, the more of a strange connection he felt to it. The more he replayed the conversation over in his head the more he felt it to be about him.

Jim tried to sit on the bed and think things through but found his behind hurt too much. He lay on his side in the pool of light from the lamp and gazed at the card. It seemed connected with the remote and mysterious and it fascinated him. What was The House of Glass, who was G. Armstrong, where was Walsham-on-Sea and what had any of it to do with him?

He lay there for hours with the card in his hand, as the house descended into silence and the noises from beyond dwindled away. He got up only once, to open the window for Corky, who scratched and mewed to be admitted from the darkness outside. The cat curled up in the crook of Jim's knees and purred himself quickly to sleep. Jim lay still, his eyes closed but his mind awake. Eventually, as he heard the grandfather clock in the dining room strike one, he got up, fetched the chair from his desk and set it under the main beam that ran across the middle of the attic. Corky sat up, yawned and watched Jim clamber, silently, up onto the huge wooden spar and then sidestep his way carefully along to the wall. He gently eased out one of the bricks and drew from the space behind it a small brown envelope. Back on the bed he emptied out the contents. There were two ten shilling notes, a half crown and three sixpences. He had earned this running errands for Giles the grocers in the high street, on the way home from school. From his desk he took the large world atlas he had been using for some geography homework and peering closely at it, under the lamp, he found Walsham-on-Sea on the south coast somewhere between Hastings and Eastbourne. He tore out the page, folded it and put it with the money.

From the top of the wardrobe he fetched down an army rucksack, used in some long forgotten war by an even longer forgotten great uncle. It was large, built on a small triangular metal frame and easily swallowed all the clothes Jim could find. He put in, besides these, a torch, a large pocket-knife with a long spike for the removal of stones from horse's hooves, one of his newer exercise books from school with some pencils and a photograph of him holding Corky, taken by Mrs Dugdale next door. He briefly picked up the Bible from his bedside table but after a second's consideration, dropped it on the bed. Finally, he placed the money in his old wallet and tucked it safely into his inside jacket pocket with the folded page from the atlas. Then he remembered his mouthpiece and fetched it from his school blazer pocket. This was the only part of a trumpet that Jim actually owned and he would sometimes practise playing little tunes on it. It was important a trumpet player did this to maintain his 'lip' in proper working order.

A long coil of rope came from the locker in the corner and Jim knotted this carefully round the carry handle at the top of the rucksack. As he lowered the bag over the edge of the dormer windowsill, Corky sat and watched it disappear down toward the cabbages in the dark below. When he felt the rope slacken, Jim pitched the end of it through the window and, after shooing Corky away, he climbed out after it.

A full moon lit the gardens and painted the edges of everything with a subtle silver line. Shadows laid a deep rich darkness across most of the gardens and not even a faint wind disturbed the tops of the poplars.

The big black pipe was so familiar, Jim made quick time down to the study window and was about to reach down his foot for the tool house roof when, with a tremendous shock, he heard the sound of his father's bedroom window being shot up. Jim froze into the shadow as the bearded head leaned out across the adjoining sill. His father looked up at the moon for a moment and then down into the garden below. He had only to turn to the right and he would be staring straight at Jim, no more than a couple of arms lengths away. When his eyes had adapted from the brightness of the moon he would find himself looking right at the rucksack, sitting on the cabbages under its pile of rope, or he would surely hear the beating of Jim's heart as it pounded his ribs.

The moment seemed to last an hour when there was a loud scrabbling sound as Corky appeared suddenly on top of the fence dividing the garden from Mrs Dugdale's next door. He had obviously made his way down to see Jim off and sat there in surprise, returning the gaze of the two humans.

Then the old man did an unexpected thing. He reached his hand towards Corky, rubbing his thumb on the side of his index finger and making little tutting noises with his tongue. For whatever reason Corky did not take to this at all. The cat rose up on his four tip toes, arched his back and with his tail fluffed up to twice its normal size and ears flattened, he spat at the old man and let out a long hiss.

This did the trick and with a murmur that may have had something to do with 'the devil', Abraham shut the window again. Jim let out a long held breath and as soon as he dared, reached again for the tool house roof with his foot.

He gathered the rucksack and rope then stashed one in the other, down the little ginnel at the side of the house before letting himself silently out of the side-gate and into the empty street. He paused only to give Corky one last rub behind the ears and a quiet 'thank you' before swinging the bag up onto his back and setting off down the street, without a single backward glance at the house.

3 - Lester and Bird

Jim knew where he was heading. A boy at school had told him how his big brother used to catch the milk train down to the coast in the early hours of the morning to see his girlfriend in Hastings. It went from Charing Cross at about four in the morning and the train guard would usually let you ride for free. Jim walked down to the main road and soon caught a night bus bound for Trafalgar Square. The lady conductor was friendly and helpful, if a little curious about Jim and where he was going on his own in the middle of the night. He murmured something about visiting an uncle by the sea and she pointed him across the broad empty square, with its huge fountains, towards the station. It was strange; being in such a famous public space and yet having the whole square and those mighty fountains all to himself. Jim stood watching the great arcs of water reach up into the night and listened to the incessant rhythms as they crashed back down into the blue tiled pools. A small group of pigeons had nestled down on the fountain wall, their beaks tucked under their wings. They barely stirred as Jim stood next to them looking up at the charging water.

Once in the station he soon found the train as it was the only place of activity under the great arched roof. Jim looked for the guard among the trundling piles of newspapers, milk crates and boxes of this and that. He was just staring into an open wagon piled high with mailbags and wondering if it would be a better idea to stow away, when a huge hand clapped him on the shoulder and spun him round. The weight of the rucksack almost unbalanced Jim but the big hands caught and held him steady. He found himself staring into the eyes of a large black man, on whose head sat a train guard's hat.

The eyes smiled and a big grin spread across the face before cracking open to show a row of blindingly white teeth and to allow the escape of a great bellowing laugh.

'What do we have here?' he asked, in what turned out to be a Jamaican accent. 'Doctor Livingstone I presume?' This joke of his must have been funnier than Jim had realised for it was followed by an even louder and longer laugh.

'I have to get to Walsham-on-Sea, sir,' said Jim trying to sound grown up but feeling smaller every second.

'Well,' said the guard. 'We don't go there but I think we can get you as far as Hastings, if that will help.'

Jim felt relieved and the guard soon had him settled down in his own compartment, while he finished directing the loading of the train. It had been made quite cosy; there was a kettle and small camping stove with a little frying pan on it. Behind the guard's chair sat a cupboard on which stood a portable record player and a pile of records. Above this a large birdcage hung from a hook in the ceiling. Jim could hear the occupant scratching around on the floor out of sight. He took off his rucksack and put it down in the corner before settling down on a pile of mailbags, which were surprisingly comfortable.

The next thing Jim knew he was woken up with a jolt as the train started forward, the guard leaning right out of the door with his flag and whistle. The platform glided slowly by becoming a little tarmac river on which the now empty trolleys floated past like so many rafts. The heavy slow clunking of the wheels on the tracks suddenly became lighter as the train emerged onto the bridge. Dawn was already brightening the eastern sky through the small window to Jim's right and the lemon yellow and blue light fell across the Thames, livening the little waves that lapped at the silent hulking barges moored in the middle of the river. Jim looked in wonder through the big open door. The first beam of sunlight had just made it over the horizon to strike the golden finial that topped Big Ben's clock tower and it shone like a jewel against the still darkened sky to the west. The jagged cliff of the Houses of Parliament stood over the choppy river and a lone red bus made its way across Westminster Bridge.

Soon the loud click clack of the bridge rails was muffled again as the train gained the solid brick viaduct that led south past the backs of houses, warehouses and factories.

Leaving the door open the guard turned and beamed to find Jim awake.

'Ah, welcome again to the land of the living!' He bent down and offered Jim a massive hand.

'Lester.'

'Jame…er, Jim,' he replied quickly correcting himself.

'Would you like a cup of coffee, Jim?' said Lester lighting the little primus stove.

'…and perhaps some fried bacon sandwich?'

Jim said 'yes please' to both of these and sat back to enjoy the view through the big open door.

He was soon distracted by a loud chirruping from the cage in the corner. Looking down at him was a bird, like a small parrot, rosy face and green and blue plumage. Jim went over and stretched up on his toes to see more closely.

'He's beautiful,' said Jim. 'What kind of bird is he?'

'He's a Lovebird.'

'Shouldn't there be two of them?' asked Jim.

'That's a very good question, young Jim. Lovebirds should always be kept in pairs but I'm afraid that Bird here is on his own 'cos that's how I found him, left on the train in a shoebox.' He passed Jim a large enamel cup of steaming hot coffee and turned back to the stove.

'Just 'Bird'?' said Jim.

'Yup, named him after Charlie 'Yardbird' Parker.'

Lester lifted his head and made a loud chirruping noise with his lips to which Bird responded immediately.

'He never make a sound until one day…'

Lester left the stove and pulled a record from the stack on the cupboard.

'…I played him this. You know why?'

'No,' said Jim.

'Well - 'Ornithology', that's the study of birds, right.'

He handed Jim the record sleeve and with much gentleness from such big hands, he placed the disc on the record player.

'And,' he added, 'just look at the title.'

The record itself was called 'Ornithology' and the cover featured a black man in a sharp looking suit playing a saxophone. Jim settled back on the mailbags and watched the back of London roll past the big open door as the first notes drifted out into the warming dawn light. By the end of the record the endless brick of London had been replaced by lush green fields and Jim knew for sure, not just because of his journey, not just because of his quest to uncover the mystery of The House of Glass, that his life would not be as he had expected it to be. The music that came from the little speaker in the rattling train had changed the way he felt inside. It was music that went anywhere it wanted, it was music that asked a million questions but had no care for the answers, it was music that seemed to break free of the bars and staves on the page and launch itself into the air.

As the record ended, Jim got to his feet and found that he was holding a cold bacon sandwich, missing only a single bite, in his hand. Lester was asleep with his boots up on the small desk and the brim of his hat down over his eyes.

'Um…'

Jim half crouched and tried to peer under the hat.

'Mr Lester…sir.'

A big finger pushed up the shiny peak an inch or so and a single eye opened.

'You like that huh, young Jim?'

Jim could only nod.

'Do you have any of this kind of music but with more trumpet, please?'

A huge laugh seemed to rock the old wooden guard's van. A couple of jackdaws flew up from the hedge and a chestnut horse in a field beside the track stopped grazing and flared its ears at the passing train.

''This kinda music!' That's *jazz,* Jim, where you been all your short life?'

Lester took the cover from him and swung round in the chair to select another record. Again he handed Jim the sleeve. It was called 'Groovin

High' and this time the guy on the front had a trumpet but the bell was bent right up at an angle as if to shoot the music up to the sky.

Jim sat and watched the country slowly awake as they trundled by, the music of Dizzy Gillespie flying out of the door to mix with the clattering wheels, the cocks crowing, farm dogs barking and the breeze, in from the nearing sea, that rustled the top of the elms along the line.

He felt like a new Jim and he knew that whatever happened, they could never bring the old one back.

**

Lester had set him down on St Leonard's station with a packet of sandwiches and directions to the Walsham Road. Jim had made sure to note down the names of Lester's records in his notebook and shook his hand one more time, before shouldering the pack and walking off towards the sea.

The huge shimmering expanse that stretched away before him had taken Jim by surprise. He had only seen the sea once before and that was in a film show at Garside. The early sun burnished a bright strip across it, running right away over the horizon. Its many subtle colours, none of them blue, were over laced by ripples and patterns which seemed to change and merge invisibly with one another. Distant ships stood still on its far edge and little fishing boats churned the water to white froth as they headed out, each one trailing a lazy gaggle of seagulls in the air behind them.

Jim sat on the pebbles and gazed out, letting the inshore breeze ruffle his hair and tasting the sea air at the back of his throat. He pulled the torn-out page of the world atlas from his pocket and studied, as far as was possible given the small scale, the route that would take him to Walsham-on-Sea. He looked west along the coast to a far headland that he thought he could identify on the map. Although it was only a fraction of the way to Walsham on the page, the point jutting out into the sea was shrouded to blue grey by the sheer distance. Jim already knew, from his short trudge onto the beach, that walking on the big oval pebbles was difficult and tiring. To make his way to Walsham that way was all but impossible. One tiny line on the map represented the road and that seemed to lead inland from Hastings before bending back towards the sea, just before Walsham. Jim trudged up the beach and set out west along the seafront.

The hotels on the front soon gave way to houses and then the houses to grassy banks that led the way uphill. Jim became mesmerised by the rhythm of his steps and the slowly changing view, the music that Lester had played him dropping into time with his stride and playing itself in his mind.

Jim used this ability, to play back in his head whatever he had heard, as the purpose of his journey came to the forefront of his mind. He searched back, to that frozen moment on the window ledge the winter before. There, where the card had flown across the room, unseen by anyone but him, the hidden watcher; there was the secret. What had it all to do with him? What was it he must 'never know'?

The strange thing was; Jim thought he did know. He felt, at least, that when he found out whatever it was, he would think he had known it all along, somehow. It was a strange feeling but he felt he was in search of the obvious. This gave him a strong notion of rightness and purpose as he strode along, uphill, under the climbing sun, the grass on the bank waving softly in the wind, the unknown road disappearing around each new bend as he advanced.

The sun was nearly overhead when Jim stopped for a rest and some food. The road crossed a small culvert of clear water for which he was thankful, as he had brought nothing to drink. When he unwrapped his sandwiches he found two half crown pieces that Lester must have hidden in the paper. That a stranger could have treated him with such kindness and asked nothing in return, not even where Jim was going on his own in the middle of the night, filled Jim with gratitude. After a short rest in the hot sun, he again hoisted his pack on his shoulders and set off along the road.

There had been very little traffic so far but after another mile or so a dark blue police car came round the bend in front of him. The driver slowed as he passed Jim and he tried not to look back at the two policemen as they drove on towards

Hastings. He wondered, for the first time, what the scene was back at home. His father would have climbed the ladder after calling him for school and discovered Jim's empty room. What had he done then? Would he have called the police straight away? It seemed unlikely and even if he had, how could he possibly have guessed where Jim had gone? They didn't know he had seen the burning of the letter through the window or found the card from The House of Glass.

As he rounded the next bend Jim found himself on a long straight for almost the first time since leaving town. Far along it in the distance an old hay wagon, piled high with bales, stood stationary at the side of the road. A big brown and white horse had been taken from the shafts and Jim could see the driver kneeling next to one of its hind legs as it grazed the grass on the verge.

As he came up he found the old farmer grumbling and cursing as he wrestled with the horse's hind leg. He had a nail in his hand and was trying to prise a stone from the huge hoof with it.

He looked crossly up at Jim.

'I don't need spectators, thank you very much,' he said gruffly. 'If you can't be no help then on yer way.'

'Is it a stone?' asked Jim.

'Well it aint a bleedin' marshmallow now is it? It's a nasty bit of flint in there and Young Tom's gone and had my tool box off the wagon,' he grumbled, more to himself than Jim.

He threw the useless nail down on the grass in disgust. 'I'll never get it out with that.'

'Maybe I can help,' said Jim.

The old farmer looked up as if puzzling for something more sarcastic to say.

'How, exactly?' he asked.

'Well…' said Jim, throwing his rucksack down on the verge. He opened one of the side pockets.

'I've got this.' He drew out the pocket-knife and unfolded the long spike opposite the main blade.

'Well I'll be a badger!' said the old man getting to his feet.

'A grockel with something useful in its pockets! Let's have a look.'

He took the knife from Jim and in what seemed like a few seconds had the stone out from the hoof. The horse gave a snort and jogged a few paces down the verge before stopping to munch at the grass again.

'Thar's better Sampson, 'ennit, my boy?' He stroked the mighty muzzle of the horse and blew into its nostrils as it raised its face to his.

'Well, young man, it looks as though I'm indebted to you there. Most of these new fangled penknives don't have a hoof pick on 'em.' He snapped the knife closed and handed it back. 'Anything I can do for you; you just let me know.'

With that he began to lead the horse back to the front of the wagon.

At just that moment Jim heard a distant crunch of gears and the whining of a car engine. He looked up to see the police car appearing round the bend from the direction from which he had come. He stepped in quickly behind the hay wagon.

'Actually, sir…'

'Yes, what is it? Anything you want, young fella.'

Jim tried to quell his panic.

'Can I hide in your hay wagon for a moment?' The farmer looked up quizzically at him and saw the police car in the distance. He looked surprised but did not hesitate at all; stepping up to the blind side of the wagon he swiftly pulled a couple of bales out onto the verge.

'In yer go lad, look lively.'

Jim almost flew into the hole that had appeared and in seconds the gap was plugged up again with a hay bale.

He heard the police car come to a stop as the farmer went about his business, getting Sampson back between the wagon shafts.

There was the sound of two doors slamming and police boots on the roadside gravel.

'Alright there, Tom?' said a voice.

Tom grumbled something inaudible back.

'Got old Sampson sorted then?'

'What's it look like?' came the reply.

Jim had a narrow view between two of the bales and it was soon filled with the dark blue uniform of the constable that had spoken. He appeared to be looking up at the wagon.

'You seen a young lad come along here, in the last few minutes? Grey shorts, rucksack?'

He took a step closer to the wagon, cutting out the light completely. Jim lay as still as he could in the darkness, holding his breath.

'Seen nothing, had my hands full with this one,' said the farmer, doing up the last buckle on the harness.

The policeman moved away down the side of the wagon and Jim realised, to his horror, that through the thin gap in the bales, he could see his rucksack still there on the verge.

'Funny,' said the second policeman. 'We saw him, not ten minutes ago, just coming to the top of Acre Hill. Must have come past you here.'

'Not that I've seen,' muttered the old man.

Jim saw him pick up his rucksack and heard it tossed onto the bales over his head; neither policeman appeared to notice.

'What's he done, this kid?' he asked.

'Ahh, police business I'm afraid,' said the first voice.

Jim began to feel a tickle in his nose. It was the hay; there was no escaping it, cocooned as he was. He held his breath and his nose as hard as he could.

'Well, best be off, see you, Tom, bye there, Sampson.'

Jim heard the footfalls head back in the direction of the car, the door opened, the tickle eased slightly and Jim let go of his nose. That was his mistake. The sneeze had been hiding too, biding its time. It leapt on him in an instant, giving Jim barely enough time to muffle it at all. He heard the car door close but the footsteps paused and came back towards the wagon.

'What was that?' asked the policeman.

4 - The House of Glass

Jim could see the constable's silver buttons as he leant against the wagon, reaching up to tug at the tarpaulin that covered the bales. Jim held his breath once more. There was a sudden snap and a growl and the light flooded in as the policeman leapt back with a big yell of surprise. Jim could see the look of shock on his face as he shook his hand, looking up into the wagon above Jim's head. Old Tom and the other policeman burst out laughing.

'You don't want to go poking young Millet there, especially when she's not well.'

He heard the policemen head back to the car, the bitten one grumbling about dangerous dogs and having Millet muzzled, or even put down. He heard the engine start and then the noise of the car dwindle into the distance.

He lay very still and after a minute or two he felt the farmer climb up on the wagon.

'You alright in there, young'un?' said the quiet gruff voice.

'Yes,' said Jim, and after a moment, 'Thank you.'

'You just lay there quiet while we go along.'

With a word from his master, Sampson gave a gentle tug and they rolled off down the road. Jim lay among the fragrant bales listening to the creak of the wagon and the steady clop of the horse's hooves. The countryside moved slowly past his narrow window and then for a while, the sea, which at least blew a pleasant breeze through his hiding place.

He must have dozed off again and was confused for a moment when awoken by Old Tom, pulling the bales of hay from around him. They had parked in an old wooden barn, lit from above by one large skylight. Jim rubbed his eyes awake and, when he opened them, found he was looking into the brown eyes of Millet. She licked his face before he could stop her and gave a small squeaky yelp. Tom laughed.

'Welcome to Highgrange Farm,' he said, pulling the final bale aside.

Jim was soon set down at the kitchen table and given a long cold glass of lemonade. It was cloudy and had none of the bubbles he had seen in the bottled lemonade from the high street. After much of the day wedged between the hot bales it seemed to Jim, undoubtedly, the finest drink ever invented by humankind. His new friend sat by watching his every sip and tipping her tail. If Jim looked down at her she would lash it enthusiastically from side to side.

'She thinks she's found a new friend,' said Old Tom. 'Had no-one to fuss her properly since Young Tom moved over to Long Acre.'

He chopped a few vegetables up and threw them into a pot which was soon bubbling gently.

'Nobody to chuck a stick or tug a piece of rope with. Have yer girl?'

He ruffled the dog's ears as he sat down at the table with Jim, placing a plate of thick buttered brown bread doorsteps between them.

Before long there followed a hot bowl of stew to dip them in and a mug like a china tankard with steaming hot tea.

'So, young…young…'

He realised, from the way Old Tom was looking at him, that this was a question.

'Jim,' he said.

'So, young Jim, where is it you're headed to, all on yer own, and with the police taking an interest?'

Jim thought for a moment.

'I don't really know,' he said. 'Well, I know I'm going to Walsham-on-Sea.'

'What for?' asked the old man directly.

Jim let his spoon sink into the stew and watched the tiny swirls of meat juice patterning the gravy. He suddenly felt a bit silly.

'That's what I'm not sure of,' he admitted.

They ate without talking for a while.

'Do you know The House of Glass? In Walsham?'

47

The old man stopped eating and looked over the top of his spoon at Jim. There was a short silence.

'Yes, I do know of it.'

'But what is it, The House of Glass? And do you know Mr G. Armstrong, the proprietor?'

The farmer said nothing more. After a while he looked solemnly at Jim.

'There's obviously a lot you need to find out, young man. I have no answers for you I'm afraid.'

When they had eaten, Old Tom took Jim outside to a small stone terrace that bordered one side of the house, where he sat and stuffed a pipe with powerful smelling dark tobacco. The view was tremendous, rolling fields running down to the sea and, sandwiched in between, as he pointed out with the stem of his pipe, were the red tiled roofs of Walsham-on-Sea.

Jim was all for hoisting up his rucksack and heading off down the long sloping fields straight away but Tom sounded a note of caution.

'That Constable Steele has already got an eye out for you, young Jim, and there's a small police station there in Walsham, that's where he'll be right now. Just you wait there a moment.'

He puffed away into the house and was back a few minutes later with a neat stack of clothes.

'Young Tom's, should fit yer, about.'

There was a pair of long trousers in rough tweed, a twill jacket with a blue collarless work shirt and lastly a peaked flat cap.

Jim changed quickly in the barn, dropping his own clothes behind one of the bales. Old Tom declared him a perfect local when he came out but suggested Jim take what he needed from the rucksack and leave it behind for the time being, as it spoiled the whole effect and made him stand out as a traveller again.

Jim selected the torch and his knife and, after putting his wallet in the inside pocket of his new jacket, he thanked Old Tom and set off down the hill, Millet bounding after him with a stick she had found somewhere.

'Don't worry about her, she'll turn back at the last stile,' called Old Tom.

For the ten minutes or so it took to walk down to the last stile, Jim felt a happiness inside that he had never known could exist there. The air was warm but fresh, he could see the far horizon with its big freighters, the sea lapping the walls of the little harbour with its wheeling gulls and down at his feet the bouncing border collie, presenting him with her stick. Every time he threw it ahead down the field she would go rocketing after it, returning seconds later for him to throw it again. If only this could be his life from now on, then maybe he would always feel this happy.

At the stile he petted Millet one more time and then threw the stick as far as he could back up the fields in the direction of the old stone farmhouse.

By the time she returned with it he had skipped over the stile. Millet stood, paws up on the gate, watching him walk away down the hill. When Jim disappeared round the bend, she gave out a quiet whine and headed back up towards the farm, still carrying her stick.

***

It was tea-time as Jim walked through the town. It wasn't a big place, the high street having half a dozen shops, most of which were closing for the day. He looked at himself in the shop windows as he passed and was surprised at how different he seemed. It wasn't just Young Tom's clothes; he looked taller, maybe stronger and definitely more confident than the young schoolboy that had left London in the early hours of that same morning. That was another thing; the time. Less than a day and he already felt half a lifetime away from Garside Secondary Modern and his room in the attic.

He hurried on towards the small pier that jutted into the sea just west of the harbour, assuming now that The House of Glass was a shop and hoping to get there before it closed too. He wanted to see this Mr Armstrong and try and find out…try and find out what exactly? Jim realised that he had not thought this through very well. What would he say? How would the conversation begin? What if the whole business with the card and the letter was nothing to do with him at all? Mr Armstrong might very well turn him in and before he knew it he would be back in the attic, waiting for an even harder lashing from his furious father.

As he got to the pier his nervousness and the feeling of anticipation were suddenly replaced by disappointment. The House of Glass was the first shop on the pier itself. It was large for a pier shop, not the usual booth and even had an upstairs at one end; but it was shut. More than shut it was shuttered up and looked like it had been for a long time. Jim walked round it one way and then back the other. He found the main doors had large wooden boards over them fixed in place with a heavy padlock and chain. He stood back and looked at the place carefully. It went from two storeys at the end nearest the land to a long single storey, which looked like a Victorian greenhouse and stretched some twenty-five to thirty feet down the pier. This far end was topped off with a small tower, like a glassed in beehive, four or five feet high. The upper storey, at the land end of the pier, was very small and might have been a flat or an office of some kind. As Jim studied the little building he felt the awful sucking feeling of disappointment rising up inside him. He was adrift, all direction suddenly gone. What had he been thinking? This was nothing to do with him, this closed up place somewhere past the back of beyond. He felt his teeth gritting together and had to close his eyes and take a deep breath to stop the tears rising.

He opened them again as a large herring gull landed on a decorative acorn, which topped out the little glass tower. It looked at him with a stern yellow eye, as if to ask him what he thought he was doing there. Then Jim noticed; just below where it sat, a little window, or more likely a ventilation flap, seemed to jut out a tiny bit. It wasn't exactly open but then it was obviously not properly shut either. Jim walked round to the end, watched by the cynical eye of the gull. The flap was small, very small. He wondered if he could fit through, even if it were possible to get up to it and prise it open.

Jim then noticed something about the other people on the pier; there weren't many of them but they all seemed to be leaving. He saw a man at the end coming down towards him with a big bunch of keys, stopping to check various doors and booths. Once again Jim found that he needed to hide, and quickly.

**

At first Jim thought there was nowhere. He looked around but apart from a slightly recessed doorway there was nothing. He began walking back down the pier towards the entrance. As he cleared the shop he looked over his shoulder and saw the caretaker cross from his side of the pier to the other. He gave a quick look round to make sure he was not observed and darted back up the pier, keeping The House of Glass between him and the caretaker. He was lucky, in a way, that the place was boarded up, or the caretaker would have seen him through the windows, running up the other side of the shop on tiptoes, so as not to make a sound on the wooden decking.

Jim squatted down at the end, tracking the caretaker through the sound of his footfalls. Before long he heard the gates being pulled across the entrance and the rattling of chains and a padlock.

Then it was silence, bar the calling of gulls and the swoosh and hiss of the waves on the pebble beach below the old iron stanchions that held the pier up over the sea.

Jim didn't have a watch but he guessed it was approaching six o'clock. Although the sun was well on its way down to the western horizon, Jim knew that it would not be properly dark for several hours now. He retreated carefully to the far end of the pier and settled down, out of sight of land, between the fortune-teller's booth and one selling bait for the fishermen who spent their days pulling dabs and flounders from the sea beyond the pier.

If boredom was a problem it was soon replaced by hunger. Jim had seen some chocolate vending machines about half way along the pier but was worried he might be spotted from the promenade if he ventured down there in daylight. He entertained himself by trying to count the circling gulls and observing the passage of a large freighter, by lining it up against one of the rail posts and seeing how long it took to pass through. A speedboat came thrillingly close, chopping the tops off the waves before heeling over dramatically and powering out towards the horizon. Jim imagined himself in it, imagined it pulling up alongside the distant freighter and climbing a big steel ladder let down from the deck, imagined heading away across the world where he, the new Jim, could be his new self and do nothing but eat coconuts and play music all day. He played some more of the tunes from Lester's wagon in his head and wondered why it was called jazz.

Eventually Jim persuaded himself it had become dark enough to sneak down the east side of the pier, in the shadow of the buildings. The first chocolate machine swallowed his sixpence but refused to budge any of its drawers the least inch in return. He had more luck with the second, and sat watching the sunset as he slowly ate the sticky squares to make them last a little longer. Even with the sun gone the sky held its light for a long time and there was another hour or so before Jim felt confident enough to move around the darkened pier without fear of being seen from the road.

He examined The House of Glass more carefully. The whole of the little building was covered in large plywood sheets, screwed firmly in place. The doors were sealed with two more, held in place by a large padlock and chain. A slow walk round soon convinced Jim that the only way in was through the little ventilation window in the beehive-like tower that he had seen earlier.

He clambered up via the boards over the front door but when he got to the roof he realised, to his dismay, that it too was made almost entirely of glass. Thin ribs of wood divided the large panes and led upwards to a central ridge that ran the length of the building. Jim removed his shoes and socks and, after tying them together he slung them round his neck and laid himself down along the upward sloping strut of wood between two of the panes. He reached up but his fingers, stretched to the limit, were still a few agonising inches short of the roof ridge. He would have to crawl up the glass and take the consequences if it failed to hold his weight.

He sat back on his haunches for a minute and thought about his position. This would probably be the only chance he would have of solving the mystery of The House of Glass and whatever connection he had to it. Jim peered down into the gloom of the shop. He could see very little, although by this time the moon had risen over his shoulder, throwing a faint silvery light. There was nothing solid visible below but, as he moved his head from side to side, strange glints and tiny highlights seemed to twinkle at him from the blackness beneath. Whatever was down there seemed unlikely to afford a soft landing should the glass panes give way. He paced out along the strut again with his hands, one in front of the other, like a cat on a narrow fence. Having gone as far as he could in this way, he lowered his body, as gently as a mother lays down a sleeping baby, putting as much weight as he could on the narrow strut and spreading the rest as widely as possible across the thin glass. Using his toes he pushed himself up again, as far as was possible and then tried to crawl gently up the glass. With a careful lizard-like action he moved towards the safety of the roof ridge. There was a long slow creak followed by the short sharp sound of cracking glass. A large portion of the pane to his left fell into the shop and smashed noisily beneath him. Jim froze, as the terror seized him. He lay there, like the chalk outline of a murder victim, waiting to fall into the darkness, accompanied by big razor shards of glass from the shattering roof panes.

5 - Discovery

After a long time Jim took his first slow breath. The rest of the pane held fast. He concentrated as much of his weight as possible along the line of his chest and reached with his right hand. It touched the ridge but came away with just a few flecks of white paint under the fingernails. Dare he push once more with his feet against the fragile glass? He took another deep breath, brought his right knee a fraction higher and spread the fingers of his hand wide, the palm flattened softly down against the glass for maximum grip. He reached again, this time with the left hand. As his fingers folded around the ridge there came another loud crack and a piece of the window to his right fell into the void below. There was a tinkling as it smashed on the floor but by then Jim had his other hand on the ridge and was hauling himself off the deadly glass crown of the shop. He sat firmly on the long wooden beam, panting away the fear and waiting for his heart to stop banging.

After a while he looked up at the bright moon and marvelled at the number of stars in the night sky, as it stretched out across the darkness of the sea. One tiny star sped through the heavens, seemingly brighter than its fellows. Jim watched it disappear towards the horizon then looked down at the answering glitter below and thought about his next move. He realised now that he had only given thought to moving forward, he had no plan of retreat. There was no way back down, if he did not go onward he would be stuck here until someone called the fire brigade the next morning.

The ridge was narrow, no more than four inches wide at most. He remembered the beam at gym lessons; that was four inches wide and many a boy, including Jim, had not made it from one end to the other without falling off. He thought he could crawl but found that not having his arms out to balance made him wobble horribly and he had to sit for a moment to regain his confidence. Standing up was hardly better; the shoes round his neck bothered him and seemed to make his balance worse. Jim sat back down and un-knotted the laces, then stood once more, holding out a shoe in each hand, as a tight ropewalker might use a pole to aid his balance. He soon found that if he kept his head up and looked straight ahead at the wooden acorn that topped out the small tower, his balance was less upset. Before long he reached its wooden frame and Jim felt his whole body relax. He realised that his jaw ached from clenching his teeth together and he shook his head from side to side to ease the tension in his neck. He looked down at the spot where he had been earlier that afternoon, and saw himself standing on the deck, as if with the sceptical gaze of the herring gull that had eyed him from just this spot.

The ventilation window was indeed slightly ajar, but rather small. Jim levered it fully open with his knife, fetched the torch from his pocket and leaned his head through. The little marble of light showed a worn stool sitting in the centre of a large circular display cabinet. A till on one side had its drawer slid out, the empty money compartments adding to the slightly abandoned air of the place. It seemed an awfully long way down but on the positive side Jim noticed that the four slender columns that held up the little beehive cupola were easily reachable.

He took off his jacket and dropped it through the hole, realising that he would never fit through the narrow opening while he had it on. Next were the boots, which bounced off the old stool and then lay on their sides in a slightly comical way, as if on the run by themselves. Jim then realised that the torch would have to go as well since it was too bulky to fit in his pocket while he squeezed through the window. He tried to drop it on top of the jacket but instead it hit the floor and went out instantly.

'Damn,' he said quietly.

He got in feet first and then, when up to his waist, he swivelled round so as to hang on to the window opening with his hands, reaching down for the nearest column with his feet. He soon had both arms round it and slid gently to the floor like a fireman.

At last Jim was inside The House of Glass.

***

He stood for a while, inside the circle of cabinets, waiting for his eyes to adjust to the dark interior. The torch was dead, the bulb probably broken in the drop, but Jim soon found he could see surprisingly well by the light of the high moon striking down through the roof panes. He replaced his shoes and jacket and went over to the nearest cabinet to peer inside.

The glimmerings and gleamings from within soon resolved themselves into a handsome crystal statue of a polar bear, about a hand high. She stood on the edge of an ice flow with two young cubs at her side and seemed to gaze nobly back at Jim through the glass. Next to her was an eagle perched on a rocky crag, his head turned to gaze across the cabinet at a pair of otters, one of which was pinning down a glistening salmon. The whole cabinet was a glass menagerie of wild creatures from all over the world. The shelf below had animals from Africa; a lion, a pair of zebra and three bounding gazelles, every part of their delicate bodies made perfectly in glass. At the bottom were some dolphins leaping clear of a wave and a seal twisting itself around after a fish.

Jim moved along the line of display cases. The next contained man made things; a country cottage with a cat on the wall, an old fashioned racing car and a small but intricate model of a sailing ship, maybe the Cutty Sark thought Jim, its sails billowing out as it sliced through the glassy sea.

Jim examined every object he could see with fascination. Those that stood in the moonlight he could make out quite clearly, but where the cabinets sat back in the gloom of the shop the little sculptures were harder to recognise.

The final cabinet contained musical instruments, a violin and its bow, a grand piano and, as he rounded the corner, a beautiful little glass trumpet. Jim stared in admiration, this was an instrument that he knew well and he could see that every last detail was present, down to the tiny valves and the mouthpiece. He stood for a long time, staring at the trumpet and feeling ever more deeply drawn into the mystery of The House of Glass. His eyes seemed to lose their focus and the instrument became a small constellation of shining stars as he heard the sound of a solo trumpet echoing in his mind. It was a tune unknown to Jim and he vaguely wondered where it came from. Although he could rehear any music he wanted to in his head, he had never before experienced new music in this way. The melody was both sweet and sad at the same time.

As he walked around the last case his footsteps boomed loudly on the wooden floor and, looking down, he noticed a brass ring set into the oak boards; Jim realised that he was standing on a trapdoor. The thought that barely an inch of wood separated him from a thirty-foot drop into the sea was unnerving and he stepped quickly off. It was then he saw the stairs; they spiralled away into the dark behind a half open door which was marked 'Private'. Leaning in and peering upwards only revealed more blackness. Jim found a light switch by his hand but dared not try it, for fear of alerting anyone who may have been looking at the pier to the presence of an intruder.

He suddenly remembered that the torch had a spare bulb, cleverly fitted into the cap of the battery compartment. After a few moments of careful fumbling he found it and was relieved when a flick of the switch sent a beam of yellow light up the stairs. Keeping it low, so as not to shine out of the windows, Jim advanced cautiously into the darkened upper storey of The House of Glass.

The first door off the landing at the top revealed a tiny kitchen with a double gas ring, a sink and plate rack that stood on a narrow drainer under the window. Opposite the kitchen was the toilet and just to his right a narrow door, probably a broom cupboard. He ignored this and chose the last door, which opened onto a fairly large room. An old iron bedstead stood under the sloping eaves at one end and a workbench ran along the wall under the windows in front of him. Peering round the door Jim saw a desk covered in papers with a couple of small framed pictures on the wall above it. The only homely touch was a large Persian carpet in the centre of the room.

He examined the workbench first. It was covered in all kinds of strange tools, which he imagined were used in the production of the glass statues downstairs. There was also a blowtorch attached to a large cylinder of gas and some drawings, which Jim's torch showed to be plans of the glass trumpet he had just been admiring. It must have been the last thing the owner had made before shutting the shop for what looked like forever.

At last Jim knew what The House of Glass was, the only mystery that remained; what on earth had it to do with him?

***

Jim crossed to the desk and shone the torch on the papers scattered across it. There were many bills and official looking letters, which he moved to one side. Under these he found a large sketchbook. It was hard to see the drawings inside properly by the light of his little torch, so Jim crossed to the window and drew the heavy curtain closed, before returning to the desk and switching on the old angle-poise lamp. He looked anxiously across the room in case any chinks should let some light slip out to give him away, and then turned his attention to the book.

There were many sketches in which he recognised the things he had seen downstairs, the leaping gazelles and the Cutty Sark in full sail. There were often several drawings before the final design had been settled on. The polar bear started out on her own, before acquiring one and then two cubs. The curious thing was the trumpet. It had pages and pages of drawings devoted to it. In many, the various parts were separated out, so that each tiny component could be seen. There were many handwritten notes in tiny scrawly writing that Jim could barely read.

In the very back of the book he found an old yellowing envelope containing a single photograph. It was of a young woman wearing a nurse's uniform, with a white hat and a watch dangling from her pocket. She was, Jim thought, very pretty and had a smile that made you want to smile back straight away. He slipped it back into the envelope and put it in his jacket pocket.

He turned the lamp upwards and examined the pictures on the wall more closely.

There was a larger version of the picture in the envelope and one of a couple, the same woman and a man, by a small sports car parked outside what looked like a country pub.

Jim removed the picture from its frame and discovered some faint writing in pencil on the reverse. He held it against the wall and peered at it in the patch of light from the angle-poise but it slipped from beneath his finger and fell down behind the desk. Jim got on hands and knees to crawl underneath and retrieve it, but found the way blocked by a large leather case. He pulled this out and set it on the desk, angling the light to get a better view.

It was rectangular and about four feet long. Jim looked at the small brass plate set in the middle under the carrying handle. The plate was oval and beautifully inscribed...with *his* name.

James Davis

At first there was shock, he felt the hairs on his neck bristle and a gasp escaped him. Then came a huge flood of relief - that he was right all along, right to run away, right to have risked everything to be here, now. Whoever George Armstrong was knew about Jim, cared even – it was as if someone had lifted the lid on the dark loneliness in which he had lived for so long, and a warm beam of light caused it to brighten a little.

The case had four strong clasps but unfortunately two of them were locked. Jim soon found some keys after rifling through the desk drawers but his hand shook as he tried to insert one into the small keyhole. After a couple of attempts the locks clicked quietly and he snapped down the catches.

He took a quick breath and opened the lid. It was the last breath he was to take for some time, for that was a moment that would live with Jim forever. There, nestling in the deepest blue velvet of the case, was a real glass trumpet.

It shone up at Jim, detailing his amazed features. The trumpet was perfect in every respect from the glassy slides and the valves, to the graceful curve of the bell. This was engraved with delicate lines and swirls. Jim lifted the instrument gingerly from its case to examine them more closely. It was light, lighter than the school's trumpet. The decoration curled around the bell and consisted of a stave of music interlaced with some words. Each spiralled around the other and the trumpet bell at the same time. Set into the velvet of the case were two mouthpieces, also made of glass. Jim fitted one into the leadpipe and raised the horn to his lips. He was scared of blowing too hard and making a loud noise, but he found that the instrument responded to the softest of breaths with a long sweet soft note. He ran it up and down the scale quietly, finding the notes easy and fluid, like running up and down a carpeted stairway in soft slippers. He wanted to play more and glanced nervously over towards the window, wondering how much the curtains would deaden the sound.

It was then he noticed the intermittent flicking blue light edging them every second or so. That could only mean one thing; a police car. Before he could even make it half way across to the window for a peek, he heard the heavy clattering noise of chains and padlocks being removed from the entrance to the pier and the sound of voices and heavy boots on the deck below.

Jim darted back across the room and put the glass trumpet back into its box before snapping it shut and running out onto the small landing. He could already hear the chains and boards being removed from the doors near the bottom of the stairs, so pulled open the narrow door of the broom cupboard and crammed himself inside. He put the case at the back and discovered a pile of blankets on a shelf. Draping one of these over his head he crouched down, making himself as small as possible.

The heavy boots came up the stairs now. He heard them pause as their owner poked his head briefly into the kitchen before crossing the landing to the big room. They returned to the top of the stairs and a loud voice shouted:

'Anything?'

'Just a lot of broken glass,' came the answering voice. 'He'd be cut to ribbons if he'd come in through the roof.'

'Well there's nothing up here,' said the near voice and it sounded as if the man was about to set off down the stairs when the footfalls suddenly paused and the door of the cupboard was opened. Jim crouched under his blanket as a bright light played over him. He tried to keep as still as possible, he tried not to breathe, he tried not to feel the fear of being taken home, to Garside, and the strap, hanging patiently from its nail on the top landing.

There was a pause and then the edge of the blanket lifted up; Jim found himself looking up the beam of a large policeman's torch.

6 - Downhill and Up

The policeman studied Jim for a moment or two and then whipped the blanket off, before ordering him out onto the landing. The other policeman trudged heavily up the stairs and Jim stood there, like a specimen, while they examined him with their torches.

The second one was a sergeant and rather fat for a policeman. When he stopped wheezing he asked:

'Are you Jim Davis of Highbury New Park, London?'

Jim nodded.

'Well you'd better come with us then, lad,' he added in a kindlier tone and started for the stairs.

The younger policeman took him by the arm but Jim cried, 'Wait!' and darted back into the broom cupboard to get the trumpet case.

'Now hang on there a minute,' said the constable.

'You can't just go helping yourself; breaking and entering is bad enough but that's burglary, and in the presence of the law!'

'But it's mine!'

'What, broke in here with it did you?' asked the sergeant.

'No,' said Jim and held out the case to show them the brass plate on which his name was inscribed.

The policemen looked at each other and the fat sergeant shrugged.

'Well, I suppose that's a positive identification at least,' he said.

When they put Jim in the back of the car he was surprised to find Old Tom there, and even more surprised to find him wearing handcuffs. The old man looked miserably at Jim.

'I'm sorry, Jim,' he said, 'but when they came looking round the farm for you all they found was your rucksack and the clothes you took off and left in my barn.' A tear seemed to glisten in the light from the streetlamps that lit the entrance to the pier.

'They accused me of the most terrible things, Jim.' His voice sounded a little choked, as if he needed to clear his throat.

'Said they were going to start digging up the garden. I had to tell them where you went.'

Jim put his hand on the old man's arm.

'I know, Tom. You had to.'

As they pulled away Old Tom asked quietly,

'Did you find what it was you were looking for, Jim?'

Jim grinned and raised the trumpet case up off his lap.

'Well I certainly found something.'

***

The police station was tiny with just a reception desk, a back room and a single cell towards which Old Tom was led as soon as they got inside. Jim was horrified.

'But he's done nothing!' he yelled. 'You've got me, why can't you just let him go?'

'Well let me see.' said the younger policeman, 'How about obstructing a police investigation for starters?'

'But he told you where I was.'

'Not when we saw him on the road yesterday. He said he hadn't seen you.'

'But he hadn't,' Jim lied.

'I climbed into his wagon while he was busy fixing the horse. When he found me all he did was make me some tea and lend me some clothes.'

The policemen looked at one another.

'Please,' said Jim quietly.

'Think of the paperwork,' said the sergeant.

'And no-one round here will thank us for prosecuting Old Tom,' the younger one added.

'Alright, Tom,' said the fat sergeant and undid the handcuffs. The old farmer came over and shook Jim's hand solemnly.

'You're a good boy, Jim, and whatever it is you're searching for, I pray that you find it, lad.'

As he walked down the station steps Jim saw Millet dart across the road from where she had been waiting in the darkness of a shop doorway.

When he had gone Jim was put in the back room and given a cup of tea. They brought his rucksack in and set it on the floor next to the trumpet case. It was a small room with a filing cabinet, a picture of the Queen on one wall and a clock on the other. A couple of magazines and a copy of yesterday's Daily Express lay on a wooden table near the door.

Outside the young policeman yelled, 'Goodnight, Sarge,' and drove off in the car. Jim listened to the sound of the engine fade away into the darkness and then heard the heavy old receiver lift and the slow dial of a trunk call.

'Hello, Inspector Sherwood please...It's Sergeant Major here...from Walsham-on-Sea.'

He paused and Jim heard faint laughter in the background from the other end, then a crackly, 'Sherwood.'

'We've got him, sir, your runaway lad; Jim Davis.'

'Oh well done, Major...' but the rest of the conversation was lost, as the better to hear the praise being lavished, the sergeant pushed the receiver firmly against his fleshy ear. He listened a while and then cut in.

'Yes, sir, we checked the pier right away, as soon as we got the call at lunchtime but there was no sign of him then. Only found him after following up a sighting by Constable Steele from this morning, sir…yes…good work…yes, thank you, sir, goodnight, sir,' and he put the handset down with a satisfied clunk.

Before long he came in with more tea and some very large ham and piccalilly sandwiches, which he shared willingly with Jim.

'Eat up son; I've loads more. Keep a little cold box under the counter there.'

He demonstrated by removing nearly half a sandwich with one enormous bite, and then informed Jim, through a tumbling mouthful of ham and piccalilly:

'Your father is being driven down to collect you; he'll be here first thing in the morning. 'Til then, young Jim, you'll stop here with me.'

He washed his food down with a deep draught of tea and looked across the table.

'What you do it for, son?'

'What?' Jim asked, alarmed.

'Run away? Why d'ya scarper? And the pier, why break into the pier?'

'I was just looking for something,' he answered.

'But what, young James, what was it you was looking for?'

Jim just about fitted a corner of the sandwich into his mouth and considered.

'I'm not really sure,' he answered honestly, after few moments thoughtful chewing.

Eventually, having demolished his sandwich, the sergeant stood up and explained to Jim that, although he wasn't a criminal, he was to be locked in the room until morning...'Just in case,' as he put it.

He allowed Jim to go to the toilet and fetched him a glass of water before turning the heavy key in the door.

Jim finished the food miserably and then sat for a long time, his chin resting on his hands, which in turn rested on the old oak table. Although he was tired he could not sleep; the thought of his father's rage filling him with dread. What would happen to the trumpet, he wondered; he could not imagine being allowed to keep it.

What had been in the letter his father had burned, how did he know where Jim was headed and most mysterious of all, why was there a glass trumpet with his own name inscribed on the case?

He thought these things through for a while before bringing out his wallet and checking the contents. Sure enough, the business card that had set him on his journey was missing. He could still picture it, lying slightly bloodied and crumpled under the light by his bed. Jim kicked himself and his head sank even lower on the table.

It was the trumpet, though, which both puzzled and excited him. Having been united with something which was destined to be his, Jim felt that he could bear the rage, bear the fierce beating he would receive; bear anything, except being parted from the glass trumpet.

He moved his chair over to the little window set high in the wall but found that he could barely reach up enough to see out of it, besides which it was firmly barred. After sitting a while longer at the table he heard, from the other side of the door, a long drawn out rattling noise. Although it sounded increasingly like an elephant blowing a raspberry, Jim soon realised that it was the snoring of the fat sergeant. He put his eye to the keyhole in the hopes of seeing exactly how this ponderous sound was created but found his view blocked by the big brass key.

Jim spun round suddenly as the idea hit him. He looked at the old newspaper still lying on the table and checked the gap under the door; it was easily big enough for what he had in mind. He took a single sheet from the paper and slid it gently under the door. On second thoughts he withdrew it, opened the whole paper out and slid that under instead. He put his eye again to the hole; the key was only turned a little clockwise. Taking the knife from his pocket he opened out the smaller of the two blades and reached this into the lock. The key rattled a little as he worked it round but there was no pause in the rhythm of the policeman's snores. When he could see the whole thing he pushed at it gently with the tip of the blade. There was a gentle thump as it landed on the newspaper outside the door. Now he had to be careful; if the key would not fit under the door he would lose it. Jim cautiously slid all but the top sheet of newspaper back under and then put his eye as close to the floor as he could. With all the care of a man defusing an unexploded bomb, he drew the key back under the door to him, and then sat back and let out a relieved sigh.

Jim put on the rucksack and moved the trumpet case over to the door. He used both hands to turn the key, trying to keep the noise of the mechanism to a minimum. Both the lock and the hinges were well oiled and he swung the door open in almost complete silence. Jim stepped through, taking the precious trumpet case with him. The policeman was leaning back in a high swivel chair, his big boots up on the counter, his chest straining at the buttons of his tunic as he snored. Jim wanted to relock the door as, left alone, it would not stay perfectly shut, but felt this would be pushing his luck a little too far. He slipped around the counter where it lifted up to allow people to pass in and out and tiptoed down the steps.

As he stole into the dark street outside a surprisingly lively breeze blew in and Jim heard the fat policeman snuffle and snort. It was then he realised his mistake in not relocking the door, as a loud voice rang out suddenly from the police station.

'Oi! Come back here, you little sod!'

Jim bolted down the road, turning for a second to see the bulky figure of the policeman come barrelling through the doors of the station. He ran on down the hill, the rucksack bouncing uncomfortably on his back, the trumpet case gripped in his hand. It was no good; the heavy boots gained a yard on him for every yard he covered.

It was, in the end, the hill that saved him. For every downhill in the whole world there is, of course, an uphill to match. Jim swerved into a little back lane and found himself running upwards between the quiet houses, the path rising a step every few yards. He soon realised that while the downhill had worked in favour of the bulky sergeant, he was now gaining ground on the policeman as the path led ever upward and the big figure, although still pursuing him, was diminishing. As he came to the end of the path he looked over his shoulder once too often and caught his toe on the last step. He stumbled headlong across the pavement and fell into the road to be instantly blinded by a pair of powerful headlights and terrified by the squealing of brakes and tyres.

When Jim had managed to un-squeeze his eyelids he found himself lying on his back, the trumpet case hugged tightly again his chest. He was looking up at the grill of a lorry, no more than a couple of feet from his face. Within a second he was up, his free hand yanking at the door handle,

'What the…!' said a cockney voice.

Jim stuffed himself into the cab.

'Drive!'

'Who's after yer, the devil himself?' laughed the driver.

'Police,' said Jim before he could think. It was, as it turned out, a lucky admission.

'Right then.' The driver jammed the lorry into gear and took off along the main road out of town.

As they passed the end of the lane Jim caught a last sight of the fat sergeant hanging onto a lamp-post a good way down the hill, stooped over and gasping for breath.

He looked round at his saviour. The driver grinned and held out his hand.

'Anyone on the run from the coppers is a friend of mine!' he said.

7 - The Tramp

'My name's Frankie, but you can call me Flynn.'

'Jim,' he panted, shaking hands.

Cockney laughter rang out over the last few houses of Walsham-on-Sea as the lorry chased its own small pool of light up the hill and out into the darkness of the countryside.

Flynn was a wiry dark haired man in his twenties. The hair was curly and quite long, for a man anyway, thought Jim. He had on a collarless white shirt and a waistcoat. Besides this he wore a red bandanna tied raffishly round his neck, which gave him a gypsy air and he held a roll-up between the fingers of his left hand where they rested on the gear knob.

He didn't ask Jim why he was running away from the police in the middle of the night, in the middle of nowhere, but instead wanted to know where Jim was headed.

Jim thought for a moment and realised that he hadn't the least idea.

'Where are *you* going?' he asked instead of answering.

Flynn laughed aloud again.

'Like that is it? You really are on the run!'

He put the cigarette in his mouth and with much grinding put the lorry into a higher gear as they reached the top of the hill that led out of town.

'I'm goin' to Billingsgate, mate.'

Jim looked none the wiser.

'Where's that?' asked Jim.

'London, by the Tower, 'ent you never heard of Billingsgate Market?'

'No,' said Jim. 'What do they sell there?'

'Take a deep breath - then you got one guess.'

Jim did as he was told.

'Oh, fish!'

'That's it, only the freshest in the whole market. I do the late run along the south coast, all the little towns, and Hastings of course. Get up to London about 'alf past five so when they gets it on the plate it's fresh as a nun's knickers.'

Jim blushed a little as Flynn continued on for some while about the intricacies of the fish business, and he felt his eyes begin to close. His long day, the noisy engine and even Flynn's continuous talking seemed to weigh them down. Only the occasional grinding of the gears, usually accompanied by Flynn shouting, 'Go on my son!' as he wrestled with the lever, stopped Jim from falling entirely asleep.

Seeing that conversation was unlikely, Flynn leant forward and switched on a radio set built into the dashboard. Jim's curiosity awoke him and he watched, fascinated, as Flynn gently turned the tuning knob, creating a lot of whooshing and wheedling sounds with the odd snatch of French or what sounded like Dutch thrown in.

'I didn't know you could have a wireless in a lorry.'

'Oh yes, can't go anywhere without my music. Cost a bit but s'worth every penny when you do the miles I do.'

The distinguished voice of a newsreader came on and announced that the Soviet Union had launched something called Sputnik Three into earth orbit.

'BBC,' said Flynn. 'You get a good signal but the music's bloody awful, anybody'd think the war was still on.'

As if to confirm this, the news ended and was replaced by a string orchestra playing a syrupy composition on what sounded like a thousand violins.

'Mantovani…again,' spat Flynn and resumed his efforts with the tuning knob, causing the fish lorry to wander around in the road alarmingly.

Eventually he found a station with a much more upbeat voice reading out something called 'The Hit Parade'.

Top of the hit parade was a new record by Connie Francis called 'Who's Sorry Now?'. The lady singing it had a nice voice, thought Jim, but he found the melody a little dull.

There followed a song called 'Jailhouse Rock' by a man called Elvis. Jim, brought up without a radio or even a gramophone in the house, had never heard anything like it. The drums were really loud and the music seemed to dance about on its own. Flynn snorted and said there wasn't really much rock and roll in prison.

'Have you been to prison then?' asked Jim.

'Yeah, done me time, four years in the Scrubbs.'

Flynn laughed when Jim asked what for.

'That's one thing you *do not* ask, inside at least. I don't mind though. Went into the family business didn't I - safecracker, like me old man. Started as the break-in boy 'cos I was small and I could climb anything. That's where I got the nickname...'In like Flynn' as they used to say,' he laughed.

'I never had his luck with the ladies though!'

Jim looked puzzled.

'You know, Errol Flynn?'

Jim shook his head and Flynn gave up.

'Trouble was I was too cocky to listen to 'im. Thought I knew it all by the time I was nineteen. Got caught, first job I did on me own.'

He paused to do battle with the gearbox again as the lorry slowed on a hill. After much crunching and grinding he relaxed and lit another cigarette.

'Not goin' back though, that's it, wasted four years of me life, gonna just concentrate on goin' straight now, build up a nice little business.'

He looked at Jim across the cab.

'Sure you aint been locked up yourself, Jim? I mean you got the cops after you and you don't seem to know nuffin' about anythin'. Never seen a radio, never heard of Errol Flynn or even Elvis! What's goin' on eh?'

'I have, kind of, I suppose,' he answered. 'My parents don't like much, except Jesus. They think it's all wicked, all the modern things.'

'And that's who you're on the run from? Yer mum and dad?'

Jim shifted awkwardly in his seat and, sensing he was unwilling to discuss the matter, Flynn changed the subject.

'So what's in the case?' he asked.

'It's my trumpet,' said Jim. As he spoke those words he felt a little swell of pride.

'*My* trumpet,' he thought and knew that he would never own anything that was as much his.

'Oh, musician are you?' said Flynn.

'Yes,' replied Jim; although he had rarely been asked anything about himself before, he found that he answered to the name of musician without a moment's hesitation.

'Let's have a look then.'

Jim didn't need to be asked twice; he pulled the case up onto his knees and snapped back the catches.

Flynn let out a long whistle as the trumpet emerged from its case and the lorry narrowly avoided the ditch that ran beside the road.

'That's incredible, can you play it?'

'I don't really know yet,' said Jim.

'Have a go then!' urged Flynn.

Jim put the instrument gingerly to his lips, somewhat nervously in case Flynn's erratic driving should pose a threat to his new possession.

He let an easy breath into the mouthpiece and ran up through an A major scale. As in The House of Glass he found the trumpet seemed to turn thought into music with the least trouble. He played some more warm-up scales and then a little Handel, then stopped and looked over at Flynn, whose mouth was wide open.

'That's incredible…just amazing…the sound! Play some more, know any jazz?'

Jim thought for a moment and put the mouthpiece back against his lips.

He recalled some of Lester's records on the milk train and blew the first few bars of 'Groovin High'.

Again the tone was delicious and the trumpet seemed to almost suck the notes out of him. It was as if it provided a bridge from his mind across which the music could flow straight out into the world and Jim, being Jim, could recall the music perfectly. Whoever had made this unique and beautiful thing, they had made it for him.

After playing for a few minutes he put the trumpet away fearing for its safety in the lurching lorry.

'Sorry,' he said. 'I'm rather tired.'

'You get your head down, son. I'll wake you when we get into town.'

Jim soon fell asleep, dreaming about the devil trying to pull the glass trumpet from his grasp and having to live on a pier but one that was far out to sea. A dark shape in the water filled him with dread.

***

He woke to find the lorry pulling over outside Waterloo Station. Flynn looked up at the big clock outside.

'Twenty-past-five, there's a café in there opens at half past and the tube starts up at six, you can get anywhere you want from 'ere.'

He held out his hand.

'Good luck, Jim.'

Jim jumped out and fetched down his bag and trumpet case. As he crossed the road towards the broad sweep of steps leading up to the station, Flynn wound down his window and called:

'You watch out fer yerself, not everyone in London's as nice as me.'

Then there was the familiar grinding of gears as he headed off towards the bridge over the Thames.

Waterloo Station was open but deserted. Jim soon found a waiting room, which was empty except for someone with no laces in their boots, asleep under a coat along one of the hard wooden benches.

It was a little cold so Jim found a jumper from his rucksack and sat down to wonder at what he was to do next. He realised, just as he had on the roof of The House of Glass a few short hours ago, that he had no plan. He knew now that he was, as Flynn had put it, 'on the run' and was unlikely to escape the police a second time if caught. Jim felt that, now he had the glass trumpet, both keeping it and finding out why it was his had become the most important things in his life.

He was longing to look at it again, in the daylight and so opened the catches and lifted the lid. It lay in its velvet-lined bed as perfect as a work of nature. He lifted it out and felt it balance in his hand. It was as if it had been made in one piece; wherever one could have been expected to find a join there were just the smooth supple shapes of glass. He examined again the strange etchings that ran in a spiral round the bell and down towards the valves.

Against the lightening sky through the grimy window of the waiting room he read:

> *There's a somebody I'm longing to see,*
> *I hope that he turns out to be,*
> *Someone who'll watch over me.*

This seemed strangely moving to Jim although he could not really understand its significance. The music he found harder to read but managed to hum it to himself after studying the winding stave for a while.

Jim was dying to play the trumpet more. He looked over at the sleeping figure and instead just rang the edge of the bell gently with a flick of his finger. It rang a perfect B flat and he listened to it die away before locking the trumpet carefully back in its case. He took a last look at the waiting room as the door swung shut behind him, just to make sure that he had left nothing behind. Although he saw the figure under the coat on the bench, he failed to notice one watery eye, watching him leave from under its dark folds.

The station clock showed five-thirty and Jim soon found the café that Flynn had told him about. He asked the lady behind the counter for a hot chocolate, and sat at one of the tables just outside on the station concourse while she heated the milk.

Jim took the photo from his pocket and studied it again. It was as if the lady in it was smiling at him from a lost world, one which Jim felt a longing to visit. He gazed at it quietly for a moment and then, as he slid it back into the envelope he realised that there was a stamp and an address on the front.

Lizzie
17 Belsize Rd
London
NW3

Jim's heart gave an extra beat. Here, at least, was something tangible. A place that must at least exist, a person who could perhaps explain to Jim what it was that he was searching for.

The lady came over with his hot chocolate and Jim asked if she could direct him to Belsize Road.

She laughed and said London was a big place but to 'hang on a tick'. She was soon back with a book called The London A-Z which had every road in the whole city mapped out. Jim found Belsize Road in the index and was soon copying the relevant piece of map into his notebook. He worked carefully, making sure that when he arrived at Kilburn High Road Station nearby, he would be sure of his route. He noted everything relevant, except perhaps the noiseless boots, with no laces, that stole closer and closer as he worked. When Jim was finally satisfied, he finished his now luke-warm hot chocolate and turned to put the little notebook back in his rucksack, only to find that it was not there. He looked to his other side and felt instant horror clutch at his insides. The trumpet case too, was gone.

***

Jim let out a quick shriek of despair, then he was on his feet running first this way and then that. Pigeons flew up and the lady came out of the café to see what the problem was. As he looked along the station concourse, past the innumerable platforms, his eye caught the slightest movement in the far corner of the vast station. Not knowing what else to do he ran in that direction. All he saw was the head and shoulders of a man going smoothly down on the escalator, but what really caught his attention was that, just as the figure was about to disappear, its head turned towards him and then ducked quickly from sight. That tiny instant spoke to Jim of one thing: guilt. He ran across the grey tarmac towards the escalator, stuffing his flapping notebook into his jacket, and feeling himself rise up onto his toes as he hit full sprint. It seemed an age before he reached the top, just in time to see the legs of someone vanish into the left hand tunnel at the bottom of the moving stairway. Jim plunged down the escalator, almost losing his balance near the bottom and sprinted along the tunnel down which the figure had disappeared. He skidded to a stop at the first set of steps he came to, leading off to his right. There, near the bottom was a single boot, lying abandoned on its side. Jim leapt the half dozen steps and found the other boot at the bottom of the next flight. As he tore along the tunnel to the next set of stairs he tried to quell his panic at what he heard. It was the sound of a train coming to a halt at the platform. Spurred on to even greater speed he rounded the corner to the final steps as he heard the hiss of the train doors opening. A last desperate bound sent him plummeting down the stairs as he missed his footing. He arrived at the bottom a tumbling mass of scuffed and scratched arms and legs. Jim got dizzily to his feet just in time to see the doors start to close. He threw himself across the platform in a last desperate attempt to make the train, but the doors shut and he bounced off them to land sitting on his bottom. There was silence but only for a second as Jim screamed:

'Noooooooooooooo!'

It was as if despair had made itself into a sound. It echoed down the empty platform and up through the endless galleries of the station. The train sat for another couple of seconds and then, with a swoosh of compressed air, the doors slid open again. Jim catapulted himself onto the train and sat there on the floor, gasping, as the doors closed once more and the train pulled out of the station.

He was familiar with the tube, having been taken on it once during a school trip to the Science Museum and he knew that the doors between the carriages in the train opened, to allow people to pass between them as the train was in motion. Ducking low he ran up to the door between his and the carriage in front. Peering cautiously through the window he caught his first sight of the man who had stolen all his belongings.

8 - Number Seventeen

The train rattled and screeched through the tunnel. It swayed from side to side as Jim eyed his opponent through the window of the connecting doors. He had no doubts that an opponent was what this man was, for Jim would never surrender the glass trumpet while he still lived. The man was thin, his feet clad only in his ragged socks. He was clean shaven but looked dirty and everything about him was grey; grey trousers and coat, grey shirt which once had been blue, lank grey hair and grimy grey fingers which were busily going through the contents of Jim's rucksack. Impatient with rummaging, Jim watched as the man upended the bag and shook everything out onto the floor. He searched through it for anything of value and sat back disgusted when he could find nothing.

Jim considered his options. It was hard to tell how tall the man was while sat down, but he certainly was not heavily built. This, Jim knew, was no guarantee that he would not fight.

Although smaller and lighter than Cracker, Jim had managed to put him down and he knew that fighting was more about spirit than strength. He had decided to wait until the next station came up and rush the man via the doors that opened onto the platform, reckoning that the element of surprise would favour him in a short fight and that all he would have to do to regain his possessions would be to eject the man from the train.

All this changed however as the tramp began to worry at the locks of the trumpet case. Jim had the keys in his pocket but the man seemed determined to get the case open somehow. It was when he picked up the pocket-knife from the pile of Jim's belongings, strewn across the floor of the train, that Jim knew he could delay acting no longer. As the tramp struggled to open the blade, Jim tore open the door and flew at him down the carriage. The man half stood as Jim caught him in the middle and they both went tumbling along the floor as the train suddenly began to slow. Skinny or not the grey man was a fighter and lashed viciously at Jim as they both struggled to gain their feet in the rocking train. Jim dodged but fell on his backside in avoiding the full force of the man's punch. Rather than press his advantage the tramp fumbled with the knife and managed to pop open the hoof pick that Jim had offered Old Tom only the day before. He leapt at Jim and it was only through grabbing the man's wrist and rolling backward that he avoided being horribly stabbed with the spike. As the weight bore down on him he drew his knees to his chest and turned his head desperately to the side as the tip of it came nearer and nearer his eye. He felt the fear course through him, sapping his strength. The horrible stench of the man filtered though his nostrils as he gasped for air. Still, the point neared his eye.

Suddenly the train burst into the next station and began braking hard. The tramp had to stick out an elbow to brace himself against the partition by the doors, and this allowed Jim just the second he needed to bring his knees up to his chin and get the flat of his feet against his opponent's chest, as the man renewed his attempt to skewer Jim with the spike. The train eased up off the brakes and as it came to a halt the doors opened and Jim saw his chance. With a mighty effort he pushed, putting every scrap of strength he had against the man's chest, propelling him backwards out of the door and across the platform, where the back of his head met a large fire extinguisher with a dull thud. He saw the tramp slide unconscious down the wall, into a grey heap, as the doors closed again.

Jim sat up, shaken, as the train moved off. He rubbed his head where the punch had connected and found that, in his surprise at being so suddenly launched from the train, the man had dropped the pocket-knife. Jim shuddered as he closed away the long sharp spike, which he had so recently examined at such close range.

He found he was shaking violently as he repacked his things into the rucksack and checked that the delicate trumpet was undamaged. As each of his scattered belongings was placed back into the bag, he felt his heart slow and his breath come more quietly. All the fear and rage that the tramp inspired seemed to coalesce into something quite else and he found, when he stood back up, that he seemed to stand a little straighter, and to sway a little less with the rocking of the train. Then he simply sat for a few stations to regain his composure while the train slowly began to acquire some early morning passengers.

***

Needing directions, Jim had to get off at the next station, Kings Cross, to have a look at one of the big tube maps on the wall. He found the directions for Kilburn High Road and set off for the correct platform. Kings Cross underground was a massive and complex warren of tunnels where four different tube lines met. As he walked along looking for the Metropolitan and Circle line, Jim began to hear snatches of music drifting up the tunnel towards him. He soon found a tall man with long black hair, through which ran a single narrow streak of white, playing the violin to the uninterested people who hurried past him on their way to work. He was dressed in full black tie and tails and was playing Vivaldi with a passion and fluency that impressed Jim. His eyes were closed and he swayed back and forth as the notes gushed from the instrument. Jim put his bags down and stood to listen, while fumbling in his pockets for a coin to drop in the open violin case that awaited donations, mostly in vain, from the swirling throng of passengers.

As the last notes died away along the echoing tunnel, the violinist opened his eyes to find Jim standing there, a trumpet case at his feet.

Before Jim could even offer the thrupenny bit he had found in his pocket the violinist's expression changed from inspired enlightenment to malevolent jealousy.

'Piss off, sonny. This is my pitch,' he hissed in a rather educated tone.

He resumed his haughty demeanour and put the fiddle back under his chin, beginning again the same piece.

At Kilburn High Road, Jim left his train and consulted the map he had drawn in his notebook, before setting off in the direction of Belsize Road. He soon discovered that the walk was a lot further than it had appeared on the map. The trumpet case was well built, to protect its delicate cargo and several times Jim had to stop and swap hands. He crossed the road to be on the side of the odd numbers and kept craning his head out to the left to see if he could yet distinguish number seventeen. As with his walk down to the pier in Walsham-on-Sea, Jim went through what he might say to the lady in order to explain his sudden and unannounced appearance at her door. He would, he decided, show her the glass trumpet and his name on the case and then ask her if she knew who Mr Armstrong was, where he might be found and if she knew why he had made him, Jim Davis, such a thing as a glass trumpet in the first place.

He passed number nineteen, passed a huge poster for Players Cigarettes and began to climb the steps of the next house. As he put down the case to ring the doorbell he was puzzled to find that he was at the door of number fifteen. He went back down and past the poster, thinking he must have misread the number of nineteen but found that he had not. The street went: number nineteen, huge poster for Players Cigarettes and then number fifteen. As Jim stood there puzzling he noticed the postman arrive at number fifteen and stopped him as he came down the steps.

'Excuse me, sir,' said Jim, 'but can you tell me where number seventeen would be?'

The postman laughed a little.

'Well, young man, it *would* be there but for it got hit by a bomb in the war, and that…' he gestured at the huge smiling sailor on the advert, '…is about all that's left.'

He dropped a handful of letters through the door of number nineteen and went on his way, leaving the young man with the leather case and the old rucksack gawping up at the puffing sailor.

***

Jim was dumbfounded. Every time he thought ahead and imagined finding an answer to one mystery or another it seemed that he was met by shuttered windows, deserted buildings or bombsites. He sat on some milk crates by the side of the road and stared up at the giant hoarding. He wondered vaguely what to do now, but it was as if the disappointment had frozen his mind and the best he could do was simply to stare blankly upwards, while iron coloured clouds slowly obscured the morning sun.

He kicked disconsolately at the white wooden panels at the bottom of the advertising hoarding. He found one was loose and pried it open to look down into the devastation that had been number seventeen Belsize Road. A set of steps, spared by the explosion, led down into a wilderness of rubble, shaded by a thin forest of saplings and the bushy purple fronds of flowering buddleia, which sprouted on every piece of abandoned land in the city.

Jim toyed briefly with the idea of rooting around to see if he could find any clues to the fate of Lizzie, but was put off by the ramshackle look of the staircase and sheer desperate hopelessness of it all.

After a while he picked up his belongings and headed wearily back towards the station. Near the junction with Abbey Road a police car passed him in the stream of traffic and, as it went across the lights, the policeman in the passenger seat leaned out of the open window and looked back in his direction. Jim dropped his head and tried to follow the car by looking upwards, almost through his eyebrows, his pace slowing to a crawl. To his horror the police car stopped a few yards over the junction with Abbey Road and the driver began waving the following traffic to pass, as if to give him room to turn around. Jim pivoted on the spot and began to walk quickly in the opposite direction, desperately scanning the street with his eyes for a place to hide. There was nothing. He looked quickly over his shoulder and saw the police car trying to make an awkward three point turn, with much waving of arms and flashing of headlights at the minor traffic jam it had created for itself.

Jim broke into a run, there was nowhere to hide, no shops, no side roads or little alleyways this time. As he approached the bomb-site he suddenly remembered the loose board. Putting the trumpet case down he clawed it open and ducked inside then dragged the case in after him and pulled the board closed with a handy rope handle that he found fixed to its inside. As he crouched in the gloom at the top of the ruined staircase he heard the police car accelerate past, its two-tone siren coming on and then disappearing into the distance.

Jim waited. Then he waited some more. Fat drops of rain began pattering the leaves of the saplings around him and before long a heavy downpour began. Jim wanted to leave his hiding place but was too shaken by what seemed a narrow escape from the police. Although he had no plan, and indeed was not even heading anywhere with a definite purpose in mind when the police car had stopped, the incident had proved that he was not willing to hand himself in yet.

He went gingerly down the crumbling staircase and found that two basement rooms, at the front of the house almost under the pavement, had survived the bomb damage and the subsequent demolition. The larger one was missing most of its back wall and so offered a view across the bomb-site through its thicket of saplings. The other, possibly a pantry or storeroom at one time, contained a few sticks of mostly broken furniture, rotting quietly away in the mildewed semi-darkness.

He sheltered from the rain, squatting on the bare concrete and looking up at the massive wooden beams that held apart the two houses that had once stood alongside number seventeen. Jim soon began to realise how hungry he was. The last food he had eaten was the ham and piccalilli sandwich given him by the fat sergeant and his guts groaned and grumbled.

As the rain subsided he ventured back up the steps, leaving his things tucked away in the storeroom below. He opened the panel a crack and then, when confident he was unobserved, he stepped quickly through and into the street. There was a grocery shop round the corner and Jim bought a few provisions with a half a crown and one of the sixpences.

As well as bread and some cheese for supper he bought a box of matches, a bottle of pop, a replacement spare bulb and some batteries for the torch. He ummed and ahhed about buying some chocolate, a rare treat he was never allowed at home but decided he should save as much of his money as possible for essentials.

He went quickly back down to the den, as he now thought of it, and hungrily ate most of the bread and all of the cheese. From the smaller of the two rooms he took some old chairs, and after some kicking and smashing, Jim had a small pile of firewood. There was a little circle of bricks where somebody had lit a fire before, but try as he might, Jim could not get the damp newspaper that he had for kindling to support a flame strong enough to fire the wood.

Eventually, as the light faded through the forest of slender young trees, he found a kind of bed in the corner of the main room, made from flattened cardboard boxes. He covered himself with as many of the clothes from his rucksack as he could, before lying down to try and sleep.

As Jim lay there, slowly getting warm under his pile of clothes, he went over the last couple of days in his head. If only, he thought, he could just stick to the Old Toms, the Flynns and the Lesters of this world, things might be all right; he would get by. The problem was avoiding the police, his father and any thieving murderous tramps in the meantime. The future he tried to avoid, feeling that the morning was always the best time to make plans. When the sun was up all things seemed possible but when it was dark, Jim felt how alone he was all the more keenly and found it best to think on the things in the world he loved, if only for the comfort that they bought him.

He fell asleep playing 'Everything Happens to Me' by Charlie Parker to himself in his head and imagining that he could feel the weight of Corky through the clothes that covered him where he lay. Despite being on the run from it he felt a strange longing for home. He wondered if his parents would be sorry now that he had run away and if they would treat him any more kindly if he were to return. He fell asleep dreaming of his own bed.

At first he didn't know what it was that woke him up so suddenly in the middle of the night, but he realised after a moment that it had been the scrape of the board that led to the street being dragged open. As he lay so still in the dark, eyes wide, his keen ears heard the sounds of footfalls, soft, on the crumbling stair.

9 - Archie

The legs appeared first. There was a patch of streetlight that shone through a gap in the advertising hoarding and lit up the small landing where the steps changed direction. Here the legs paused, as if unsure, before carefully stalking their way down into the basement where Jim lay, silent and still, beneath his pile of clothes.

He could not make out their owner as it was so pitch dark, but could see a vague shape as it turned at the bottom step and began pacing slowly towards him. It was another tramp.

Jim froze, the fear gripping him as he pulled his head in under the heap of clothes, praying that he would not be noticed in the darkness. The tramp paused and Jim saw him in profile against the patch of streetlight. The face looked thin and was tilted upwards, towards the street above, as if listening. Jim held his breath. There was the outline of a scrubby beard and on the head was a hat, the old fashioned type like detectives used to wear.

The tramp stood there, unmoving, for what seemed a long time and then produced something from his pocket and held it up. There was a clink, some sparks and then he was standing in the faint candle-like radiance of a cigarette lighter, held high up over his head.

He disappeared into the dark shadow of the other room, taking his little circle of light with him and soon returned, carrying an old chair with the seat broken through. He put this next to the circle of bricks and placed a short piece of wood on it before sitting down and bending over to examine Jim's attempt at a fire. The light snapped out and then Jim heard the rustling of newspaper being scrunched up and his fire being rearranged. Before long the lighter came back on, gently touching the newspaper into small flames around the edge, then the wood caught and the crackling blaze lit the dark basement room with its wavering orange glow.

Jim could see the tramp by its light now. He leaned over his fire and stared, unmoving, as the flames flickered before him. He had on shoes rather than boots and trousers with turn-ups, in which Jim could make out the faded remains of a pin stripe. The long rain mac was draped over the shoulders and he leaned forward, his chin resting on the heel of his hand, the hat tipped down over his eyes.

For a long time he sat like that, moving only once to add a piece of wood to the fire. Jim watched through a small tunnel in the pile of clothes that covered him.

After a long while the tramp raised his head slightly and the eyes, glittering in the firelight, seemed to stare straight into Jim's, invisible as he was under his pile of clothes in the dark far corner of the room. Jim looked at the face and felt a surge of sorrow well up inside him. This face looked desolate, like an abandoned house on a windy moor, its empty windows opening on a bare waste, the path leading to its broken gate overgrown and unused. It was a face unvisited by human kindness, forgetful of itself and uncaring of the slow depredations of nature. It was the face of a soul locked in solitary confinement so long that freedom barely beckoned anymore.

Then the face spoke. It said, in a quiet baritone voice: 'Why not warm yourself by the fire? It will burn out soon enough.'

Jim was shocked, thinking that he must surely be impossible to see, away in the shadows and buried as he was. After a few seconds he sat up slowly, warily and then got to his feet.

'How did you know I was there?' he asked.

'It was the eyes, James. I saw them catch the light of the fire.'

The answer left Jim even more dumbfounded.

'And how do you know my name?' he said, with a tone both suspicious and amazed.

'Your name is on your luggage, so poorly hidden, in the other room.'

They regarded each other across the fire.

'It is your luggage I take it?' said the man.

'Yes.'

Jim crouched down by the fire for a while and they both stared into the flaring embers.

'And it's okay if I stay here for a while?'

'I suppose so.'

He poked at the fire with a chair leg for a moment before dropping it into the flames that rose up. From an inside pocket he took a half bottle of spirits and unscrewed the lid before taking a long swig.

'You get some sleep, I tend to stay up.'

He nodded toward the pile of clothes and Jim stood, feeling as if dismissed.

'Oh,' added the man, holding out his hand across the fire, '…and you can call me Archie.'

'Jim,' said Jim shaking it.

He rearranged the clothes that were his blankets, climbed in and went to sleep. He slept the rest of that night without dreaming and as soundly as if he had been in a feather bed at The Ritz.

***

He woke to the sound of pigeons cooing loudly and looked across the floor of the basement room to see Archie, legs crossed ankle on knee, an open book pinned down with one hand and a bread roll in the other, from which he occasionally flicked crumbs at a crowd of many sparrows and a few scruffy pigeons that had gathered about him. An unlit pipe protruded from the corner of his mouth and the whisky bottle from last night stood empty at his heel.

Jim sat up, rubbed his eyes and said 'Good morning'.

Archie looked up from his book.

'You slept well, Jim. Not a peep out of you all night.'

'Yes,' said Jim, coming over to squat down by the embers. He rubbed his arms and looked up at Archie.

And then: 'Thank you', although he was not quite sure why.

Archie shut the book, a slim volume that Jim did not manage to see the title of, and stretched. He gave a big yawn and threw his hat across the room to land neatly on an old peg still attached to the wall.

'Well I'm going to turn in, Jim,' he said, and then added:

'If you wouldn't mind clearing your stuff off my bed.'

Jim, slightly embarrassed at not having realised that the cardboard boxes were Archie's bed, quickly repacked his rucksack and then went to check on the trumpet case. He felt that he trusted this man and part of him wanted to show off the trumpet; indeed he was dying to play it again.

He looked round to see Archie settling, rearranging his bed, and thought better of it, for now anyway. Instead he hid the case better, finding an old fireplace covered by the rampaging buddleia, into which it fitted perfectly.

In the other room, Archie had removed his coat and was rolling his jacket up to use as a pillow. He then sat and removed his shoes, placing them neatly together at the foot of his bed, lay down and fell immediately to sleep.

Jim breakfasted on a fried egg sandwich at the local café. As the lady served him he asked if she knew anything about number seventeen and what had happened there during the war.

'Not me,' she said. 'I only moved here when it was all over.'

As he went up to pay she added, 'You should ask old Renee, she was born round the corner and she's lived here all her life.'

'Do you know where she lives?' asked Jim.

'I'm not sure, love but she always has half a stout in The Bell at opening time. You'll find her there at six on the dot or my name's not Marilyn Monroe.'

This raised a small cheer and some ribald comments from the workmen, who were eating massive plates of sausage, eggs and bacon in the little café.

Jim left, slightly puzzled, and went in search of The Bell.

He found the pub nearby but, being so early, it was closed. Walking the streets made Jim nervous after his narrow brush with the police car the day before. He decided to change his clothes as those given him by Old Tom seemed out of place here in the city and he did not like to stand out any more than necessary. He spent a couple of hours in some local thrift shops and furnished himself with a sports jacket, some men's slacks and a rather snazzy yellow jersey in lambswool with blue diamond shapes. Since he found he could only donate his old clothes rather than exchange them, all this hit Jim's pocket hard and he left the shop with only one of his ten-shilling notes and half a crown left.

After asking directions he found the local library off West End Lane and began looking through the old newspapers on file to see if he could learn anything more about the fate of number seventeen and its occupants during the war. After several hours of fruitless searching he finally came across a report in the Ham and High about a stray bomb that had destroyed a house in Belsize Road in September 1943. There was a picture of a pile of rubble and the article said it was believed there had been three casualties, but there was no mention of their names. He also looked through the relevant London telephone directory but there was no entry under Armstrong at that address. The rest of the time was filled by looking through the various newspapers and magazines on view and then, as the library closed, he headed off to The Bell.

His father had decried pubs as houses of iniquity and sin and Jim had always tried to catch a glimpse of what went on inside whenever he passed the open door of one, so there was a thrill of fascinated trepidation on entering the public bar of The Bell. The landlord had just opened up and the place was deserted, Jim was rather disappointed to find no more than a slightly tatty room with an old carpet and worn furniture. He ordered half a mild in his deepest voice and sat down in a far corner to await the arrival of Renee. Before long he heard the door of the snug bar swing open and the barmaid greeted an old lady, all in black, with what sounded like a familiar greeting.

'Usual?'

'Please, dear.'

Jim moved around to the other bar and found her seated alone in a big beam of amber light that shone through the wavy glass of the single window.

'Excuse me.'

The old lady looked up through her thick bottle glass spectacles. She seemed surprised.

'I was talking to Marilyn in the café this morning and she said you might be able to help me.'

The old lady's wrinkled brow knitted further.

'Marilyn, Marilyn who?' she said suspiciously.

'Marilyn Monroe.'

The old lady's head pulled back and the corners of her mouth turned down. She studied Jim, his sports jacket and fancy jumper.

'Are you one of those confidence tricksters, young man? I may be getting on but I've still got my wits about me,' she said loudly.

Jim felt flustered; this was not going to plan. The landlord suddenly appeared at the bar.

'Is this young man annoying you, Renee?'

Jim fought the impulse to run.

'It's about the war, I just wanted to ask you about the war,' he said desperately.

'Ah well then,' the old lady almost sang, 'come and sit down next to me, I can tell you all about that!'

Jim smiled nervously at the landlord who stood polishing a glass, with a wary expression. He sat down next to Renee who squeezed his knee surprisingly hard with a bony hand.

'Now, which war was it, young man? I've been through 'em all you know, the Boer War, the Great War, the last one.'

'Well it's the last one really, I was wondering…'

'I was in Portsmouth when it started, my 'usband, that's my second 'usband of course, he was a mid-shipman in the Merchant Marine, lovely man, younger than me y'know…'

Jim sat and listened. He leaned forward to try and ask Renee a question but she waved him away and carried on about the state of the house she had and the 'terrible long time' that her husband spent away from her at sea. After a few minutes he even looked up at the landlord for help but it was no use. He just smiled knowingly, placed a final glass on the shelf and moved off to serve someone in the other bar.

In a final desperate effort to get a word in, Jim asked Renee if she would like another drink. She heard this immediately and sent Jim up to the bar for another half a stout, only to change her order to a 'nice glass of port' once the stout had been poured.

'Medicinal you know,' she confided.

'Are you the one's got Renee taking about the war?' the barmaid asked, laughing. 'You'll be here all night!'

Jim sighed and took both drinks over to the table. He thought to have the stout for himself as it had been poured in error and he had had to pay for it, but Renee started on this no sooner than he had put it down.

Eventually, by constant interruption he managed to bring her to the point.

'Do you know about the bomb that hit seventeen Belsize Road?'

'Course I do, I was living at number twenty. Blew me clean out of bed it did. I should have been at work but I 'ad the flu...'

'Yes Renee but did you know the people who were in the house? Do you know who it was that was killed?'

She thought for a moment. The snug was quiet, motes of dust drifted slowly around in the beam of light from over her shoulder.

After a moment she spoke. Her voice had lost its stridency and for once she spoke slowly.

'They was all killed; blown to bits they were.'

She was silent.

'That poor woman.'

'What was her name?' asked Jim

She sat quietly, staring at the table.

'Her name, Renee, what was her name?'

'Can't recall now. Beautiful girl she was. So lively.'

She sat there sadly, the words, such a torrent so recently, entirely tailed off with the sadness of remembering.

'Was it Lizzie by any chance, Renee?'

Renee suddenly sat up straight and put her hand over Jim's.

'Elizabeth - that's what it was! But yes…mostly people called her Lizzie,' her eyes stared unseeing through her bottle glasses.

'Yes, that was it. That was her! How did you know that?'

She studied him for a minute through her wine bottle glasses. Her expression seemed to cloud over with apprehension and then she suddenly announced:

'I have to go, look at the time, *look* at the time.'

She got up and bustled out of the door.

The barmaid came over to collect the empties and wipe the table down.

'What's the matter wiv' her? She seen a ghost? Not like Renee to leave a full glass of port.'

'I'll have that,' said Jim, grabbing it before she could pick up the glass.

10 - Someone to Watch Over Me

Jim got back to the den feeling slightly light headed. He had never tasted port before, or indeed any other alcoholic drink, and despite an upbringing indicating that he was now destined for the fiery pits of hell, he quite enjoyed the slight sensation of giddiness it had induced. He sat down and considered the position of his soul. However much he tried to feel guilty he found that he couldn't. The port had been quite delicious, and how that, or music that touched your innermost feelings, could make God send you to hell for all eternity he couldn't imagine; it just didn't make any sense. The very thought that these things may not be true began to fill Jim with a heady sense of freedom and excitement.

Archie had left and he relished the chance to finally try out the glass trumpet properly. He took it from the case and for the first time got to examine it in full daylight and at leisure. His eyes and fingers traced the glistening curves of the bell and the fine intricacies of the valves and fittings. It seemed the only parts of the trumpet not fabricated from glass were the valve springs, and these were so fine and of such highly polished silver that they may as well have been. They returned each valve to its open position with a smooth, light and very satisfying action.

He started with some simple scales and the warm up exercises that he had learned in the school orchestra. These completed, he began the cadenza from Haydn's Trumpet Concerto, the one that he would have played on his trip to Leeds with the school orchestra. It was exhilarating. More than any other man made object, an instrument of the highest quality can seem to possess magical powers. Although an inanimate thing, it gives its user abilities that he never felt he possessed before. Passages where Jim previously felt he had to push the notes out of the trumpet seemed to just flow. Wherever he had doubts about the quality of his tone before, the trumpet sounded lyrical. He could tighten his lip and produce a sharp incisive tone or round it and almost imitate a French horn. The instrument needed less air than any he had played before; you felt as if you could open up a phrase with one breath and then play the piece almost to the end.

The music rose up through the leaves of the saplings and echoed slightly in the natural courtyard made by the sides and backs of the houses bordering the bomb-site. Jim closed his eyes and saw instead the receding rows of seats in the concert hall where he had been due to play. Although completely alone he felt the joy of connecting, through the music, to all the people sharing the evening with the orchestra and then felt that humble kind of pride you get when everyone applauds.

As it died away in his mind Jim realised that there was still one person clapping alone. He opened his eyes with a start to see Archie, halfway down the steps on the little landing, applauding and looking at him with a kind of earnest amusement on his worn face.

'Bravo, my boy.'

Archie came down the last few steps and over to Jim, placing a hand on his shoulder and holding Jim's eyes with his own.

'That,' he said, nodding slightly, 'was truly beautiful.'

He bent over to examine more closely the intricacies of the glass trumpet.

'My God, and so is this! And this is what brings you here, is it?'

Jim looked into the face that last night had frightened him with its desolation and saw only warmth and kindness.

'I suppose it is,' he said.

'Well...' cried Archie straightening up, '...musicians must be fed!'

From various pockets in his voluminous coat, Archie now produced the makings of dinner. He started the fire and, when it had settled, raked some embers to the side and began grilling bacon on an old fridge shelf set over them. A couple of eggs went into a small tin plate used as a frying pan.

Jim held the trumpet up to the light once more and peered at the tiny stave of music which curled around the bell. With much twisting around he managed to read it to the end, then put the trumpet to his lips and blew the tune straight out of it. It was beautiful and melancholy, the style readily suggesting itself from the music.

As dinner was about ready he put the instrument reluctantly away and sat down, finding his host strangely choked and, apparently, with something in his eye.

'Sorry old man…' said Archie clearing his throat and running a dirty sleeve across his cheek.

'That's such a lovely tune…we used to listen to a lot in the war. 'Someone to Watch Over Me', we could all do with that eh?'

Jim recognised the title from some of the words etched into the trumpet but let it go at that, as Archie seemed both upset, and embarrassed that he was.

He smiled, if a little sadly and handed Jim his plate of egg and bacon.

'Breakfast is served,' he said with a flourish.

'But it's dinner time,' Jim pointed out.

'Not for me.' Archie crouched down to put an old tin full of water on the fire.

'I'm on New Zealand time, old boy.'

They ate together in silence. Jim looked at Archie more closely now. Although he was a tramp he spoke quite properly, with an accent that would not have been out of place in a country house. He was, Jim decided, not quite as old as he had at first thought, mid to late forties perhaps. The clothes he wore, although old, tattered and none too clean, were well cut and looked to be made from good cloth. The overall impression was of a city gent, recently dug from the rubble of a bomb-site, possibly the one in which he now sat eating his dinner, which he called breakfast.

As they finished eating, the water in the tin can came to the boil and Archie made them both tea, using two more cans for cups.

'Have you always lived here?' Jim asked after a time.

Archie laughed and was thoughtful for a moment.

'I don't really 'live' here, Jim. This is just my West Hampstead residence. I come up here when the hurly-burly of the West End gets tiresome.'

'Where *do* you come from then?' asked Jim.

Archie handed Jim a tin cup that was so hot Jim almost dropped it immediately.

'Let me give you a tip, Jim. It's best not to ask people, people you meet on the road, as it were, about their past. Why they're here and so on. If they want to tell you then they will. Mostly we just don't want to talk about it.'

'A bit like prison?' Jim suggested helpfully.

He looked up at Jim with a raised eyebrow.

'What do you know about prison, young Jim?'

'I thought you weren't meant to ask.'

They both laughed a little.

'Nothing really, it's just something someone said to me.'

Archie went through his pockets again and produced a half bottle of whisky and a silver hip flask. He carefully poured the whisky into this and then returned the bottle to his pocket. Jim could not help but notice that his hand trembled while he did this and a little of the warm brown liquid ran down the side of the flask onto the floor.

***

He awoke the next morning to find Archie asleep, sitting up in the old chair by the fire, the whisky bottle, now empty, stood by the smouldering ashes. Archie sat leaning back in the chair with his head hanging down a little. As Jim came closer he could hear a faint muttering and realised that Archie was talking in his sleep. He stood before him, unsure of what to do. After a moment he gently jogged Archie's elbow and called his name softly. The result was a nasty shock.

Archie sprung suddenly to life and struck out wildly at Jim, he yelled and screamed incoherently while his eyes bulged with fear. Jim toppled backwards and nearly fell into the hot embers, finally coming to rest on the floor near his bed. The fit seemed to pass as quickly as it had begun and left Archie on his feet, panting and gasping. He looked wildly around him and then appeared to notice Jim, as if for the first time. All the strength went out of him and Archie fell back onto his chair, breathing rapidly. His head went into his hands. Jim saw the shoulders shaking slightly and realised that Archie was crying.

He didn't know what to do. The only adult he had seen cry was his mother and although that had happened fairly often it hadn't prepared him for this. He approached the figure of Archie cautiously and laid a tentative hand on his shoulder. Archie placed a hand over his and after a minute or so he looked up. His red eyes met Jim's, wide with alarm and Jim saw that his cheeks were wet with tears.

'I'm sorry, Jim, I didn't mean to frighten you.'

He took the boy's hand between his own and held it for a minute before looking back up at him.

'Never wake me, Jim. If you find me asleep leave me. I don't just mean leave me alone, I mean leave. Leave here, go away and come back later when I'm awake.'

Jim studied the worn face.

'Is that in case you go...you go...'

'Mad, Jim? No it's not so bad as all that really, I suppose. It's only dreams, bad dreams. Nothing for you to worry about. It's just best not to disturb me when I'm having one. Don't know where I am when I wake up you see.'

Archie still seemed shaken and Jim led him over to the bed and helped him from his coat and to lie down. He rekindled the ashes of the fire and put some water on to boil but found Archie fast asleep by the time he had made some tea.

He drank a cup by himself wondering what to do. He was keen to play some more but could not do it here in the den for fear of waking Archie. Also money was a worry. Plying Renee with drinks the evening before had drained away most of what he had left. Jim felt the first pangs of hunger as he finished his tea. He took the trumpet case from its hiding place and went up to the street. He wandered around for a while looking for another bomb-site so that he could play unobserved but could find none. In the end he settled for a small, quite secluded park that had nobody in it on a weekday morning.

He lifted out the trumpet and took some time examining its intricacies before running through his warm-up scales and then a little Mozart. The first couple of times somebody walked past he stopped playing and sat, embarrassed, as he waited for them to pass. On the third occasion however he had closed his eyes to recall some of the music from Lester's wagon. He found himself playing the opening bars to 'Crazeology', the twisty opening run spilling from the bell of the trumpet like so much water from a tipped up jug. He did not notice the approaching pedestrian until too late and opened his eyes again just in time to see a well-dressed man dropping what turned out to be a two-shilling piece on his jacket as he walked past.

Jim was surprised as he studied the coin but left it where it was. A few minutes later and there were two more; Jim played on. As lunchtime came the park saw more visitors, either bringing their sandwiches out into the sunshine or simply passing through. Jim's haul of coins grew. Some people even stopped to admire the sight of a young man making music on such an unusual instrument. Just when Jim had begun to think that his money worries were over, he found himself confronted by the authoritative figure of the park keeper.

'Pack that bloody thing away and off with yer.'

'But I'm only practising,' explained Jim.

This was not good enough for a stickler such as the park keeper.

'If you care to read the Borough Park Bylaws, section eight, which are properly displayed *at* the entrance to the park, *as* required by section eleven *of* the said bylaws, you will find that, and here I quote: 'The playing of musical instruments *for* the purposes of entertaining an audience or for financial gain of any sort *is* prohibited.' And I may well point out to you, young man, that it is within the power of the local magistrates to confiscate musical instruments and other related equipment *from* persistent offenders and that they have had recourse to this expedient in the not too distant past.'

Jim goggled up at the man and wondered what he was talking about. Whatever it was it seemed to include the possible stealing of the glass trumpet from him, so he was up and packed away in a flash. He did, however, leave the park with the happy sound of many coins jangling in his pocket.

He went to the local grocery store and bought provisions for 'breakfast' that evening, even pushing his luck and managing to buy a small bottle of whisky for Archie. The shopkeeper rolled his eyes just enough to indicate to Jim that he knew very well that he was underage and that the words '…for my father,' tacked on the end of his request were barely worth the breath it took to say them, but he sold Jim the whisky anyway.

Returning happily to the den, he found Archie newly woken, rubbing his eyes, stretching and yawning. Jim laid the provisions proudly before him, saving the bottle of whisky until last. This did, as Jim had hoped, please Archie greatly, and he looked at Jim with what Jim thought might just be a touch of admiration.

They ate the feast as Jim explained to Archie how he had come by the money, and indeed, a way of earning it from now on.

'Busker eh?' said Archie.

Jim had never heard the expression before but it sounded right enough. He tried it to himself a couple of times as he ate his supper, and thought of where he would busk next. He had seen the violinist in the underground and settled on that as the venue for his next performance.

***

It was with some apprehension that Jim carried the trumpet case to the bottom of the long escalator at Kings Cross. He had woken early that morning and left quietly, taking care not to disturb Archie who was dozing by the fire again.

He found a good spot, near the bottom of two escalators and in front of a poster of a well proportioned lady, advertising corsets. The rush hour was just beginning to get going and hundreds of people hurried past as he took out the trumpet and stood behind the open case, feeling exposed. It was as if you moved from being a private person to one whose business everybody knew by taking out an instrument in public.

He began playing from Haydn's Trumpet Concerto again, as a warm up but people immediately started dropping money into the open case. Jim became increasingly amazed at the interest he aroused. When he played the solo some people actually stopped to watch. They formed a little knot in front of him and eventually became a nuisance as, once a crowd forms that is large enough to block from view the object of their interest, passers-by want to know what is causing all the excitement, and the crowd gets ever larger as they stop to join.

This was all very well but the main effect was to dry up the regular tinkle of money falling into Jim's case, as people at the back could only see him by jostling others and peering over their shoulders. The solution, Jim discovered, was to stop playing altogether and pretend to start packing away the trumpet. This he had to do every few minutes in order to prevent his crowd of onlookers from blocking the way.

After an hour or so Jim heard the strident voice of the stationmaster asking the crowd to 'Please move along,' as they were blocking the way. Remembering the threats of the park keeper the day before, to have his trumpet confiscated, Jim put it hurriedly back in the case and disappeared into the crowd he had created, causing the stationmaster some confusion when he finally pushed his way through to find the space occupied by the centre of attention completely empty. He was left staring at the picture of the lady in the corset as the crowd dispersed around him.

Jim jumped on a Circle Line train and went along a stop to Euston where he set up again. This time it was another busker who tried to end the performance. A large grizzled man with a battered guitar pushed his way to the front of Jim's small audience.

'On yer way, sonny, this is my pitch,' he said, starting to push the trumpet case aside with one foot.

'Leave him alone, you bully!' said a woman's voice from the crowd. It was immediately joined by more voices agreeing, and amid a lot of jostling and pushing, someone threatened to do something quite horrible to him with his own guitar. In a moment or two he had been ejected from the crowd and went off issuing dire threats about what he was likely to do to next time he found Jim on 'his pitch'.

Jim played on for a few more minutes and then thought it best to quit while he was ahead, or the busker came back and found him without his protective crowd of admirers.

He caught a train back to what had now become 'home' in his mind and stopped to do some shopping on the way back from the station. This time he bought a full bottle of whisky and some chocolate for himself as well as a handsome stock of provisions for the den. He also bought Archie a newspaper and some pipe tobacco, figuring that the den was Archie's really and this would count towards his 'keep'.

When Jim reached the den he found Archie still asleep so he stashed the trumpet case in its hiding place, before taking the older man's advice and leaving him well alone. There was still plenty of money left so Jim gave himself a treat and caught the bus up to Swiss Cottage, where he went to the pictures and watched a film called Passport to Pimlico, about a lot of ordinary people declaring independence for their part of London. It was rather funny and heart-warming and the mood stayed with Jim all the way back on the bus.

When he got back to the den he found Archie wide awake reading the newspaper Jim had bought him, with the fire already going, some sausages sizzling away on the griddle and some water boiling for tea.

It was only after they had eaten that Archie called him over, the newspaper open on his lap.

'I think you'd better take a look at this, Jim.'

There, near the bottom of the page was an article with a small headline:

'Police Fear for Missing Boy', and a picture of Jim, taken in his Garside school uniform.

11 - Cologne

Jim was dumbfounded. He stared at the photo in shock and then read the article beneath.

Police yesterday issued this photograph of James Davis, who has been missing from his home in Highbury for the past four days. He is fourteen years of age with dark hair and brown eyes, five feet seven inches tall and described as shy and quietly spoken. His parents, Abraham and Emily Davis said yesterday that they were 'praying for his safe return'.
Anyone with any information as to James' whereabouts should contact Detective Inspector Sherwood at Scotland Yard on Whitehall 2737.

He sat down on an old orange box next to Archie's chair, staring at the article. Jim had felt hunted enough since escaping the police in Walsham-on-Sea but he now feared that setting foot outside the den could lead to an immediate end to his quest.

Archie regarded him silently, filling his pipe from an old silver tobacco tin. Eventually he asked:

'What are you going to do, Jim?' and blew out a large puff of smoke which was seized by the hot air rising from the fire and turned into a little mushroom cloud. Jim watched it billowing up to the ceiling.

'I can't go back. Not now.'

'When then?' asked Archie.

'No I didn't mean that. I didn't mean I might want to go back later, I mean I can't go back ever, after what's happened.'

'And why's that, Jim?'

'Well since I've discovered the glass trumpet, and being able to play it, and wondering who made it - and why they made it for me.'

Jim found himself telling Archie the story of his escape from home, his discovery of The House of Glass and the glass trumpet with his name on the case. He described his home life, his parents, mostly his father and the Church and the Great Schism and the beatings. He felt ashamed of these and found himself trying to persuade Archie that he somehow deserved them, that his father was doing it for his own good. Archie just harrumphed a bit and knocked his pipe out against his shoe. As it all came tumbling out of him Jim recognised his own life, as if for the first time. For some reason he felt tears rising, but kept his head low and stared into the fire as they ran down his cheeks, thinking that were he to wipe them away then Archie would be bound to notice that he was crying.

He finished his tale and leaned closer to the flaring embers so as to dry them more quickly and for a while there was quiet, save for the crackling fire.

After some time Archie seemed to make his mind up about something.

'What I'm going to tell you, Jim is something I've never told anyone before.'

He took a glass tumbler from his pocket and poured a generous tot of whisky into it.

'Not that it's a secret or anything, it's just that I've never put it into words before. Never explained it to anyone.'

There then came a silence so long that Jim thought Archie had changed his mind. Just as he was about to say something, Archie began.

'During the war…'

'The Second World War?' asked Jim.

'Yes, Jim, I'm not old enough for any other war, in spite of how I might appear. I was born just after the end of the First World War, which was just called the Great War back then, the War to End All Wars.' Archie laughed sardonically.

'And during the second 'War to End All Wars' I was a pilot in the RAF. I flew bombers, Lancasters.'

Jim was impressed; he had seen photographs of these huge machines and knew something of the dangers of flying in the Second World War.

'You mustn't forget, Jim, that we had been bombed pretty thoroughly by the Germans during the blitz. Our Chief, Bomber Harris, made up some line about how the Nazis, having "sown the wind" would "reap the whirlwind"'.

'No,' said Jim.

'No?'

'Well he didn't make it up anyway, it's Hosea from the Old Testament, chapter eight I think.'

'Oh, well, thank you for that, Minister,' chuckled Archie.

Jim blushed and made a mental note to try and ignore the many Bible quotations that littered everyday speech.

'Everyone, well nearly everyone in the country wanted us to strike back, for revenge I suppose, that and to help us win the war as quickly as possible. As it was, the war went on for many years, six altogether, and we certainly repaid the Germans for what they had done to us, and a lot more besides. We used to bomb them at night and during the day the Americans would take over.

'The problem we had with night bombing was accuracy. It was hard enough to hit a tank factory from thirty thousand feet in broad daylight but at night it was impossible.

'We used a technique called carpet-bombing, obliteration bombing some people called it. We would bomb a whole city and wipe out not only the factories, but all the housing for the workers and probably a lot of the workers too…and their wives…and their children.'

Archie paused to poke the fire back to life and take another drink of his whisky.

'And our chaps died by the cartload too. The chances of surviving a tour of thirty missions over Germany, without being shot down, was about four to one against. I made it through forty-nine missions.'

He sat, silent for a while, toying with his glass, swirling his drink around and watching the light of the fire through it.

'So did you retire then, after flying all those missions?'

'No, Jim. I wish I had. I was shot down on my fiftieth and final mission. It was over Cologne.'

Archie paused for another large bolt of whisky.

'We were on the final approach to the target; you're at your most vulnerable then. The air around the plane is filled with anti-aircraft fire. Huge bangs and great bursts of shrapnel everywhere. If you escaped that there were always the night-fighters waiting. You have to hold the aircraft very steady and straight, the bomb doors open and the bomb aimer giving you directions over the intercom. We had just dropped ours when an anti aircraft shell exploded near the starboard wing. It started a fire which began to spread pretty quickly. I managed to hold the aircraft more or less level while the crew jumped but by then the searchlights had us and every anti-aircraft gun in Cologne was shooting at us. I think a shell must have hit one of the fuel tanks because the whole aircraft more or less exploded. Somehow I managed to bail out but only just before she went in. I found myself floating down right over the target. It was awful. Terrifying. It was like being lowered slowly down into hell. I even heard bombs whistling past and saw them explode below. I felt the blast hit me and as I got lower I felt the heat from the thousands of fires. Somehow I managed to land in between them on a huge pile of smoking rubble. I rolled up my parachute as we had been trained and hid in one of the wrecked buildings on which I'd landed.'

Archie paused again, for such a long time that Jim thought he'd heard the whole story, or as much of it as Archie was prepared to tell. Finally he cleared his throat and leaned down, even closer to the fire.

'It was then I got to experience the other side of bombing. I thought I had been scared before, as a pilot, but it was nothing like this. Cologne was a thousand bomber raid, the first one ever, and my squadron was probably about halfway down the bomber stream. I cowered in this wrecked building while the bombs from another five hundred aircraft dropped around me. Once the fires had been started, you see, all the bombers would line up their bomb runs on them. They call it a stick of bombs because they land in a long line but there's only a few seconds between the first and last bomb going off. The explosions seem to race towards you at incredible speed and you know you're about to die and there's nothing on God's earth you can do to stop them. It's like a string of Chinese crackers going off but each cracker is a five hundred pound bomb. Whole buildings disappear in a blink. Trucks get thrown into the air with bodies and bits of bodies. All you can hear are the bombers overhead and the never-ending explosions. They were bombing the rubble. The raid seemed to last for hours though in fact it was only about an hour and a half. They must have dropped another ten thousand bombs on the city. By the end of it I was practically insane. I couldn't remember who I was or what I was doing there. I had lost the hearing in one ear and I was shaking uncontrollably. The last thing I remember that night was screaming as a stick of bombs ran towards me.'

Jim stole a look up at Archie and tried to imagine him screaming in terror. The face was deeply lined and the eyes stared into the fire, as if it were the remains of a bombed out city. Sitting as they were, in the ruins of number seventeen, with the crackle and smell of burning wood and the great piles of bricks everywhere, it was as if Archie had never escaped from his personal hell, as if he had taken it with him and recreated it wherever he was. Jim threw a couple of chair legs onto the fire and waited for Archie to continue.

'I came to at dawn. I was in the basement under a pile of bricks and timbers. I had been knocked out. Calling for help was impossible; my mouth was full of brick dust. Eventually I managed to get free and crawl up the rubble. I was desperate for water. There was a lot of shouting from outside and I climbed up to look out of a window hole.

'There was a crowd of Germans, civilians. They were mostly women and children with a few older men. They had hold of someone and were pushing him along. He was stumbling and tripping across the rubble. I tried to call out to them but my mouth and throat were so full of the brick dust no sound came. Then I realised that the man they had was in RAF flying gear. As they got closer I saw it was Billy Fraser, he was the bomb aimer from my crew.

'Then he tripped and fell down and they started to beat him. A German army lorry pulled up and some soldiers climbed out but they didn't try and stop the crowd. They were kicking him and punching him. I saw a hand, holding a brick go down again and again in the centre of the mob. Eventually an officer in charge of the soldiers fired a shot in the air and they cleared the crowd away. Billy just lay there all broken up. His head was caved in, probably by the brick. His arms and legs all stuck out at strange angles where they were broken. The soldiers came up and started to drag Billy's body away. He had been my best friend on the crew. We had been together since flying school.'

Archie paused to refill his glass and stare into the ashes. He seemed lost in his memories, as if Jim had not been there at all.

'What did you do?' he asked after a while.

'I hid. I realised the only chance I had of survival was to surrender to a German officer and hope that he wouldn't turn me over to the crowd. There was a broken water pipe in the basement of the building I was hiding in, so I managed to get a drink.

'Later I saw another German army lorry stop a few hundred yards away. As I struggled out from a gap in the rubble an old woman saw me. She started screaming 'Flieger, Flieger' and all the civilians picking through the remains of the buildings for survivors began to converge on me. I ran for it across the rubble. An old man blocked my path and I had to punch him on the jaw to get past. I remember the officer just standing there watching me come, his hands on his hips, as the crowd chased me. I think he was prepared to let them have their way if they could catch me. As it was I fell at his feet just as they were about to get me. He had to fire several shots in the air to get them back. Then his soldiers picked me up off the ground and just threw me in the back of the lorry.'

Archie dropped another couple of chair legs on the fire and they watched the flames leap up and lick around them.

'That's why I have to sleep on my own and in the day you see. It's the nightmares. I have them often and it's always the same. It's either the stick of bombs coming towards me or the mob. Funny thing is, Jim, I don't really blame them for what they did to Billy. Having been through it with them I could understand. They were mad with the fear of it. And they had all the grief too; it was their families under all that rubble.'

'What happened then?' Jim asked.

'Prisoner of war camp. It was pretty terrible. Once the war was nearly over they forced us to march away from the advancing British and American armies. There was little or no food and we were even attacked by our own aircraft, who mistook us for a retreating German army.'

'But when you got back to England, then what happened?'

'Well that's another story, Jim, and not one for tonight.'

Archie broke off as he was seized by a fit of coughing. Jim had noticed Archie cough before but nothing like this. The man was bent double in the chair, his eyes squeezed shut and coughing so hard he barely had time to draw breath between one bout and the next.

Finally it finished and Jim saw that Archie was exhausted. The old tramp looked as if he'd had the life wrung out of him. Jim stood up, took Archie by the arm and led him over to the bed.

'No, Jim, can't sleep in the night, that's when the dreams come. It's always worse in the night-time and sometimes I don't realise that the dream has finished when I wake up. I'm scared. Scared that I might...' Archie trailed off as he was seized by another bout of terrible coughing.

He was so tired there seemed no other option besides putting him to bed. As the hacking subsided Jim got him onto the pile of flattened boxes and covered him up with his coat. Archie seized him by the arm and looked up at him through bloodshot eyes.

'Don't stay here. Not tonight, not while I'm asleep. Promise me.'

Jim promised and Archie fell instantly to sleep, his body relaxing and his breathing becoming slower and easier.

He looked around, the fire was guttering and Archie's bottle of whisky stood near, almost finished as well. It was still relatively early in the evening and Jim wondered what to do, having promised Archie not to stay in the den.

On checking his money, Jim found that the evening's expenses had depleted it severely. Flushed by his success busking, Jim decided to try the evening crowd and see if they were as generous as the commuters.

He took the trumpet, borrowed Archie's hat, which had fallen to the floor during his coughing fit and headed for the West End.

***

Jim arrived at Piccadilly Circus somewhere in between the end of the rush hour and the arrival of the 'evening out' crowd. He found a good pitch and stood up behind his trumpet case with a lot more confidence than the day before, hoping that the combination of having Archie's hat on his head and a trumpet in front of his face would avoid him being recognised from his picture in that evening's paper.

Business was brisk and as the station got busier the money started to rattle into the case with satisfying regularity. He still had to use his ruse of pretending to pack up once in a while, when his new fans threatened to obscure him from his paying audience and once, when he looked up into their faces, he saw the frowning features of the violinist he had seen playing a few days before. Jim was tempted to wink but decided instead to ignore the competition. He was playing more and more jazz now, stuff he had heard from Lester's collection on the train journey, but with little additions of his own. Although he had only listened to this once, Jim's ability to recall anything he had heard, as if it were playing back to him in his head, meant that he had become very familiar with Dizzy Gillespie and Charlie Parker over the last few days.

If anything, the evening crowd were more generous than the daytime travellers. Jim took a break to buy himself some food and resumed playing on a different pitch when he returned, as another busker had taken the first.

He had been playing for some time when the people before him were shouldered aside by a large figure in blue. Jim's blood froze; it was a policeman. He had Jim by the collar before he'd even had time to put the trumpet down.

'Right, son, put that away, you're coming with me.'

12 - Harry Brisk

*A*s he was miserably packing away his trumpet, one of his audience, a broad man in a beautifully cut camel-hair coat, came to a stop by the escalator. He turned and started back towards Jim and the policeman. He removed his hat, to make it harder to identify him as one of the crowd that had been standing around Jim when the policeman had arrived.

Jim was just clicking the catches shut on his case as he came striding up to them.

'What's the problem here, officer?' he asked, his voice fairly crackling with charm.

'He's been busking, sir. That's an offence under the London Transport bylaws.'

The broad man shook his head regretfully and then bent over Jim and said gently:

'I've warned you this would happen, Steven; it's not what your mother would have wanted.'

As he spoke he gave Jim a sly wink. Jim did not know much about sly winks but he knew that this one meant: 'play along.' Jim hung his head and almost without a thought said, 'Sorry.'

'Is this your son, sir?'

He swung round to face the policeman.

'Nephew, officer, I'm terribly sorry about this but…'

He led the constable away a few steps and spoke to him in a conspiratorial tone for a minute or so. The policeman looked over at Jim a couple of times during their conversation and nodded. There was a swift handshake and then he strode off, slipping his hand into his trouser pocket as he went.

The broad man put his hat back on his head, stuffed his paper under his arm and came back over to Jim.

'Right, young fella, you're coming with me, quick as you can now.'

He picked up the trumpet case himself and swung off down one of the tunnels, beckoning Jim to follow. Within a minute or so they came up into the street where the stranger waved down a taxi with his newspaper and helped Jim into the back of it.

'Black Cat Bar and Grill please, driver,' he called as he settled down comfortably in his seat.

'So, James, I find you at last.'

Jim looked up at the face lit by the passing lights of the city. It was a strong looking face, and Jim was reminded of the giant statues of Easter Island he had seen on the cover of one of the books he used to look through, back in the days when he spent his lunch-hours hiding from Cracker in the school library.

The wide mouth smiled but Jim noticed that the eyes didn't join in.

'Who are you?' he asked nervously.

'I, Jim, am your new manager; Harry Brisk.'

Jim was surprised by this but made no comment.

The man held out a hand that nearly crushed Jim's own as they shook.

'But how do you know who I am?' he asked.

'Oh that's easy.' He snapped open the paper and folding it, handed it to Jim, the photograph of himself uppermost.

'I don't suppose you've seen that or you wouldn't have risked busking down the West End,' he chuckled. Jim felt foolish and said nothing.

'One of my blokes came in this evening and said he'd seen some kid playing some very passable jazz on a glass trumpet down the tube. Well, I'm not the kind of man, James, who lets things such as that just pass me by. And blow me down if when I finally find you, aint you the spit of the kid in this evening's paper. I was just going to introduce myself when the copper turns up. Still, we made short work of him, eh?'

The cab pulled up outside the bar and grill where an enormous man in a dinner jacket swung open a wide black plate-glass door on which was outlined the head of a cat, its right eye winking.

'Evening, Mr Brisk,' he said, taking his boss's coat from his shoulders.

'Eugene,' he replied, dropping his hat in his hands and leading Jim into the club.

He took Jim up a wide curving set of steps which had lights built into them and swung open the door at the top for him. Jim gasped quietly as he stepped into the club. The space swept away from him towards a stage as wide as the room itself. The edge of it was an elegant curve and set before it, in the velvety darkness, were many round tables, each with its own soft light in the centre. Further tiny lights dotted the ceiling and secluded booths ringed the perimeter of the place. On the far side a barman in an immaculate white jacket polished tumblers and placed each on a glass shelf with a neat click. There was a smell of leather and deep carpet. For the first time in his life Jim understood the meaning of the word luxury.

The quietness of the scene was suddenly undone by the sound of female voices and, from the right side of the stage, a string of girls in glittering costumes, with almost impossibly long legs appeared and formed a line.

From out of sight behind them came a fussy voice.

'Okay, girls, now remember Lily sets the height and I want it *high*!'

A piano started and straight away, the girls, linked arm over arm, began to high kick in perfect tempo. Jim's mouth fell open and stayed that way.

Eventually Harry Brisk came back from talking to his barman and led Jim away past the front of the stage and through a door marked 'Private'.

'Come on,' he said. 'There'll be plenty of time for eyeing up the birds later.'

Jim flushed red as he followed Mr Brisk upstairs and entered a large office. There was one small grimy window, with mismatched panes of frosted and plain glass, which let in so little light it was as though the place existed in permanent night-time. Posters all over the walls showed similar lines of dancing girls to those downstairs, all glittering costumes and tall plumed headdresses. There was a picture of lady with a snake and a man with a glass in one hand and a cigar in the other, singing in a lone spotlight. Set in the back wall behind the desk was a long illuminated tank that contained a single large fish, a miniature ruined castle and some fronds, which waved slowly back and forth in a stream of bubbles. With a jerk of fear, Jim saw a revolver lying at one end of the desk.

Mr Brisk put the trumpet case on the other end and sat down heavily in the deeply buttoned leather swivel chair, his back to the morose looking fish in the tank.

'Now then, James, I'm willing to take you on here at The Black Cat; there'll be no more busking for you.' He reached into a drawer and withdrew a piece of paper, on which there was a lot of very tiny writing.

'Providing my musical director agrees, you can start tomorrow night. There's a show on the hour every other hour, the hour in between is for the girls to get to know our clientele better. You see…James,' Mr Brisk cocked his head on one side, as if to examine the imitation chandelier that lit the room, '*intimacy*' is the watchword here; we like to create an *intimate* place for our regular gentlemen customers. You can play with the main band during the show and, as long as Barney agrees, you can play with the trio during the intervals, they provide what we call the mood music, they help set the right atmosphere, you know, a *friendly and warm* atmosphere, James.'

It seemed as if he was trying to explain something; something other than what he was actually saying, but Jim was not sure exactly what.

Mr Brisk signed the bottom of the piece of paper before turning it round and sliding it across the desk, handing Jim his large gold fountain pen. Jim looked at the tiny writing. He tried to read it but not only were the words very small, they were very confusing. There were many 'hereinafters' and 'theretofores', all the sentences seemed extremely long and many mentioned several other sentences and paragraphs as they went along.

'Any questions? No I thought not. You sign…'

Here Mr Brisk planted a thick finger on the page next to his own signature.

'Just there.'

Jim wavered, the pen heavy in his hand.

He looked at Mr Brisk across the desk. He had such an air of confidence that it seemed impossible for Jim to do anything other than what he was told.

'How much will I get paid?' asked Jim tentatively.

'James, James, all your financial affairs will be looked after by the Brisk organisation, it's all part of the management service that we offer. As a minor you will naturally get a suitable living allowance and of course something for your travel. The rest we will invest in your future. Think of this as a kind of…of,' here Harry Brisk looked again to the ceiling as if seeking the right word. His fingers drummed against one another, a ruby ring flashed briefly in the light from the chandelier.

'…apprenticeship, James, in the business. We're here to teach you all there is to know about show business.'

'Can I think about it?' asked Jim.

'Yes,' said Mr Brisk, but there was something in his tone, a touch of surprise that Jim should even ask such a question and there was a slightly mocking note as well.

'You, just…think about it…young James.'

Mr Brisk leaned back in his swivel chair and produced a bottle of whisky from one of the desk draws, then poured himself a drink and took a cigar from an ornate carved box. He rolled it between his big fingers and then picked up the gun. Jim realised with relief that it was a lighter and having fired up his cigar Mr Brisk settled back with his feet up on the end of his desk and pretended to re-read the article about the young runaway.

'What if I don't want to do show business?' asked Jim after a while.

'Well, Jim, I think in that case we should have to, in your best interests of course, hand you over to those who are looking so hard for you. Can't leave you wandering the streets of London can we? There's all sorts out there!'

Jim sat there, still, holding the pen and staring suspiciously at Mr Brisk.

'And as for this…' he tapped the tip of his shoe against the side of the trumpet case, '…must be worth a small fortune, something like that! We wouldn't want to risk something beautiful and rare like that getting broken would we now, James?'

Jim said nothing

'Would we?'

Jim knew then that he had no choice, but realising that Mr Brisk had no idea what his signature would look like, he switched the pen to his left hand, before signing the document with an extraordinary series of flourishes. Harry Brisk looked dubiously at the contract, before filing it in the cabinet by the desk. He picked up the trumpet case and opened the office door, ushering Jim down the stairs.

'The girls will have finished rehearsal for now; I'll introduce you to your new boss, James.'

He led the way backstage and opened the door on a small grubby room, lit by a single bare bulb. In it sat three middle-aged men, one reading the paper and the other two playing cards. They all looked up in surprise at Harry Brisk and Jim.

'What's this?' said the oldest, looking over his half moon glasses and squinting through the smoke rising from his cigarette.

'This, as you put it, Barney, is the first instalment of that brass section I promised you, or should I say…glass section.' Harry Brisk chuckled at his own joke and at the confusion it caused Barney.

He introduced Jim and then left immediately. The three musicians looked at each other, then they looked back at Jim, then Barney jumped up and ran out of the room after Harry Brisk.

'Now hang on a minute, Harry!' Jim heard him say.

There followed a brief conversation from which Jim overheard the phrase 'Just a kid!' more than once. After a minute Barney's voice went silent and Jim heard the much lower, quieter tones of Harry Brisk, then Barney was back in the room looking a little pale. He ground out his cigarette, which had already been down to the filter tip when he dashed after Harry Brisk, and looked up at Jim.

'C'mon kid, follow me, let's see what you got,' he said wearily.

He led Jim out onto the stage where he was instantly dazzled by the lights. From the darkness beyond came a loud wolf-whistle and some raucous female laughter.

'Brought us a new plaything, Barney?' shouted a woman's voice with a cockney accent. The girls had finished their rehearsal and were gathered around the bar. There followed more laughter and some more remarks that made Jim flush red again.

'Aw, Alice, you've made 'im blush!'

Barney sat down at a beautiful black Bechstien grand piano, near the side of the stage.

'Right,' he said looking at the case in Jim's hand. 'Did you bring anything with you, any music?'

Jim shook his head.

'Okay, we'll start off easy.' He shuffled through some music manuscripts on top of the piano.

Jim looked on nervously. Although he could sight-read music he didn't think that this would work very well with the jazz that was probably required here.

'Do you know 'Groovin High?' he asked Barney.

'Course I do, kid but let's keep our feet on the ground here, what are you sixteen, seventeen?'

'Fifteen,' lied Jim. 'Nearly sixteen.'

Barney didn't look up at Jim, just shook his head and went on through his manuscripts.

'I haven't got the music here, I know the piano part anyway but what are you goin' to do?'

Jim was kneeling down, flicking open the catches on the trumpet case.

As he lifted it out into the light there was a gasp from the girls gathered round the bar near the back of the club. Jim felt himself grow a couple of inches with pride. Barney stopped riffling through his music scores and goggled at the sight of it.

'What the bleedin' heck? Are you having a laugh or something?'

'No, it's a real trumpet,' said Jim, 'it's just made of glass, that's all.'

He slid a mouthpiece into position and stood up.

'The first part is a duet with sax but I can just play that part my own if you'd like.'

He raised the glass trumpet to his lips and began to reel off the intro to 'Groovin High'. Again the trumpet amazed Jim. All his nerves blew away with the first few notes and from then it seemed to just play the music Jim heard in his head. Thought and action were one and the transparency of the horn itself made it seem as if it were not there at all. It was as if Jim had applied a valve to his lips and the liquid music flowed out, and across the dark plush acre of The Black Cat.

Before the first few bars of the song were out, the girls had gathered at the foot of the stage and the other two members of the trio appeared curiously in the wings. Barney beckoned them over with a wave of his head.

The younger of the two played bass, he was quite tall and gangling with red hair that stuck out here and there. The other, who was shorter and of similar age to Barney, settled behind the drums and began rattling out the rhythm with a set of brushes.

There was no doubt about it now, they swung from the get go. The girls were clicking their fingers and two of them began to dance with each other. When Jim finally pointed the trumpet up at

151

the ceiling and brought the number to an end with a long high note, everyone, even the hardened old hand that was Barney, burst into spontaneous applause.

'Well you got something there kid, that's for sure.'

He introduced Jim to the band, Oscar on bass and 'Snap' who turned out to be American, on drums. They both smiled at Jim as they shook his hand and for the first time in his life he felt as if he was one of them, a grown up, even if Barney did only ever seem to call him 'kid'.

They played on, through the rest of Jim's small jazz repertoire, and he felt himself stepping through that big door that had opened to him on Lester's train just the other morning. Music was another place, Jim had always known that, but he'd never known that it was somewhere you could have such freedom, where you could hold your horses or let them run, where one player could pose a question and the other respond with another and then they could play the answer together. They finished up playing 'Tenderly', a Chet Baker tune from some sheet music that Barney had. It was, he explained, a style more in keeping with the ambience of The Black Cat.

As they finished Jim found the club coming back into focus, Snap and Oscar shaking his hand and Barney clapping him on the back. They all examined the glass trumpet in amazement and asked him where he had come by it. Jim just shrugged and told them it was a long story.

Barney agreed that Jim could start the next night so he would have a chance to learn the band's set. He dropped most of the sheet music he had on the piano into a worn attaché case for Jim to practise with and then went up to see Mr Brisk.

Jim, having put the glass trumpet carefully away, found himself being dragged over to the bar by the girls. They asked him what he wanted to drink and laughed at him when he said lemonade. They sat him on a stool and teased him about his hair which, they said, needed cutting. They flirted with him and made him blush, for which they teased him, which made him blush some more. The bossiest one said her name was Camille, but her friend whispered in Jim's ear that it was Edna really and that her name was Olive but that he should call her Suzie.

They made Danny the barman give him a whisky and when Jim couldn't drink any of it they gave him lemonade, but had Danny slip a shot of vodka in it when his back was turned. When it was all getting a little too much for Jim he was rescued by a small dark-haired girl who pointed out, in a strong Irish accent, that it was opening time in five minutes and there would be trouble if Mr Brisk were to catch them at the bar. They all went clattering off backstage together in their high heels for a 'touch-up' and left Jim, his head spinning slightly, sat at the bar with just his rescuer for company.

'Hello. I'm Molly,' she said, putting a tray of cigarettes and cigars down and holding out a hand.

She was pretty, with almost black hair and a pointy little nose over a big smile. Her blue eyes were as pale as her skin and her voice was deeper than one would have expected from someone so petite, and had a sort of break in it, which made Jim feel a bit funny. He shook her hand, which was warm with immaculate long red fingernails, and introduced himself as Jim.

'Don't worry about them,' she said of the retreating chorus girls. 'They love to embarrass men.'

She slid onto a bar stool and asked Danny for a ginger ale. Jim stared at her and wondered at the strange feeling of being referred to as a man for the first time in his life. He looked at her. The black hair was tucked behind her ear on one side and she had to run it back into place with a quick trace of her fingernail every now and again. Her mouth pursed slightly as she sorted through her handbag for some lipstick, which she then put on with the help of a tiny mirror. She turned to talk to Jim and he wondered at how neat and precise it made her mouth look and the shape her lips made in forming the words. When her voice ceased Jim realised, that although she had been talking to him, he hadn't listened to a single word. He squeezed his eyes shut and replayed the sound of her voice:

'So where did you learn to play jazz? Everyone our age just wants to play rock and roll or skiffle these days,' she had said.

When he opened them again she was looking askance at him over her ginger ale.

'Are you okay?' she asked.

'Oh, yes, I ummm…I just picked it up from some records I heard.'

'Well I suppose you had to, I can't imagine it's possible to write stuff like that down!'

They both laughed and Jim searched his brain for something to say. Nothing came. Molly called over to Danny to put her bag behind the bar and then got down and waved Jim over to one of the darker seating booths in the corner of the club. He took the trumpet case and joined her in the gloom.

'Where did Harry find you then?' she asked, her voice low.

Jim decided to be honest.

'The tube, I was nearly arrested for busking.'

'And what's the deal?'

'The deal?'

'Yes, the deal with Harry, how many shows, what's he going to pay you?'

'Well he said I could play with the band and between the shows with the trio. He didn't say much about money, just that it was a sort of apprenticeship. Oh, and that he would be my manager.'

Molly snorted at this.

'Well listen, Jim; you be careful. I've been here for months and I was meant to be singing but all he's let me do so far is peddle fags to the punters. It's always 'when we can get the new show up' and 'when I get a new musical director' and crap like that. With talent like yours you don't need

Harry Brisk but once he gets his claws into you, well, it's hard to get them out again.'

She reached across the small table and took Jim by the wrist, dropping her chin and looking at him out of the top of her eyes for emphasis.

'You need to be careful, Jim.'

'How do you mean?'

He noticed her eyes flicker over his shoulder.

'Hang on….Hello, Eugene.'

The big doorman came over and gave Jim the attaché case of music.

'Barney has told Mr Brisk that he wants you to start tomorrow. That's the music for the set and…'

He reached into his pocket and pulled out a large note.

'There's a fiver for your first week.'

Jim got up to go. He reached down to pick up the trumpet case but found a large foot placed on its top.

'The trumpet…' Eugene said with an air of finality, '…stays here.'

13 - Breakfast with Molly

Jim looked up at him.

'No, it can't, it can't stay here, how can it? I need to practise, besides it's mine.'

Jim reached for the handle but found his arm wrenched away.

'Mr Brisk says it stays…so it stays.'

'Now, Eugene,' said Molly.

'You stay out of this, it's orders.'

Jim suddenly lost all reason, he howled and screamed, he became a flurry of wind-milling fists but Eugene just laughed and kept him at bay by planting a large hand on his forehead. Danny the barman put away his cloth and came over while Molly sat looking on in horror, both hands covering her mouth.

'It's no good, shrimp…' Eugene laughed, '…you'll never lay a fing…'

Jim had suddenly twisted his head away causing him to lurch past Eugene's extended arm. One of his flailing fists connected somewhere below the belt and the big man let out a bellow like a bull.

Despite the pain Eugene still managed to pick up Jim and stuff him under one arm like a naughty toddler, before carrying him down the stairs and throwing him into the back alley. As he dusted off his hands he explained what exactly was required of Jim, if he were ever to see his precious trumpet again. This was fairly straightforward and went something along the lines of:

'Mr Brisk, he's the boss, you'll do what he wants or you'll be sorry.'

Eugene slammed the stage door shut and left Jim lying between the bins under a sign that said: 'Strictly No Loitering'.

He lay there a moment, feeling a little ridiculous in his sports jacket, the tears welling up, the fury battling the anger and not a little pain where he had hit the ground so hard. The absence of the trumpet case felt like a hole in his side.

He rattled the door and looked up at the drainpipes, which scaled the gloom, wondering if he could break back in. After a while he became calmer, he had not, after all, so much lost the trumpet as found a job. If it meant working for Mr Brisk then he would just have to overcome his misgivings. Besides, there was bound to be an opportunity to escape his grip, trumpet and all.

He circled the building and came back to the front where Eugene waved him away, telling him to come back tomorrow.

Jim caught a bus back up towards the den, stopping for fish and chips on the way. He found Archie awake by the fire and they sat and shared the meal in silence before Jim made them both a tin cup of tea.

'How did you get on today?' Archie eventually asked him.

'Fine, I think I may have got a job,' answered Jim. 'Playing.'

Archie didn't press him for details but ruffled his hair and sent him to bed.

'Well done, Jim, best get some sleep, I'll take the night watch, as usual.'

Jim settled down in the corner feeling strangely at home in the bomb crater that was number seventeen.

He spent the next day trying to change his appearance some more, buying some scissors from the corner shop and having Archie cut his hair. He also bought some hair dye but after reading the instructions realised that he would need a fully functioning bathroom to use it.

The new haircut did not prevent Renee recognising him in the street. She stopped him by the post office and said she had something he should see, something to do with '…that poor woman', as she put it. Jim was intrigued but could not get her to say more on the subject.

'I'll see you at six in The Bell, young man,' was all she would say. Jim tried to explain that he had an appointment and ask her if they could rearrange but the old lady just carried on chuntering on about 'terrible shame' and 'that poor woman' as she bustled away to get her pension.

Jim explained his problem to Archie and at his suggestion agreed that Archie should go instead.

He got the bus down to Piccadilly in the rush hour and was at The Black Cat by six. Eugene let him in with no mention of the scenes of the night before and Jim was soon sat in the back room with the band going through the set for the evening. Just before they took to the stage the door opened and Barney introduced him to Stanley, a sax player from 'way back'. Stanley had a shock of blond hair that stood up from his forehead like a wave and a smile as bright and quick as a light bulb.

'I've been hearing great things, thought I'd barge in,' he said, shaking Jim by the hand. They took the stage from the girls and set about 'Night in Tunisia', Stanley's opening phrase sending a ripple up Jim's spine that made his hair stand on end.

They played a new show tune for the girls to dance to and then Barney motioned to the small dark figure of Molly at the back of the bar.

'C'mon, darling, we've got it all here, let's do it, I don't give a fig what Harry says.' Molly put down her cigarettes on the edge of the stage and took a microphone from the wings. Barney wouldn't start until someone manned the follow spot and then they launched into 'My Heart Belongs to Daddy'. Jim was surprised at the huge sound from the slight figure of Molly and how she actually seemed to grow in the power of the beam, until she owned the whole stage and the room beyond it.

She split him off from the band as the rehearsal broke up and took him backstage where she and the other girls attempted to rescue some semblance of a style from the haircut that Archie had given him. They put his head over a sink and used the whole bottle of hair dye that he had brought with him. He finished the process looking like a blond bottle-brush but still with his own dark eye-brows. Molly found him an old evening suit which she and the girls took in crudely with a few stitches and by the time the band were due on at ten he had at least begun to look the part.

***

Jim's first ever hour on stage in front of an audience was less nerve racking than he might have expected. The place filled up slowly as shadowy figures were led to various tables and booths around the club. Barney introduced each jazz standard and he and the band would play through it quietly. Once or twice he turned to them and gestured 'softly, softly' with the palm of his hand turned down.

After nearly an hour the club was reasonably full and a man with slick black hair took the mike and introduced himself as Max 'West End' Williams.

'Your host for this wonderful evening.'

With a sweep of his hand and a fanfare from the band the girls came on doing the high kick that Jim had seen in rehearsal, while the band blew a big showtune. Jim ran through the set with no problems, casting barely an eye over the score and even playing a short quiet solo at one point.

***

After an hour or so they had an intermission while a comedian took a turn. Barney sat them down in the band room and tried to explain, particularly to Stanley, the low key required.

'It's mood, Stanley, that's all Brisk wants. He just wants a jazz atmosphere; these punters of his, they don't know nothing about real jazz, it's just a style thing.'

He handed the sax player a whisky and lit them both cigarettes.

'You get up there and start blowing like I know you can and I'll be out of a job before you can say Dizzy Gillespie.'

'So why bother with a band at all then?' asked Stanley, reasonably enough.

'He could play some bloody elevator music and save himself a few bob.'

'It's all image, Stanley, image, mate. That's why he likes the kid here, with 'is glass trumpet. What's important about The Black Cat is the business that's done here. All that talk in dark corners, that's what it's all about. That's why he runs the place. This is where the deals are done. Stuff we're better off knowing nothing about, right?'

Despite Barney's wishes the band began to wind up more and more during the evening and seemed to gain the audience's blessing, the muted applause growing with each number and even a few cheers from the darkness at the end of 'Slow Boat to China'.

As Jim clicked the catches shut after the last number he was disappointed to find Eugene standing over him waiting to take the trumpet case upstairs, to the safe in Mr Brisk's office. The club closed at three-thirty and Jim found himself leaving though the stage door with Molly, scuffing through the litter-strewn alley to Kingly Street. She stopped him just as they were about to part.

'Where are you living, Jim?'

'With a friend, up in Kilburn.'

She straightened his jacket and brushed her fingers brusquely through his home-grown haircut.

'It's just that…well…is there a bathroom, Jim?'

Jim looked at his shoes and shook his head.

'Thought not,' she said and waved her hand under her nose. They both laughed, Jim with embarrassment.

'Well I'm taking you home with me, let's see if we can't polish you up some more.'

As they were about to leave, the stage door opened and Katie, one of the chorus girls, came stumbling out. She seemed upset and Molly made Jim walk behind while she took her friend's arm and they went down towards Piccadilly Circus. Molly soon had them in a black cab and Jim sat shyly in the corner while Katie sobbed into a succession of tissues provided by Molly.

'How could he?' was all she seemed able to say.

The girls shared a large room in a house in Camden, and it appeared that Jim was to have used Katie's bed, as she had expected to spend the night elsewhere. As it was, Molly made him a bed of couch cushions on the floor and gave him Katie's fur coat as a cover. He drifted off as the eastern sky lightened in the tall windows and the dawn chorus began to tune up.

He was woken by Molly shaking his shoulder and found himself staring at a steaming cup of tea and a rather black piece of toast.

'I've run you a bath, I'm off to the launderette with this lot...' she waved his clothes at him, '...you can wear my dressing gown 'til I get back.'

Jim locked the bathroom door behind him and then started a little at the sudden appearance of a stranger, who turned out to be his own reflection, in the mirror. He looked at the blond hedgehog haircut and his now even more slender figure. The face was the biggest surprise; his boyish features had been sharpened and hardened, perhaps with hunger, perhaps by experience. The feeling of looking at someone else was uncanny and Jim realised that he had never really considered before the person that he was. Was it this stranger in the mirror? Is that what Molly saw when she looked at him? He tried to put on a more adult expression, a knowing smile and then a cool look, the kind of thing that belonged on the face of a real jazz musician. Leaning forward he realised with a shock that he would need a razor for the first time.

He climbed into the bath, an enormous affair, with ball and claw feet. Molly had filled it with sudsy water to such a degree that Jim found that he had to sit bolt upright. Any attempt to rest back found him sliding beneath the surface, his head going all the way under before his feet found the end. Jim sat a long time, this being a rare treat; his father had viewed a hot bath as the beginning of a long slippery slope towards damnation.

Eventually he made his way back up to Molly's room on the landing above and sat on her bed wrapped in her dressing gown, watching the lunchtime traffic circulate outside. Before long Katie began to stir and she was soon sitting up in bed rubbing her eyes. She said a sleepy good morning to Jim and as he turned to wish her the same she threw back the covers and got out of bed. Jim realised with a shock that she was completely naked as she walked across the room to her wardrobe. He snapped back round to the window feeling the blood flushing his face completely red.

'Ah, Jim...' she said coming across the room to him and tying up her robe...'you've never seen a woman naked before have you?'

She laughed and planted a kiss on his forehead.

'First time for everything…' she said in a sing-song voice as she headed for the bathroom, passing Molly coming back into the room with a bulging laundry bag.

Molly looked after her, dropped her bag and came straight over to Jim

'What did she…'

Jim pointed at his forehead where there was a faint mark left by last night's lipstick.

'That girl!' said Molly shaking her head and polishing it off with a hanky and some spit.

'Right, I've washed your stuff and found you a few bits and pieces down the market. You can pay me back later.' She brought out a succession of second hand shirts, collars and trousers, all of which seemed to fit Jim well enough. There was a pair of Oxfords, which Molly buffed up and replaced the laces of before declaring that Jim 'would do'.

She took him to a café round the corner and ordered them both breakfast, although it was nearly lunchtime.

'So…' she said over her coffee, '…this friend, the one you live with, doesn't he care for little things like laundry, or a bath?'

Jim shook his head.

'Not really. He doesn't seem to care for…' Jim thought for a moment, '…well, much really. He had a bit of a rough time in the war.'

'Family friend?'

'No. My family don't really have any friends.'

Molly said nothing but just looked at him over her coffee cup. Jim had finished his own and Molly's silence seemed like a question; a question about everything. He found himself continuing, he told her about his father and the Church and the Great Schism and Garside and his flight to the coast to find out about The House of Glass. Molly ordered more coffee and kept him talking with her special way of saying nothing, except 'Go on' with her eyes. Jim found he wanted to tell her everything, just because having her attention suddenly seemed more important than almost anything else.

He found his own voice difficult. It no longer seemed to know what key it was in, and kept swapping lower, gruffer notes for his normal ones.

In the end Jim finished his story and excused himself from talking more by asking her about Katie and why she had been upset.

Molly lit a cigarette and offered one to Jim. He took a light from her, wanting to join in, but had to give up after disturbing the peace of the café by nearly coughing himself unconscious. She stubbed it out for him remarking: 'Never mind, they say it's bad for you anyway.'

When he had recovered she told him, in confidential tones, all about Katie. She was relatively new at The Black Cat having come up to London from Devon to audition for one of the big West End shows. When she had failed to get the part, one of Harry's side-kicks had consoled her by bringing her along to The Black Cat and fixing her up with a place in the chorus. Molly had just taken on the room in Camden and was in need of someone to share the rent, so Katie had moved in straight away. She had barely spent a night there since. She was 'Harry's favourite girl', and as such spent most nights at his flat overlooking Hyde Park and often had evenings off escorting Harry to 'business meetings' or 'charity evenings'.

Molly had seen this process before and had tried to warn Katie but was just waved away.

'Harry's a sweetie,' was all Katie would say. After a few weeks she had even begun to talk about; 'When we're engaged,' and nothing Molly could say would make the slightest difference.

Last night Harry had not only failed to take her home to Hyde Park but had actually tried to 'fix her up', as she put it, with one of his visiting business associates. When Katie had remonstrated with him backstage all she received was a slap round the face and instructions to make sure this friend of Harry's 'enjoyed his stay in London'. Instead, she had got her coat and fled into the night with Molly and Jim.

'There'll be trouble tonight,' said Molly ominously, stubbing out her cigarette and going up to pay for their breakfast.

Molly, it was to turn out, was more right than she could possibly have known.

14 - The V.I.P.

Jim left the girls at five as he had promised Barney he would come in early for another rehearsal. The fact is he would have come in even earlier if there had been anyone available to let him in and free the glass trumpet from Harry Brisk's safe. Time spent away from his precious instrument left Jim feeling anxious and unsettled and he had even taken to carrying one of the glass mouthpieces wrapped in a handkerchief in his pocket. He would take this out and play gently to himself when alone, helping to maintain his trumpet player's lip in good working order.

He found Stanley there already with a pile of jazz records he wanted Jim to listen to. 'You need to know this stuff, Jim, this is our history, this is where it all comes from.'

They started with some dixieland on old 78's and began working their way through some of jazz's greatest trumpet and sax players. Stanley, as it turned out, was not only an excellent jazz musician himself but a walking talking encyclopedia on the whole subject.

Of particular fascination to Stanley was Jim's ability to hear something as complex as 'Groovin High' and render it back to him note for note.

'You've got a photographic memory, Jim, but for music. I've not seen anything like it. It's like…' he searched for a word, '…a phonographic memory. That's it!' He laughed at his own cleverness.

Jim just said 'Thanks' and stared at the floor. Praise was something he had little practice in dealing with and he felt his cheeks fire up.

Stanley played him Louis Armstrong's Potato Head Blues, traditional Dixieland jazz but where the first true solos started to appear.

They listened to the big bands from the wartime era, Glenn Miller's signature tune 'A String of Pearls' where each instrument would break out of the close harmony to take a turn at playing its own solo.

They talked about improvisation, which was, Stanley said, the very heart of what jazz was all about. He played Jim several versions of 'Night in Tunisia' and they listened to the way Dizzy or Stan Getz handled the rhythm or the key.

Jim was familiar with improvising from days lying on his back in the attic, adding little extras to the music he heard in his head from the day's lessons and it was a revelation realising that other people had always done this.

Barney and the boys turned up at eight and they rehearsed right through until the doors of the club opened at ten. Without Harry Brisk in the building, Barney gave the band its head and let Jim wow them with the new inspiration provided by his evening of jazz history and the new freedom he felt, to add whatever he had running through his head into the mix. The range of tone available from the glass trumpet seemed endless, from the refined lilt of Chet Baker all the way to the raucous bellow of Louis Armstrong. Jim even managed to produce a breathy tone in imitation of Stanley's sax and amused the band by doing impressions of Stanley himself.

At the end of the last number, 'Crazeology', Molly emerged from the darkness of the club clapping her hands and smiling up at Jim so much he had to look away. She took him to the bar while Stanley beckoned Barney backstage for a chat in the band room.

'What…' he asked the pianist, '…have we got here, Barney? I've never known anything like it, and he's just a kid!'

'I know, Stan, I know, it's a waste but…' he held out his hands with a 'but what can I do?' expression.

'We have to get him out of here B, let me take him over to The Flamingo for an audition; they'll grab him in a gnat's crotchet.'

Barney sank into a chair and searched his jacket wearily for cigarettes.

'I don't think you understand Harry Brisk, Stanley.' Barney blew a long column of grey smoke up at the bare light bulb.

'He's set himself up as the boy's manager. You don't take from Harry Brisk that which he considers to be rightfully his, not if you value your own neck anyway.'

'Well I'll suggest it to Brisk,' said Stanley looking through the battered cupboard for Barney's bottle of cheap whisky.

'I wouldn't, Stan, there's something else; the boy's a runaway. Eugene saw him busking in the tube and Brisk only just got to him before the coppers took him off.'

He held out his glass as Stanley divided the last of the whisky between them.

***

The band played a longer set that night, as Mr Brisk turned up with a 'very important guest' for the second night in a row and wanted the girls to act as hostesses. Most of the men, burley Americans, sat in the main part of the club drinking Mr Brisk's best bourbon and chatting to the girls in their sequined stage outfits. Their boss occupied the only box in the club with Harry Brisk and a couple of girls from the show. From where he stood on that side of the stage Jim noticed that one of them was Katie. She sat there morosely examining her nails, occasionally glaring at Harry Brisk and emptying any glass that was put in front of her. After an hour or so she attempted to make Harry jealous by sitting on his guest's lap, feeding him champagne and delicacies by hand, and before much longer she was obviously drunk. Jim caught Molly's eye as she left the box having brought in yet another bottle of champagne and she shook her head, powerless and exasperated.

Jim enjoyed playing that night as the insistent shouts from the Americans, who obviously knew their jazz, gave Barney the license the band needed to cut loose and play some of the stuff they had been doing in rehearsal. They ended the evening with many of their guests rising to applaud and Jim began to feel like the 'real deal' as he locked the trumpet away in its case for the night.

His mood was soon altered as Molly dragged him out of the band room.

'It's Katie, Jim; I don't know what to do. She's spent the whole evening getting completely legless trying to make Brisk jealous with that fat American creep and now, of course, he wants to take her home and she's gone completely loopy.'

Jim pulled a face and shrugged.

Molly thought for a moment and then sent Jim out through the stage door to try and find a cab.

'If I can get her away from them we'll just take her home.'

She was to be disappointed. They could only stand and watch as Eugene held the stage door open and Katie, after screaming abuse at an embarrassed Harry Brisk, was put in the back of the visiting American's long black car and driven off into the night.

'Well…' she said to Jim as they left in the taxi he had found, 'at least you'll have a bed for the night.'

'Actually, Molly, I wanted to go and see Archie tonight.'

She looked at him, puzzled.

'You know, the friend I was staying with, the one without a bath.'

He asked the driver for Kilburn and they sat in silence for most of the journey, Jim spinning through the evening's set in his mind and Molly worrying about Katie.

***

Jim heard the coughing as soon as they alighted from the cab. He had the loose panel open and was down the crumbling steps before Molly had even found the fare. He discovered Archie lying on the ground by the guttering fire; his eyes squeezed shut and his knees drawn up to his chest where he lay on his side. His cough sounded like someone tearing up carpet and it echoed horribly round the bare brick walls of the bomb-site. Jim tried to get Archie upright but the weight was too much. He found some water and when Molly had arrived they got him into a sitting position and tried to give him some from one of the tin can cups. Archie just coughed it up in another huge spasm and curled back into a ball of convulsions. They looked at each other across the wracked form.

'Hospital,' said Molly and with a mighty effort they got him to his feet and with one of them under each arm they guided Archie up the steps towards the street. It took a tremendous amount of heaving and pulling to get him through the gap in the hoarding and onto the pavement, and Jim was worried that Archie might actually pass out or even die right there.

Rather than search for a phone box and wait for an ambulance they flagged down the first taxi that passed and managed to get Archie into the back.

'Nearest hospital,' shouted Jim at the driver.

'This aint no bleedin' ambulance,' he said looking doubtfully at the shabby figure on his back seat. Molly stuck her head through the partition.

'Just do it!'

One look in her fierce blue eyes was enough.

'Royal Free it is then,' he said, swinging the cab round in the road.

They never made it to the hospital. After a few minutes Archie came to himself, putting his head to the window and gasping the fresh air into his tortured lungs. He sat back between them and waved his hand back and forth.

'No…hospital,' he croaked.

'But, Archie,' said Jim.

'No. No hospital. Be alright, just the smoke from that dammed fire. Driver!'

The cabbie swung round, a 'what now?' expression on his face.

'Holland Park, 28 Holland Park.'

Once again the cab swung round in the road, despite some muttering about tramps and toffs from behind the wheel.

'Where are we going, Archie?' asked Jim, perplexed, but he was just met by another wave of the hand.

'No…talk…now,' wheezed Archie fighting off another attack of coughing. 'Wait…be alright.'

Eventually the taxi pulled up halfway down Holland Park, in front of the only totally dark house among the high walls, clipped hedges and carriage lamps that characterise the area.

Archie, just about walking, now heaved open a heavy gate and stumbled up a somewhat overgrown path towards the steps to a large house, towering into the darkness.

He reached up and found a key above the ornate double doors and passed this to Jim. He and Molly looked at each other, amazed.

'Open up, Jim,' gasped Archie.

Jim turned the key, pushed at the door and the three stepped inside, past a small hill of unopened post. Molly found a light switch and it was her and Jim's turn to gasp, as they found themselves standing on the diamond checkerboard tiled floor of a large entrance hall. A wrought iron banister swept round towards a first floor gallery, and several large mahogany doors led away in different directions.

Archie began another coughing fit and gestured towards the stairs.

'Archie we really should get you to hospital,' Molly told him.

The exhausted tramp pointed out a telephone on the hall table and gasped out the words 'Doctor' and 'Savage' in between coughs.

Molly helped him up the stairs while Jim looked through the address file next to the big old bakelite telephone, and began to dial the doctor's number.

A very tired and rather irritable voice answered 'Savage' after what seemed an age.

'Hello, Doctor, I'm calling from …from…Archie's house and I wondered if you could come out.'

'Good God, it's nearly four in the morning! Who is this, Archie who?'

Jim realised that he had no idea what Archie's last name was.

'Well I found your number in his address book.'

'Address book, what address?'

Jim became confused.

'It's in Holland Park, number twenty-eight I think.'

There was a pause.

'Twenty-eight Holland Park? That's the Hargrove House.'

There was a longer pause.

'Are you telling me, young man, that Archie Hargrove is actually there, at Holland Park?'

'Well…yes, and he's dreadfully ill, Doctor.'

Jim went on to explain about Archie's coughing fits and how they had tried to get him to go to hospital but was interrupted when the doctor merely said:

'Ten minutes,' and hung up the phone.

Jim followed the sound of his friend's coughing up the stairs and found Molly putting him to bed in a large four-poster in one of the first floor rooms.

Archie sat up against the cushions, his breathing fast and shallow as he fought to suppress another fit. Jim went to fetch a glass of water from an adjoining bathroom but had to run the tap a while before he could get the water to come clean of rust.

'This place must have been shut up years,' he said to Molly as Archie took small sips from the glass.

They managed to get him to lie back a little and close his eyes but his breathing wouldn't slow and he still twitched with the need to cough.

The doctor, in a rather tousled state and with his pyjama top still visible under his jacket, arrived in a few minutes and looked at Archie incredulously.

'Well I never thought to see you again, young Archie,' he said, shining a small torch into his patient's eyes.

He sent Jim out to his car for a tank of oxygen and a face-mask and asked Molly to boil some water.

'What for?' asked Molly.

'Tea, young lady. I certainly need a cup and I dare say you do too.'

Molly eventually discovered the kitchen in the back of the house and soon brought the doctor a cup of rather stale tea whitened with some milk powder, which must have been left over from the war.

They left him tending to Archie and went on to explore the house, finding room after room and staircase after staircase.

'So this is the friend without a bath?' she asked Jim as they opened yet another door on yet another en-suite bathroom.

'And I thought he was just another tramp,' marvelled Jim.

'And so he is!' answered Molly. 'Just because you come from money, it doesn't make you any better than anyone else.'

She chose a room along the landing from Archie's and then they went to see how Doctor Savage was doing.

They found him softly closing the bedroom door.

'I've given him a sedative so he should sleep. I'll be back in the morning to give him a thorough going over, I just hope it's not TB. Where did you find him, you do know he's been missing nearly ten years don't you?'

'I met him in Kilburn. He looked after me, for a while,' said Jim.

'Kilburn! Archie's relatives have searched the world for him and he was in Kilburn?'

'I think he moved around a bit,' said Jim, 'but only in London. He had a bit of a rough time in the war I think.'

The doctor looked at Jim sagely and then led the way to the staircase.

'Did he tell you what happened to him during the war?'

'Yes, all about the bombing and being trapped in the rubble.'

'Well, do you know, young man…' the old doctor put his arm round Jim's shoulders as they came to the entrance hall, '…you are the first person I've ever heard him tell of his wartime experiences? He would never talk about it. That was what caused all the trouble, I always thought. That's why Celia left him, the drinking and the night time raging.'

He opened the heavy door and stepped out.

'Well I shall see you in the morning, or should I say, later on this morning.'

***

Jim spent the night on the settee in Archie's room. Although he had no more coughing fits that night he did wake just before dawn shouting and screaming: 'Bale out! Bale out!' Jim found him sat bolt upright in bed, his eyes staring while he clawed at the oxygen mask Doctor Savage had left strapped to his face. Jim managed to remove this and calm Archie down. He fell back to sleep, without having fully awoken, but Jim just lay there listening to the dawn chorus build and then the sound of the local milkman beginning his deliveries.

He went downstairs in the vain hope of finding some breakfast and decided to explore the rest of the house. The first door off the entrance hall led to a huge panelled sitting room, which was furnished after the fashion of a gentleman's club. Deep button chesterfield sofas and armchairs stood around, gazed down upon by the glassy eyes of many a stuffed and mounted animal head. There was a vast wall of books and several ornate clocks, all stopped at different times.

He opened a door at the back of the room and found a much lighter airier room, with a long dining table and a great many paintings on the wall. Beyond this there was a door to what was obviously the kitchens.

As he stepped through it he had a sense, for just a second, that someone was in the room with him, but before he could turn even half-way round, he was clubbed, heavily, on the back of the head. Jim was unconscious before he hit the floor.

15 – Headlines

There was a long tunnel and some light that swam at the end of it, as if it finished in a fish tank or under the sea. There were some people talking and they were somehow managing to hold a conversation under the water. The back of Jim's head was wet although he hadn't yet reached the end of the tunnel. He took a deep breath, a gasp ready for going under.

'He's come round,' said a woman's voice and Jim found himself looking into her face. It was a kindly face, quite lined with age and framed with grey-white hair. Beyond this, a man of a similar age was coming towards him across a stone flagged floor. He felt incredibly dizzy, as if the room was whirling round with him at the centre, everything seeming to slide to the side as he looked at it. The pain in the back of his head lit up like an electric fire and his eyes felt as if they were throbbing. The man's face took the place of the woman's.

'Ello, you thieving little sod,' he said waving a heavy silver candlestick in Jim's face.

Jim thought he was going to fall off the chair and then realised that he was tied to it.

'Any trouble from you, sonny, and you'll get another one of these round the back of yer 'ead.'

Jim tried to speak but the words got tangled on the way from his brain to his mouth. There was a sudden loud ring that made the man and the woman jump and Jim wince in pain.

'Is that the police already?' asked the woman in surprise.

'Can't be, I aint called 'em yet, 'ave I?'

The man left the room still carrying his candlestick and Jim heard the front door open.

'Ah, Higgson, long time no see, how's the patient?'

There was brief surprised silence.

'Doctor Savage! He's through here... but...how...did, how did...I didn't call....'

As he entered the room, the doctor's business-like expression was replaced by one of astonishment.

'Good God man, what have you done?' He dropped his bag on the table and came over to Jim.

'Untie him immediately!'

The room slipped sideways and Jim felt himself going into the blackness again.

Next time he opened his eyes he was in a bed.

'Well hello,' said Molly's voice softly. He felt his hand being held and when he squeezed she squeezed back. He went to sit up but she tried to stop him.

'No, Molly, it's alright.'

She fattened some pillows to put behind him.

'What happened?' he asked her.

'It seems that Mr Higgson, the caretaker of the house – he and his wife live in the mews cottage across the garden - mistook you for a burglar and tried to stave in your skull with some of the family silver.'

Jim raised his hand to his head and found a heavy bandage running round it.

'Luckily the doctor came or you'd be waking up in a police cell right now,' she added.

'How do you feel?'

'Hungry,' said Jim. 'Starving.'

'Well that's a good sign I suppose.'

She rang down and asked Mrs Higgson for some soup which was promptly delivered by both of the Higgsons, who seemed determined to apologise to Jim the whole time he spent eating it. After he had said it was fine, he was fine and agreed that it was an easy mistake to have made and 'no harm done' he managed to change their tack by asking after Archie.

'Oh we haven't seen him yet, Doctor Savage is still in with him,' said Mrs Higgson and then began to thank Jim for Archie's safe return, in even more expansive terms than she had apologised for her husband trying to brain him with a candlestick. Jim finished his soup and said he felt tired, giving Molly the cue she needed to usher the couple out.

As soon as they were gone Jim was up and looking for his clothes.

'And what d'you think you're doing?' asked Molly in her most matronly voice.

'I'm fine, really Molly, I just couldn't stand any more 'sorrys' and 'thank yous'. I want to see Archie, what does the doctor say? Is he going to be okay?'

'You'll not find any clothes; Mrs Higgson has them all in the laundry. The doctor says you're to rest a couple of days at least.'

'We'll see about that,' said Jim triumphantly pulling open the door of a large wardrobe in the corner of the room. Each hanger he pulled out, however, supported a cocktail dress more splendid than the last.

'Very nice,' said Molly. And 'Ohh, lovely! Matches your eyes. Now that goes very well with your bandage.'

Jim gave up and let her put them away again.

'I'll ask the good doctor if he'll come and look at you when he's finished with Archie, though I'm certain he's going to want you a couple of days in bed; that was one hell of a crack on the head, Jim.'

She crossed the room and tapped softly at a door next to the bed. Jim heard the doctor call 'Come in' and realised that he must be in a room adjoining Archie's.

Molly was gone a few minutes and then opened the door again to beckon Jim in. He found a dressing gown in one of the cupboards and went through.

Archie was sitting up in bed looking a lot healthier than Jim had seen him before. He'd had a shave and there was even a little colour in his usually sallow cheeks. He held out a hand for Jim but ended up pulling him in and giving him a hug, an act as yet unknown to Jim.

Thanks, old man,' he muttered quietly.

Archie then held Jim out at arm's length. He looked at the bandage running round his head and let out a short laugh. 'God, Higgson really did fetch you one with that candlestick didn't he?'

'It's not so bad now,' Jim said. 'I was a bit dizzy for a while there though.'

He sat down on the edge of the bed.

'So, how are you, Archie?'

'Well Doc Savage says it's not TB, which is a surprise really.' He paused. 'Listen, Molly, would you pop down and ask Mrs Higgson to bring us up some tea and what-not?'

Molly left and took Doctor Savage down with her, after he had extracted promises from both Archie and Jim regarding the blowing of trumpets and the consumption of whisky and cigarettes.

'But...' Jim struggled to phrase his next question. He looked around the well-appointed room.

Archie laughed quietly to himself.

'I know, Jim. Why was I slowly killing myself living on cheap whisky in a bomb-site when I had a house all the time?'

Jim nodded.

Archie sat for a moment, looking at Jim, as though considering how much to tell him. Eventually he began.

'Well, after the war and what happened at Cologne, you remember don't you, I told you?'

Jim nodded again.

'Well I came home and tried to get on. I took a position in one of my father's firms and married Celia, a girl I'd known since childhood. We lived here and we tried, well I tried, to be, well, normal I suppose. Nobody talked about the war. Everyone was sick of it and the general feeling was that we just wanted to put it behind us and get on with life, you know.'

He was silent again as there was a tap on the door and Mrs Higgson brought in a tea tray with a large plate of biscuits.

'Mrs Higgson, hello.'

'Oh sir, Mr Archie, sir,' she said putting the tray down and wiping away a tear. 'Where have you been, Mr Archie? We all thought you was dead, sir.'

'I'm sorry, Mrs Higgson, I had to go away.'

He looked up at her and gave a soft smile.

'I'm home now, I shall stay this time.'

'I'm so glad, sir, shall I pour?'

'No, leave it; Jim can manage. Tell Mr Higgson I'll see him after Jim and I have finished.'

She left them and Archie continued his story.

'It wasn't the drinking so much, I found if I drank enough before bed I stood a chance of getting through the night. Celia didn't like this of course and begged me to stop, to get help, but by then I was already an alcoholic.' He gestured to the tea tray and Jim set about pouring.

'Bit different from the old bean cans eh?' he said as Jim passed him the delicate china cup. Jim noticed it rattle on the saucer as Archie took it from him.

'But why did you leave?' he asked.

'I had to, Jim. One night she tried to wake me from one of my nightmares. I remember it so clearly. I was dreaming that the mob in Cologne had cornered me, just like Billy Fraser, and they were kicking and beating me. I got hold of one of them and I was screaming blue murder and had my hands locked round his throat. When I came to I had Celia by the neck.'

He paused for a moment and then looked up at Jim.

'She was unconscious, she was nearly dead.'

They sat in silence for a moment, save the slight rattling of Archie's cup against the saucer, which he quietened by taking a sip of tea.

'I had to leave.'

'Where is she now?' asked Jim.

'Oh she ran off to South Africa with one of my oldest friends. Can't blame her really. I didn't contest the divorce.'

'So why did you stay out there?' Jim gestured towards the window.

'What, why become a tramp?' Archie laughed softly. 'Because nobody minds what you do when you're a tramp. Nobody cares if you're a drunk; it's almost expected of you.'

He paused for some more tea.

'To be honest, I didn't really care what happened to me. I'd probably have jumped under a train if I'd been brave enough.'

There was quietness for a while.

'That changed though, when I met you. I began to worry about you, when you were off with that trumpet of yours. That was the first time I'd even thought about another human being for ten years.'

He passed Jim his teacup and reached for the phone by the bed.

'Ah, Mrs Higgson, what happened to the clothes I had when I arrived?' Archie listened for a moment.

'And did you check the pockets before you burnt them?'

Jim could just hear Mrs Higgson's high voice from the receiver.

'Thank goodness,' said Archie. 'Could you bring that last item up to me?'

He replaced the telephone.

'Forgive me forgetting, Jim, but your friend Renee gave me something for you, and with all the goings on last night I clean forgot about it.'

Mrs Higgson tapped lightly on the door and brought Archie a brown envelope.

He looked at the front and then passed it over to Jim.

It had 'Jim' written across it in a bold hand.

'Quite a character, your Renee, think she wanted to make me husband number three. I've not opened it as it was addressed to you.'

Jim thanked Archie and took the envelope off to his room where he tore it open carefully and pulled out a newspaper clipping. He felt a lump in his throat as he took in the whole thing, the picture and the headline at the same moment.

ARP Seek Help Identifying Expectant Mother Killed By German Bomb

And beneath, a picture of the same young nurse from the photograph he had found in The House of Glass. This one had been obviously cut from a group snapshot. She was wearing civilian clothes and laughing at the camera. Someone's hand was on her shoulder and another, in the foreground, held a half-full pint of beer. The date 'Sept. '43' had been roughly hand-written in the margin.

Tragedy struck in the early hours of the morning of September 15th when a stray German bomb hit a house in Belsize Road. The house was so utterly destroyed that ARP wardens said last night that they were unlikely to be able to recover some of the bodies at the address for burial.
Police are trying to trace the relatives of an expectant mother lodging temporarily at the address, number seventeen. The young lady, known to her neighbours only as Elizabeth or Lizzie, arrived in May, her particulars being known only to her landlord, who also perished in the explosion. If anyone can identify the young lady from the photograph above, which was found in the wreckage, please contact the Chief Warden for the Belsize Ward on Maida Vale 1805.

Jim took a deep breath and held it, hoping to keep his disappointment at bay. Whoever she was, Lizzie had touched him, and the thought that her trail had now run cold and he was unlikely ever to discover more about her, or Mr G Armstrong, left an empty feeling in his middle.

***

Molly arrived back at teatime the next day, hardly noticing Jim's mood, as she was still so worried about Katie, who had not returned to the Camden flat. She ate supper with them and afterwards, when she and Jim were alone in the clubroom she quizzed him about Archie and how he had gone from 'here to the gutter'.

'Was it the drink?' she asked.

'Not really, that had something to do with it. It was the war, Molly. I think he came back a bit mad from the war.' But he didn't feel like telling her the details. After all, he reasoned, this was a story Archie had not even shared with his wife.

Jim was keen to return to the club again and throw himself back into the music, but Molly insisted that he was not yet fit enough.

'Barney says he won't have you back 'til you're totally better, you'll only give yourself a splitting headache blowing that horn of yours!' she laughed.

As she walked off down the drive that evening, Jim realised that he missed her almost as much as the glass trumpet.

He flopped back down in one of the large chesterfield sofas and spent a while looking through the newspapers that Mr Higgson had bought that day. Eventually he came to a copy of the Evening Standard. For the second time in twenty-four hours his heart was almost brought to a halt by a newspaper headline:

Mystery Blonde in Canal Murder

There was an artist's impression of the victim, done from the body. It was, Jim had no doubt, a picture of Katie.

He remembered the last time they had seen her, at the rear entrance to The Black Cat, the only witnesses to her being dragged into the car of Harry Brisk's very important guest.

'Oh my God! Molly!' he said, springing for the door.

16 – Gun

*B*y the time Jim's cab arrived at The Black Cat it was just gone half past eight and he couldn't be sure whether or not he'd beaten Molly, who was travelling by bus. He hung around Kingly Street - taking care that he was not spotted by Eugene - for a good half hour or so before he became sure that she must be inside.

At twenty past nine he saw Ginny, one of the chorus girls, emerge and head towards the fish and chip shop up near Great Marlborough Street. Not wanting to pass the doors of The Black Cat, Jim raced off in the opposite direction, sprinting down Beak Street and cutting round the back of the club via Carnaby Street. He caught up with her just as she was leaving the shop with a large bundle of fish and chips.

'Ginny,' he gasped.

'Jim, sweetie! How are you, how's your head?'

'Fine, fine.'

'C'mon you can walk back with me.'

Um, Ginny, is Molly in yet?'

Ginny looked suspicious and interested at the same time.

'Yes, why?'

'Can you give her a message from me?'

'Why don't you come in with me and see her yourself?'

'I can't explain, Ginny. Just ask her to meet me by the stage door straight away could you?'

'Okay, sweetie.' She gave him a peck on the cheek. 'I hope you're not leaving us Jim, all the girls love your horn, darling!'

'Not a word to anyone, Ginny.'

She promised and headed back down Kingly Street into the falling darkness.

Jim doubled back again and waited furtively by the 'No Loitering' sign in the back alley.

After a few minutes the stage door opened but it was Ginny again.

'She's in with Mr Brisk, sweetie. Eugene's up there as well, don't know why. They're not to be disturbed. What's going on, Jim?'

He wondered whether to ask if any of them had seen the Evening Standard but thought better of it.

'Nothing, Ginny, just don't mention that you've seen me, to anyone, okay?'

She agreed and turned back into the building. Jim caught the door and wedged an old cigarette packet in place to stop it closing fully, then stood in the alley and pondered his options.

He could simply turn up for work and take his chances at getting himself and Molly away. This he soon dismissed as wishful thinking; the very fact that they had Molly in there meant she was considered a witness, and he had stood beside her as they watched Katie being put in the back of the car.

He looked up at the back of the building as he had done the first time he was here, when Eugene had thrown him into the alley and he had wanted to get his trumpet back so badly.

The pipes spread up the walls like so many black shiny roots. He could make out the little square window with the odd patch of clear glass, which was the only one in Harry Brisk's office.

Jim took off his jacket and began the climb. It was, if anything, easier than his escape route at home. The pipes were numerous and there were many ledges and sills, offering easy hand and foot holds. After a few minutes he was able, cautiously, to peer in through the single clear pane into the office. What little he could see confirmed his worst fears. Molly was sitting facing what Jim knew to be Harry Brisk's place across the desk, Eugene's mighty bulk stood against the door. He saw Molly shake her head and hold her hands out with an 'I don't know' expression. Jim peered hopelessly in through the window and wondered what to do. He could perhaps climb down and go to the police, but that would mean being returned to his father and almost certainly giving up hope of ever seeing his glass trumpet again.

Harry Brisk appeared from the blind side of the room. He paused threateningly over Molly before leaving the office with Eugene. As the door shut behind him Molly was immediately up and pounding on it. It opened again, only enough for Eugene to lean in and point a threatening finger at her, which he then raised to his lips before pointing at the chair. The door closed again and Molly sat down, head in hands.

Jim waited a moment or two until he was sure they would not return and then tapped lightly on the glass with his fingernail. Molly had to look around a few times before locating Jim at the window. It opened reluctantly having been shut for so long and Jim realised that Molly had been crying.

'Jim, my God, what are you doing out there?'

'What are you doing *in* there?'

'I don't know, they keep asking all these questions about Katie, and about you - do I know where she is, do I know where you are? I've no idea what they want.'

'Did you tell them about Archie's?'

'No, I just said that I'd been at home or out shopping. What is it they want, Jim? I've no idea.'

He looked for a nice way to tell her but he couldn't find one, hanging as he was, twenty feet up on a drainpipe.

'Molly, Katie's dead. It was in the paper.'

Molly's hands went to her face and her pale blue eyes widened with shock.

'Oh God, no!'

Then she suddenly understood her own situation.

'And we were the last people to see her alive – we saw her leave with that fat American. That's why they want to know where you are as well.'

She looked Jim in the eyes.

'Oh, Jim, I'm scared.'

'Can you get through here, Molly?'

She pulled her chair across to the window but found it too high and small to have a chance of climbing through.

'Anyway, heights are the only thing I'm afraid of Jim, that and Harry Brisk.'

'Have they left the key in the door?' asked Jim, remembering his trick in the police station.

'No, it's on that huge bunch he carries around with him. You know the stupid thing is I've got a key for this room. I got one cut when I was opening up for a couple of nights. It's on my key-ring in my bag.'

'Where's the bag?' asked Jim.

'It's in the girls' changing rooms, under the make-up mirror on the far left. But Jim, they'll nab you as soon as you come up the stairs.'

'Pass me that gun cigarette lighter, it should be on the end of the desk.'

She passed it through asking, 'What are you going to do, Jim? I'm worried.'

'Just sit tight and be ready to run,' he said setting off back down towards the ground.

Just inside the stage door and up a few steps Jim found the large electrical junction box that brought power into the building. He had noticed it before with its warning signs of 'Danger' and

'High Voltage'. He considered his options; he could simply throw the big lever switch and take advantage of the couple of minutes of darkness and confusion that would result, or he could try and wrench the fat cable clean out of the box, meaning that there would be no way that Harry Brisk could get the lights back on.

Like everything that was out of sight at The Black Cat, the cable fixing seemed dilapidated and crumbling, several of the brackets missing or hanging loose. Jim reached up, grasped the cable and squeezed his eyes shut, mentally picturing his route through the club to the girls' changing room. Then, putting his foot against the wall for extra purchase, he tore at the cable with all his strength. The result was immediate. The building was tipped into darkness and filled with the sudden screams of the chorus girls and the shouting of men. Jim lay on the floor terrified by a deluge of sparks where the cable came to rest against the iron handrail. He kicked it away and it fell to the floor completing the blackness and then Jim was on his feet running into the club. He found the wings of the stage and took his bearings across it from the curtains, which thankfully had been left closed. As he scuttled down the short corridor to the changing room he could tell the door had been yanked open by the sudden increase in volume from within. He flattened himself against the wall as a string of chorus girls dashed into the passageway yelling and shouting. One of them, Veronica, was screaming, 'Don't panic!' at the top of her voice and he could hear Ginny telling everyone to hold hands.

Finally they passed and began falling over each other out near the stage. Jim ducked into their dressing room and pulled the gun lighter from his pocket. Despite the feebleness of its light he found Molly's bag and the keys in it with no trouble and set off towards the office, anxious to free her before someone could find a torch.

As he regained the far wing of the stage he heard a man's heavy tread very close and shrank down under the stage manager's table as it passed.

'I'm going to check the mains, Mr Brisk,' Eugene's voice boomed out of the blackness.

'There should be a torch in the stage manager's cupboard,' he heard Mr Brisk reply from the back of the auditorium. Jim held his breath and thankfully heard Eugene's steps going off toward the back stairs.

He bolted up the steps to Harry Brisk's office and called Molly, with the loudest whisper he dared.

'I'm here,' she replied from the other side of the office door. Jim examined the bunch of keys with the lighter.

'Which one is it, Molly?' he asked.

'It's one of the two brass mortice lock keys.'

Jim found the first and fitted it to the lock; it went in but would not turn. He had just fitted the second when the voice of Harry Brisk from the bottom of the stairs made him stiffen with fear. He had heard the keys rattling in the lock.

'What's going on up there?' came the suspicious enquiry.

The heavy steps of Harry Brisk followed rapidly on the wooden treads. Jim slid away across the floor and made himself as small as possible.

Molly had cottoned on to what was happening and began rattling the door handle, banging and shouting to be let out. With much fumbling in the dark Harry Brisk found his own key and swung the door open viciously, knocking her to the floor.

'You just stay where you are,' he said, a nasty rasp in his voice. 'We'll finish our chat later.' His tone made the hairs on the back of Jim's neck bristle with fear. He realised that if he and Molly were not to escape The Black Cat then they were certain to share Katie's fate. Harry Brisk slammed the door and relocked it, apparently convinced that it was Molly making the noise.

As he turned, Jim summoned up all his bravery and took a chance; he stuck his leg across the top of the stairway. There was a light kick against it from Harry Brisk's leg, a brief cry of surprise and fear, followed by a satisfyingly loud crashing and banging as Mr Brisk cartwheeled to the bottom of the stairs.

Jim, who already had the correct key in hand, had the door open in seconds.

'Molly!' he hissed.

He could see across the office by the faintest of lights from the small window. Molly found him in the gloom and gave him a swift hug and a kiss on the forehead. Jim had not thought up to that point that his heart could beat any harder.

'Was that Brisk falling downstairs?'

'Yup.'

Jim darted across the office to the safe; it was locked solid. He examined the front of it with the lighter.

'Dammit, it's a combination.'

'Jim, we've got to go,' came Molly's urgent voice from near the door.

'But, my trumpet,' he said desperately.

'If you don't come now they'll bury us both in the same hole. Jim, we *have* to go!'

She took his hand and they went as cautiously and quickly as they could down the stairs. Jim trod on Harry Brisk's keys halfway down and lobbed them back up to the top landing. They got safely to the bottom, but as Molly stepped over the unconscious Harry Brisk there was a groan and she felt a hand grasp at her ankle.

'Get the…' she kicked out hard and Jim propelled her across the wings towards the exit.

He yanked open the doors to the back stairs and they galloped down the last few steps, past the dead junction box, and ran towards the faint light shining through the dirty panes of the stage door. It was not to be so simple; Jim jerked open the door only to find the mighty bulk of Eugene blocking the way.

'You, you little…'

He seized Jim by the lapel and forced him back into the building and up the stairs, knocking Molly over in the process. He drew back a mighty fist but before he could deliver one of his jaw smashing punches, he found himself looking down the barrel of a gun held in both Jim's hands and pointing straight at his face. He dropped Jim, who fell on top of Molly, and slowly raised his hands.

'Where on earth did a little brat like you...' he paused for a moment as Jim got shakily to his feet. A sneer came across his face, 'You wouldn't dare!'

He took a step towards them. Jim thrust the gun out further, tensing his grip on the trigger. That was his mistake. There was a faint click and a tiny flame appeared from the muzzle of the gun.

17 – Billingsgate

'Ahh,' said Eugene, looking at the little tongue of flame licking the end of the muzzle, then, without a word, he half stooped and punched Jim hard enough in the stomach to double him over. As the gun-lighter hit the floor he came forward and neatly collected the collapsing boy in a fireman's carry, over his shoulder.

'Back in, you!' he said to Molly giving her a shove towards the interior doors.

Although still gasping from Eugene's heavyweight punch, Jim saw one last chance for him and Molly to escape as he was carried up the stairs. Reaching down, he closed his fingers lightly around the thick power cable where it had come away from the wall, letting it run through his hand as Eugene took him up towards the darkness of The Black Cat. As he came in reach of the end he grabbed it and with a sudden twist he jammed the bare copper wires, which protruded from the very end of the cable, into the side of Eugene's enormous neck. The result was painful but effective; there was a loud cry as the jolt coursed through both their bodies and Eugene threw Jim, involuntarily, hard against the double doors that led into the club. Jim lay there winded for a moment but Eugene, his head surrounded by a thin wreath of foul smelling smoke, toppled slowly backwards, like a felled tree. There was a brief crack as the back of his skull met the bottom step and then a moment of silence.

'Quick!' said Molly, dragging Jim to his feet and bundling him out of the doors and into the alley.

He ran erratically down the narrow passage hanging onto her arm and then, before Jim really knew what was happening, she had him in the back of a passing cab and they swept off through Piccadilly Circus and up Shaftsbury Avenue. Molly watched intently out of the back window.

'Where are we going?' asked Jim, blearily, as the cab passed Tottenham Court Road tube station.

'Back to mine,' answered Molly, giving up her reconnaissance and lifting Jim's chin with her finger, to look into his eyes with concern. 'Are you okay? That was a hell of a jolt you took.'

Jim stared back into the blue eyes, lit intermittently as they were by the passing lights of the West End, her look of concern reviving him a little.

'I expect I'm better than Eugene,' he answered.

'God, you did brilliantly getting us both out of there,' she paused and placed a kiss on his forehead. 'You're my hero.'

Molly pulled the cab over at Goodge Street and bought an evening paper. She gasped when she saw the artist's impression of Katie, and a large tear from her eye stained the page while they sat and read the story as best they could in the dim light.

'Bastards,' she muttered, sitting back in her seat and biting her knuckle when they had finished. Katie's body had been found nearly naked, floating in the Regents canal two days before. She had been strangled.

Molly tried to make Jim wait in the cab while she ran into the flat to grab some things, but since he had now been accorded the status of hero, he felt he should stay by her side.

'We've got to be quick, God knows but it won't take Harry Brisk long to be up and after us,' she said, her keys at the ready as she got to the first floor landing. They weren't needed; the door was splintered at the lock and everything inside had been overturned and smashed. Molly gave a shriek and dived across the room, frantically windmilling through the torn and scattered clothes and bedding. As Jim got to her she let out a groan of relief and sat down on her bed clutching something to her chest.

'What is it? he asked.

She opened her crossed arms to reveal a picture in a shattered frame. In it a man wearing farm clothing stood by a stone wall, seriously regarding the photographer. He was dark haired and looked small but strong. The frame and the glass were broken but Molly didn't seem to mind, she looked down at the photo.

'That's the only picture of me dad there is,' she said.

Jim found a suitcase and Molly hopped round the room, selecting a few things and wadding them in with the precious picture.

They were back in the cab within minutes, Molly ordering the driver down to nearby Kings Cross where they paid him and set off into the station.

'Where are we going Molly?'

'It's just a ruse, Jim,' she said, marching them straight out of the side entrance to the taxi rank by the Great Northern Hotel. 'Brisk knows most of the regular cabbies in the rank by the club, this way, if he finds out anything it'll be that we left town.'

They climbed straight into another black cab and headed for Archie's.

***

As they arrived, Doctor Savage was in the hallway, being helped into his coat by Mr Higgson. He looked at Jim questioningly.

'Are you all right, young man?' he asked, leaning across and peering owlishly into Jim's eyes, one after the other.

'Yes, fine,' answered Jim. 'Just had a bit of a shock, that's all.'

He felt Molly dig him in the ribs; they had decided not to mention the goings on at The Black Cat so as not to drag Archie into the affair.

'Good rest, make sure he gets a good rest,' he called after them as Molly led Jim up the stairs. 'I'm not entirely sure he's recovered from that concussion you gave him!' they heard him say to Higgson as he stepped out through the front doors.

'It's true, Jim,' Molly agreed as they went along the landing towards Jim's bedroom. 'You've had quite a battering lately.'

She hung his coat up as he lay down on the bed, closing his eyes and resting his hands atop his head with a thumb lightly on each temple. Molly sat down beside him and stroked his chest.

'You should lay up for a day or two, get some rest like the doctor says.'

'I won't sleep Molly, not while they've got my trumpet.'

'Jim, think about it; we can't go back in there, not if we don't want to end up like Katie. Harry Brisk knows that you and I are the only people who saw where she went that night. Whatever the police's suspicions about Brisk, it's only us who can link him to her murder.'

'What do you think happened to her, Molly?'

'Well, I talked to her while you were in the bath at my house that morning. It was pretty clear to me that her honeymoon period with Harry was over but she just didn't get it. She was determined to 'win him back' she said…by whatever means. You probably saw how drunk she got that night. She thought that if she flirted with the fat yank long enough Harry would become jealous. She didn't really believe that Harry wanted her to go with someone else, that he was finished with her. I've seen it before. It's what he always does. Pretty new girl comes in; he takes up with her, when he's bored he palms her off on one of his gangster mates; in this case a very big important gangster mate. All Katie's flirting did was make it worse. I was serving the drinks; I saw it all in great horrible close up. Harry knew what she was doing but the yank, he was lapping it up. He must have been terribly disappointed when he got her in the car and she wouldn't 'play ball'. Men like that aren't used to having woman dressed as show girls say 'no' to them.'

She kicked off her shoes and laid her head on the pillow next to his, her hands together as if in prayer between the linen and her cheek.

'We'll have to get you another glass trumpet, Jim,' she said, a little sleepily.

He thought about it, about the finding of it and its mysterious maker, about the sleek tone and the raspy tone and all the tones in between, about its sheer beauty and about how fragile it was. He knew what it had done for his playing, how it had ruined him for anything made of mere metal.

'There's not another in the whole world, Molly.'

She answered with the faintest of murmurs and he realised that she had fallen asleep. He looked at her in repose, the dark hair framing her face, the still red lips and the delicately cut nostrils that seemed to tremble and flair slightly as she fell from consciousness. After a while he shuffled over a little and managed to replace the pillow with his shoulder, to feel her breath slow and deepen and her whole body relax against his.

Jim lay there in wonder, not knowing whether he felt more keenly that which he had almost certainly lost, or that which he so nearly possessed.

He too began to fall asleep, reliving the voyage from his lonely attic to here, the cold journey down the drainpipe, the discovery of Lester and his world of music, he reheard Dizzy Gillespie for the first time to the clatter of train wheels and the alarm calls of blackbirds and magpies. He remembered Old Tom and Millet, and that first meeting with the idea of happiness, on the hill down to the sea.

***

'That's it!'

Jim sprang suddenly awake, startling Molly, who was wrapped round him for warmth where she had fallen asleep. She looked at him, a little surprised and then regained her composure, sitting up on the bed, rounding up stray hairs and straightening herself out.

'God, Jim, what is it? You startled me, I must have fallen asleep.'

'What time is it?'

She looked past him at the bedside clock.

'Nearly three in the morning.'

Jim got up off the bed and started pulling his shoes on.

'Are you mad, where are you going?' she said through a couple of hairpins held in her mouth, her fingers searching out and redeploying others.

'I know how we can do it, Molly. I know how we can get it back.'

'The trumpet?'

'Yes,' he looked at her, his eyes shining. 'I'm sure we can do it.'

'Jim...is there any skin left on those teeth of yours?' She took the last hairpin from her mouth and slid it into position. 'Go on.'

As Jim had fallen asleep, and just before the remembering of his adventures began to turn slowly into dreams, he had come to his journey in the fish lorry with Flynn. He explained it all to Molly finishing with:

'He's a safe cracker, Molly, from a long line of safe crackers!'

'And what if they've changed all the locks in The Black Cat and you can't get in?'

'I doubt it; I left Brisk's keys there on purpose so they wouldn't know that you had a set; besides, Flynn's a safe cracker, I'm sure a few locks wouldn't be much of a problem.'

Although finding a cab going back into town at that time of night had not been easy, the journey through the silent city was at least swift. They arrived to find Billingsgate; a long line of stone arches stretching away into the darkness along the Thames, bustling with porters carrying boxes of fish on their heads, or on old-fashioned wooden barrows. Molly sat on a wall while Jim searched among the many lorries, parked in a line under the bright lights, for the one that had brought him to London, what seemed like an age ago. Having no luck he entered the building and began searching among the careening fish boxes, amid the unfamiliar cries of the merchants, dodging barrows and slithering about on the chipped ice, which was spilled everywhere. The names of the various dealers were written, usually in gold, on boards above their stalls but Jim could not remember which of them had been painted on the front of the lorry that had nearly run him down in Walsham-on-Sea. Everyone was far too busy to listen to vague questions about a man called Flynn who drove a lorry up from somewhere on the south coast for someone or other. Jim remembered that Flynn had told him that he usually arrived at about five-thirty and was just beginning to lose heart at ten-to-six, when he saw, from the very edge of his eye, the flash of red that reminded him of the bandanna Flynn had worn around his neck. He spun round just as a dark haired figure disappeared through one of the arches back out into the street where all the lorries were parked.

'Flynn!' he shouted at the very top of his voice but the figure neither hesitated nor turned.

Jim began to run and, being an agile young man, he managed to avoid most of the porters bustling around the busy market on the slippery chipped ice, balancing stacks of fish boxes on their heads. The angry shouts, of those that he didn't, pursued him out onto Lower Thames Street as he skidded to a halt, looking desperately up and down the street for Flynn's back.

He saw the red bandanna disappear once more, where the lights of the market ran out towards Tower Hill and pursuing it, this time along the road to avoid upsetting more fish and porters, he soon caught up with Flynn.

'Jim!' he cried, seizing him by the hand. 'I often wondered what happened to you and that trumpet of yours. How've you been?' He took a step back and looked him all the way up and down. 'You've…grown, well…changed a bit.'

'Yeah, I've…' said Jim sheepishly, 'I'm blond now anyway.'

There was a short pause during which Flynn realised that this meeting with Jim, in the early hours of the morning, in an out-of-the way part of London, was unlikely to be accidental.

'So…what can I do for you?' He feigned looking up and down the street. 'No police after you this time?'

'No,' Jim laughed. 'It's something I remember you saying to me on the way up here.'

He suddenly felt overwhelmed with awkwardness; what had seemed obvious back at Archie's just a couple of hours ago now appeared impossible. He thought it best to get straight to it.

'Well, it's about the trumpet. You see someone's got it locked in a safe and won't give it back to me. I was wondering if you could help?'

They walked along together a little.

'Help?'

'Yes, with the safe, I remember you saying that you came from a long line of safe crackers.'

'Whoa son, steady boy. I also said I done several years in the nick for it if you remember.'

'Yes but this is different, Flynn. It's not stealing; the trumpet's mine. You'd just be helping me get it back.'

'Well maybe I could get some mates of mine to have a bit of a word with this bloke, you know, 'explain' to him how it's your trumpet and all that. What's his name anyway?'

'Harry Brisk.'

Flynn stopped walking. He looked at Jim in silence for a moment.

'You are jokin', aren't you?'

Jim remained silent and tried to pull what he thought might be his most appealing face.

'Harry Brisk! He's king of half the bloody hoodlums in the West End! I'm sorry mate,' he looked at Jim and shook his head sadly. 'Good luck, Jim, but I wouldn't touch it with somebody else's bargepole.'

18 - The Plan

$\mathcal{A}$ tug, somewhere on the river, let out a long doleful note and as it died away, Flynn gave Jim a conciliatory pat on the arm and turned to go. He was surprised by the small purposeful figure of a woman arriving out of the darkness.

'Molly,' she said simply, thrusting out a hand.

'Flynn,' he said, taking it while shooting a surprised and questioning look at Jim.

'Oh yes, I forget to mention, Molly is a friend of mine from The Black Cat.'

'So?' she asked. 'What's the plan?'

'No plan, Flynn says he can't do it.'

Molly dropped the hand and took Jim's arm, as if to offer some comfort.

'Ah well, Jim…' She turned them both round and they began to walk away. 'I did say that you wouldn't get much luck with a fish delivery boy.'

Flynn dropped into step beside them.

'Look, Jim, I'm sorry but you know…Harry Brisk and all that.'

'You wouldn't be the first lad afraid of Harry Brisk now,' said Molly. 'He's a professional, and that's what we need, Jim, not some Cod Walloper from the back of beyond,' she added, looking dismissively at Flynn as they walked along.

'Well actually,' here Flynn paused to look over his shoulder, as if to add an air of conspiracy, 'I do come from a long line…'

'Of fish delivery boys?' finished Molly for him, the laughing tone just dimpling the surface of her voice.

'Flynn, this is a safe we need cracked, not some costermonger's petty cash box.'

'What kind of safe?'

'I dunno,' said Molly, 'big grey thing, like a wardrobe crossed with a tank, in the upstairs office.'

'Key or combination?'

'Combination I think, isn't it?' She looked up at Jim again. He nodded.

'One dial or two?'

'Two, I think,' said Jim.

'Make?'

'God, I don't know.'

'Milner?'

'No.'

'Chatwood?'

'No.'

Jim thought about the heavy plate above the right hand dial with the maker's name embossed on it.

'There's a plate with a picture of a lion on it.'

'Withers then?'

'Yes! That's it, Withers, I remember now because it's the same name as a part of a horse and I wondered, "Does a Lion have withers too?" It's standing on a crown.'

'Later one then.' Flynn pondered a minute longer.

'Does it have a big brass handle on each door, just below the dials?'

'Yes, yes it does,' said Jim, excited now.

'Samuel Withers Seven Lever Double Combination probably,' said Flynn, stopping and opening the door of the lorry they had come to.

'Hop in, let's get some breakfast and I'll at least have a think about it.'

Molly sat in the middle and they drove to Smithfield, the meat market; Flynn said it would be better as no-one knew him there.

Over huge plates of bacon, egg, sausage, tomato, beans, mushrooms and fried bread, Flynn asked more questions: where the safe was, who was in the building and when, if it was quiet or noisy and a host of other details.

Eventually he fell silent and sat back, picking his teeth with a matchstick and drumming his fingers quietly in intricate patterns on the edge of the table. He asked Jim to go up for more tea rather than wait 'til the middle of next week' for a waitress in the busy café.

When he came back with the three deep steaming mugs he found Molly and Flynn laughing together, though neither offered to share the joke.

Flynn hoisted his mug and offered it as a toast; Molly and Jim raised theirs in return.

'To old Mr Withers.'

Molly and Jim returned the toast and the three clinked mugs and supped.

'Family tradition,' said Flynn in answer to their questioning looks. 'Always drink to the maker's name to seal the deal; brings good luck.'

'So…so…' Jim stuttered.

'He'll do it, Jim!' cut in Molly.

A huge grin shot across Jim's face, he banged his tea down on the table and seized Flynn by the hand.

'Thanks Flynn, but what will I owe you? I've not got much money.'

'Don't worry, Jim, I've done a deal with Molly here.'

Jim looked at her, surprised.

'Are you going to pay him?'

'No,' she answered and looked across at Flynn with a laugh and a twinkle.

'I'm going to let him take me to the pictures!'

The pair talked about what they might go and see as Flynn made himself a roll-up and they finished their tea.

Jim sat there and listened to them talk, he felt odd; a kind of reversal of how he had felt at Archie's in the early hours of that morning, lying there with Molly asleep on his shoulder; he was pleased that he might well be going to get his trumpet back but had an uneasy feeling that something else, that he had never quite had within his grasp, was slipping away.

***

They spent the rest of that morning planning in a quiet corner of the market porter's pub over the road. It was agreed that the job was best done quickly, before the trumpet was moved or the locks were changed at The Black Cat.

The club usually shut at half-past-three and was locked up and left by four in the morning. Jim would ring and knock on the front door twenty minutes after the last person had left, and then hide. At the same time, Flynn would observe the rear of the building to see if there was any sign of movement. If it was all clear they would enter by the stage door, Flynn picking the locks if they had been changed.

He studied the plan of the nightclub that Jim and Molly had drawn for him on the back of an out of date play-bill taken from the wall. The one thing he was unhappy about was the lack of an alternative way out, should anyone come up the stairs to Brisk's office.

'That's what cost me four years in the Scrubbs, not having an escape route,' he said pensively, tapping the end of the pencil on the plan.

In the end they decided that a rope tied up and ready to go at the small window would do, as both he and Jim were wiry and agile enough to get through it, should the necessity be absolute.

Molly would stay back at Archie's in Holland Park, she being unnecessary for the operation. It was agreed that, as a last resort, she would call the police if she had not heard from them by six o'clock. Although this meant Flynn risked prison and Jim being returned to his parents, it was still reckoned to be better than the alternative likely to be offered by Harry Brisk. Flynn said he would miss out his last two pick-ups tomorrow night and meet Jim at Billingsgate for three o'clock. Finally, he gave Jim a list of things to bring, including torches, china-graph pencils, sticky tape and the rope, on the strict understanding that if anything were forgotten the job was off.

After shopping for these in nearby Clerkenwell they returned to Holland Park and found Archie sitting up in bed while Mrs Higgson packed a bag for him. Doctor Savage had arranged, he explained, for him to spend a short time at a sanatorium in Switzerland. After Mrs Higgson had left, he bade Molly sit down and asked her if she would mind staying on in the house 'to keep an eye on things', as he put it.

'But surely, that's what Mr and Mrs Higgson are for?' she said.

'Well, Molly, I'm afraid Mrs Higgson, or at least her cooking, is part of the problem. I've placed an advert for a cook in the London Evening News and now, since I have to go away, I was wondering if you would be good enough to interview the applicants for me. You'd be, kind of…unofficial housekeeper I suppose. I've made arrangements with the bank for you to draw any money you might need – I do hope that's alright.'

'Well,' said Molly, smiling, shrugging, shaking her head and agreeing all at the same time. 'I suppose it is.' She laughed and avoided Archie's outstretched hand to give him a hug.

'Thank you, Archie, we'll be fine here, 'til you get back.'

She kissed him on the cheek and then they left him to catch up on the sleep they had missed the night before.

Jim lingered at Molly's door for a while talking about the 'Mission' as it had become known between them. When he ran out of things to say she kissed him gently on the cheek and shut the door.

***

Jim awoke as the light from the high window faded across the room. After dressing he went to see Archie but found he had already left for Switzerland. As it was suppertime he went to wake Molly, who was still fast asleep, in a beautiful silk dressing gown that must have belonged to Archie's wife. He couldn't resist staring at her in silence for a minute or so, her nearly black hair scattered on the pillow and the soft rising and falling of her chest made the moment hard to break. Eventually she opened her eyes and stared at Jim for a few seconds, as if from somewhere far away. She held out her hand and Jim took it and sat on the edge of her bed.

'Jim…' she said, in a slightly poignant tone that promised advice, or possibly admonishment, but she didn't continue. His name just died away quietly in the dusky room. The picture of her father stood on the bedside table and Jim looked at him through the broken glass of the frame. He realised now who it was the figure reminded him of; it was Flynn; same wiry frame and dark hair, and although he stood there in the serious manner of all photos from the time, there still seemed the hint of a twinkle in his eye.

Eventually he said:

'It's dinnertime but I'm not sure if I could eat anything, Molly, and it's still hours until I have to meet Flynn.'

'Well,' said Molly, swinging her legs off the bed, 'let's do something to take our minds off it; how about the pictures?'

'Don't I have to rob a bank or something, before I can take you to the pictures?'

She laughed and tweaked his cheek.

'No, we can go anytime we like. Now go and tell Mrs Higgson I'll be down in ten minutes.'

After some fairly well burned chops, some barely boiled potatoes and cabbage that was almost reduced to liquid, they set off to walk to Notting Hill and the cinema. Molly took Jim's arm as the first proper fog of the year closed around them, giving shape to the beams of the street lamps and hiding the big houses on the hill even deeper in their gardens.

'So, how was your dinner, Jim?'

Jim considered.

'Well, she burned the chops and drowned the cabbage, it was like a natural disaster on a plate to be honest!'

'I know, wasn't it awful? One of the 'little jobs' Archie has asked me to do while he's away is to find him a cook. Mrs Higgson is just the caretaker's wife after all. It's not really fair for us to disparage the poor woman for her cooking, though how the unfortunate Mr Higgson has survived all these years is a wonder!'

Jim laughed.

'Are you going to do it?'

'God, Jim, I don't know, I've told Archie I will so I suppose so. It's all a bit much for me this high-living business. My mother *was* a cook for a while and now I'm being asked to interview them!'

They found the Coronet cinema near the top of the hill and decided to watch 'The Mummy', a horror film in which three archaeologists were endlessly pursued by a giant hulking figure wrapped in tattered bandages. It succeeded in taking their minds off what was to come that night, and caused Molly to cling satisfyingly tight to Jim's arm almost from the beginning. After the film they settled into the snug bar of a back street pub for Jim to accumulate what Molly described as a little 'Dutch courage'.

His nerves calmed, she took him back to the house and ran him a bath, while Jim checked and packed all the equipment that Flynn had asked him to collect for the job. Then he sat in the hot suds, playing the spare mouthpiece that he had brought from home, his heart beating the rhythm, his head longing for the tumult of jazz he would make, once he had the glass trumpet back in his hands.

19 - The Safe

Billingsgate loomed from the fog, a constellation of softened lights drifting towards him down Lower Thames Street. Even the raucous sounds of the market seemed muted by the deathly white mist shrouding the old building on the river. Jim paid off the cab, hefted his rucksack and went in search of Flynn among the lorries.

He found him parked in more or less the same spot as the night before, engine ticking over for warmth.

Jim climbed in with the bag and they moved off immediately, into the fog.

'Good night for it,' said Flynn.

'Is it? What if we get lost?'

'Not to worry, Jim, mis-spent my life running around the West End, in fogs worse than this an' all. Much better a job in the fog. You've only gotta make five yards on someone and you're as good as gone!'

He pulled the lorry over in a side street and ran through the checklist, getting Jim to pull the items from the bag as he named them. Eventually he seemed satisfied that everything necessary was present and told him to put on one of the pairs of gloves from his own small bag on the floor.

'Right, there's a soft cloth in there as well; I want you polish everything we've got that might possibly carry a fingerprint.'

When he was done, Flynn made him check it thoroughly for anything that could be used to track them down if they had to leave his rucksack behind.

'You don't wanna leave 'em an 'alfpenny chew,' he said.

'I don't even like halfpenny chews,' said Jim, puzzled.

'Alfpenny chew - clue Jim, it's rhyming slang, innit? One bloke me Dad knew, name of Johnny Slater, he stuck up a bank and they found he'd written the note – "Put the money in the bag or you're all dead" - on the back of his gas bill envelope! The coppers were waiting when he got back home, plastered from the pub, celebrating the success of the job. You had to laugh, even if he did get nine years!'

There was a sudden loud thump from behind, which made Jim start.

'Not to worry,' said Flynn looking out the back window at the single large box on the bed of the lorry. 'Just a specimen I've gotta deliver after we done the job.'

'Specimen?'

'Yeah, for the zoo, one of my regulars caught a seven and 'alf foot conger eel last night. I've got one of the curators up the London Zoo gives me good money for things like that.'

'But tonight, Flynn...of all nights...an eel?'

'Well you're not exactly paying top dollar are ya, Jim?'

He looked over his shoulder at the box again.

'And they'll only last so long in a wet box, it's a *live* eel the bloke wants.'

He ground the lorry back into gear and headed towards the West End. Jim soon realised that Flynn had not been exaggerating when he said he knew his way round London; even in the heavy fog he picked out one turn after another, bustling the little flat-bed along with barely a pause.

They arrived in good time and parked within view of the front doors of The Black Cat, switching off the engine and settling low in their seats to watch as the last few guests were helped into their cabs.

Shortly after the main doors were shut and the entrance lights and sign were put out, Jim saw a tall hulking shape emerge from the club and begin walking up the street towards them.

'That's Eugene,' he whispered, feeling his stomach tighten as he sank lower in his seat.

'Cor, you weren't kiddin, he *is* a big boy 'ent he!?'

'I don't know what he's doing out here, he normally leaves the back way with Mr Brisk,' said Jim, trying to keep his voice level.

As he came up Kingly Street, Eugene crossed over to the pavement on their side and Jim felt the fear grip his abdomen, squeezing a funny taste into his mouth. He wanted to slide off the seat onto the floor.

'Easy, son,' said Flynn's calm voice. 'He's not looking for us.'

As he came alongside the cab, Jim noticed the flash of a white bandage between Eugene's collar and hat, and then he was gone. Jim let out a huge breath and Flynn laughed.

'Well at least you didn't kill 'im, Jim. Looks like you did a fair job with the electric cable though, that's quite a bandage!'

They soon saw the reason for Eugene's unusual behaviour; within a few minutes he returned, at the wheel of Harry Brisk's black Jaguar. He held open the door as his boss emerged swiftly from The Black Cat and climbed into the back.

'There's something going on tonight, he usually gets a taxi home,' said Jim.

'Well as long as he stays gone for a while, Jim, I don't care where he goes.' They sat tight and waited until Edith, the cashier, came out, locked the door and left the club in darkness.

'That's unusual too,' said Jim as she disappeared down the street. 'It's one of Eugene's jobs to walk her to the night safe round the corner on Regent Street.'

'Mmmmmm,' said Flynn, his tone rising and falling in a mixture anticipation and surprise. 'Might get more than a trip to the pictures out of this after all,' he mused.

They waited the agreed half hour and then left the lorry and took up their positions. When Flynn had had enough time to get round the back, from where he could observe the rear of the building, Jim went over and pressed the front doorbell and rapped his knuckles on the plate glass door before retreating into the shadows up the street. Nothing, no light, no movement from inside the club. He collected his rucksack from the lorry and set off into the ever-deepening fog to join Flynn by the stage door.

'There's a slight problem,' Flynn whispered from his position crouched in the gloom.

'Is someone still inside?' asked Jim.

'No, but there is someone there,' he nodded down the little alley in the direction of the stage door.

Jim looked but could see nothing bar the slight halo of light around the stage door sign. Then he heard a giggle and the low imploring tone of a man's voice.

'No…' said a girl. 'It's freezing!'

'I'll get rid of 'em,' whispered Flynn. He pulled the big torch from Jim's rucksack and stood up.

'What's going on here?' he said in his most policemanly voice, shining it down the alley.

There was a squeak of panic, and after a very short pause, two figures ran awkwardly from the alleyway and off into the night.

'Right then, let's go,' he said.

It took a little while to identify the right key on the large bunch of spares that Molly had given them, and then they were inside. Jim looked at the fat electrical cable that had, probably, saved his and Molly's lives; it had been refitted into the wall with a bright new clip. They decided against using any of the club's lights, so as not alert anyone who might return that they were inside.

'It's best to know about them before they know about you,' as Flynn said.

The first hitch was the door to the office; try every key they might, nothing would work.

'They must have changed the lock after I got Molly out of there,' Jim surmised.

'Funny they didn't do the whole lot if they thought you might have keys.'

'What shall we do Flynn, kick it in?'

'Nah, it's a heavy one, take ages and make a hell of a noise, also...' he swung the torch across the narrow landing, 'no room for a run up. Not to worry.'

Flynn produced a key ring with some little rods and levers on. 'Lock picking's junior school stuff for a safe cracker!'

He knelt down and began fiddling his little sticks in and out of the lock.

'Cor, bit stiff; new lock.'

After a few minutes the door swung open and they were inside Harry Brisk's office. Flynn inspected the safe, stroking it gently with a gloved hand and murmuring quietly under his breath. Jim searched the desk, finding his old friend the gun lighter, which he put back in his pocket, making a mental note not to squeeze the trigger so hard next time.

He took the rope from the rucksack and tied it to one of the legs of the desk while Flynn tried the small window to make sure it would open if necessary. He shook his head as he looked briefly out into the back alley.

'Cor, bit tight, even for me.'

Having secured their escape route, Flynn now produced a doctor's stethoscope and a cardboard dial, with pointers like clock hands, from his bag. He stuck this to the safe 'to track the tumblers' he said, and applied the stethoscope to his patient, offering more gently soothing words. He began, with infinite care, to rotate the dials, stopping every now and then, to alter the incline of his head slightly and relocate the dial on his home made pointer. After a while he spoke to Jim:

'Right, get our pad out, first number is twenty-five left.'

Jim wrote this down carefully and sat waiting for the next; it was a long time coming.

'These old ones are often harder, they're so worn there's not much to go on.'

Jim went through the desk drawers, finding Harry Brisk's bottle of whisky and a collection of recent newspapers, with the story of Katie prominent. There was also the Evening Standard with the story about him. He looked at the picture of the schoolboy by the dim light of the fish tank and struggled to remember who it was he had been back then. He thought about taking it with him, but dropped it back into the drawer with the others, little realising how much he would come to regret that decision later on.

'Thirty-three right,' said Flynn standing up and blowing out his cheeks. He took a few steps round the office to get the circulation back into his legs and then resumed his crouching stance beside the grey hulk of the safe.

Jim sat and tried to outstare the giant gourami, trying to clear his mind of the fear that seeing Eugene again had stirred in him. The big fish seemed to sink down in the tank, as if relishing the contest. It fanned its fins slowly and pointed its big ugly forehead at Jim's; Jim thought of the big white bandage round Eugene's neck, of the terrible, humiliating telling off that Harry Brisk would have subjected him to for letting Jim escape with Molly. He shuddered and looked away from the fish, trying to think ahead.

'Okay, forty-six left,' said Flynn. 'So, check this for me, Jim, that's twenty-five left...' he carefully rotated the dial, 'Thirty-three right and then forty-six left.'

'That's it,' said Jim.

There was a faint click and Flynn reached surely for the handle.

'Here we go.'

It turned and Flynn gave a quiet yell of triumph as he swung open the heavy door. With a huge sigh of relief Jim saw the trumpet case on the bottom shelf. He pulled it out and placed it on the desk, flicking back the catches and opening the lid. There, safely nestled in its satin blue interior, was the glass trumpet. He drew it out and Flynn gave a whistle.

'That, Jim, is a beautiful thing,' he said, and then; 'You dare!' as Jim raised it towards his lips.

'I can play it very softly,' implored Jim, longing to feel the cool glass of the mouthpiece against his lip and to run through a couple of scales.

'There'll be plenty of time for that, pass me the bag.'

He began to fill the rucksack with paperwork and envelopes from the safe, grabbing everything indiscriminately and stuffing it into the bag.

'What do you want all that stuff for?' asked Jim.

'Dunno yet, may be a bit of insurance in here, bound to be some stuff Brisk doesn't want anyone to know about. Never know, may just save our necks if he catches up with us,' he said with a grin that Jim didn't feel like returning.

'And finally…' Flynn hefted a large cash box onto the desk and pulled out his picks again.

'Bit big for the bag, best open it here.'

Jim was getting edgy, especially after the thought of Harry Brisk catching up with them had been aired.

'Can't we just go, Flynn?'

'Only take a minute, besides, Jim, we might need the money, once we're on the run!'

He chortled to himself at Jim's obvious discomfort.

'Look, Jim, be sensible, if we only take the trumpet Brisk will know it's us. Anyone who robs the safe is gonna take everything, stands to reason. You untie that rope and pack it away while I see to this.'

He knelt down and focused all his attention on the little keyhole.

'Ah-ha! There we go.' He opened the lid and whistled.

'Jackpot, Jim!' The box bulged with notes, mainly in high denominations. Flynn grabbed an empty cash bag from the safe and began stuffing in the money.

'Cor, that's not just takings, can't be! Your Mr Brisk is getting all this cash ready for something, you can bet your trumpet on that.'

By the time they had finished, the old army rucksack was fairly bulging with money and documents.

'Right,' said Flynn, hoisting it onto his shoulders, 'as they always say in the movies; Let's get outta here!'

Rather than risk walking the streets with one bag of safe cracking equipment and another stuffed with money, they decided that Flynn would fetch the lorry up to the front and Jim would leave through the main entrance as soon as he pulled up.

This was accomplished without incident and Jim relocked the front doors of the club, leaving the back doors unlocked as if they had been picked, in the hope of throwing Harry Brisk off the scent or at least persuading him that it was not necessarily an 'inside job'.

It was only as they drove away that the tension pent up in the two of them turned to jubilation. Jim wanted to throw his arms around Flynn for the sheer relief and joy of having been reunited with the glass trumpet. Flynn was, for himself, delighted at what was easily his 'biggest payday ever' and 'all crook's money as well', which seemed to make it even better.

They drove back towards Holland Park through the fog, Flynn laughing and musing about what he would take Molly to see at the pictures.

Jim was pensive again as they pulled up in front of Archie's house.

'What's wrong, young Jim, shine worn off already? You don't mind me taking Molly to the flicks do yer? She's a woman, Jim, and well, with respect, you're just a lad.'

Jim sat very still and stared past Flynn out of the window.

'It's not that. It's just…'

He nodded into the gloom across the road towards the house.

'…That's Harry Brisk's car.'

20 - Conger

The Jag sat low, crouched in the fog. There was no doubt that it was the same one they had seen earlier outside The Black Cat; it had Harry Brisk's personal number plate CAT 1 and the same American whitewall tyres, favoured by men of Harry's occupation across the Atlantic.

Jim stared at it, shock and surprise prickling the hairs on his neck, questions skidding across his brain; 'How had Brisk found Archie's house, was he inside, what would he be doing?'

He looked up the driveway towards the house, and wondered what to do himself. It was still dark, only the light from the two carriage lamps either side of the front door penetrating the fog. Jim took a deep breath and consciously took control of his pounding heart. He reached into the rucksack on the floor and took out the crowbar, the only thing they had on them that resembled a weapon of any kind.

'You stay here in case they come out. If they try and drive off with Molly then stop them.'

'How exactly?' posed Flynn.

'I don't care, ram them if you have to.'

Jim climbed out of the cab and slipped away down the side of the house into the fog. He could easily reach the garden and hoped to slip inside, unnoticed, through the back of the house.

He found the scullery door, used by the Higgsons, unlocked and proceeded through the kitchen, stealing quietly across the tiles while listening intently for any noise from the house.

As he emerged into the darkness of the main entrance hall, from behind the green baize servant's door, Jim heard quietened voices and muffled footsteps from above. He shrank back, leaving open a crack through which he could just about see most of the hall and the front door.

Two figures appeared from the direction of the staircase, carrying a large sack between them; Jim shuddered, praying that if it contained Molly, she was still alive. The larger figure took the sack, slung it over his shoulder, and stood upright. Jim saw that it could only be Eugene. The other one opened the door for him and said in hushed tones:

'You put her in the car, and then come back here; we'll have one last look for the boy.' It was the unmistakable voice of Harry Brisk.

Eugene disappeared out into the now lightening fog and Harry Brisk turned and went back up the stairs. Jim considered his options. If he were serious about tackling Harry Brisk it would have to be now, before Eugene came back. Unless he did something, he knew he would never see Molly again. He crept from behind the green baize door and went silently up the stairs, his grip tightening involuntarily on the heavy steel crowbar.

**

Outside, Flynn sank lower in his seat as the lumbering figure of Eugene came down the path, the heavy sack over his shoulder. He looked cautiously each way, the few yards he could see down the street, before emerging fully from between the gates and approaching the car. He opened a rear door and threw his bundle heavily onto the back seat before locking the car and heading back to the house.

'I'll fix you, you evil sods,' said Flynn to himself, slipping quietly out of the cab and moving round to the back of the lorry.

**

Jim heard Brisk pass the principal bedrooms on the first floor and set off up the stairs at the end of the corridor. He left it a few seconds and then darted after him, keeping to the edge of the landing, where he thought the less creaky floorboards would be.

As he came to the second floor, Jim saw that all the doors along the landing had been opened. He ducked his head back out of sight just in time, as the hulking figure of Harry Brisk emerged from the furthest one. Jim steeled himself but heard Harry continue on round the corner at the far end of the corridor, where there were more guest bedrooms.

Jim took a deep breath and tried to stiffen both his resolve and his wobbly legs. He tapped the cold steel of the crowbar into the palm of his hand and wondered if Molly were even alive. He looked again along the landing and decided the best point of ambush would be behind a life-size marble bust which stood on a pillar where the corridor turned left. He stole along the carpeted landing and tried to hide behind the impassive goddess, half crouched, the metal bar raised.

What Jim had failed to realise was the room he had chosen to stand outside had another entrance round the corner; there was a sudden noise at his back as the door opened. He spun round, just in time to see an equally surprised Harry Brisk raising the pistol at his side.

***

The shot rang out just as Flynn returned to his side of the cab. He froze at the sound of it for a moment and then jumped in and started the engine. The comatose figure of Molly slumped along the bench seat, a small matted clot of blood near the crown of her dark hair.

'Come onnnnn,' he muttered through clenched teeth, hoping against all reason that Jim was alright.

***

It was the surprise that had stopped Harry Brisk, but only for a split second. It was the fear that had triggered Jim's reaction and just as the gun had come up he had brought the crowbar down hard. There was a crunch as Harry Brisk's thumb was smashed against the stock of the gun. The bullet went into the doorframe and Jim was gone, along the corridor and down the stairs almost before the gun hit the floor.

'Eugeeeeeeeene!' came the angry shout following him as he bolted down through the house. The giant form appeared from the clubroom and blocked the open front door just as Jim reached the bottom of the stairs. Impulsively he ran straight at Eugene who, unused to such bravado, instinctively braced himself to stop Jim dead. Just at the point of impact however Jim collapsed his legs, and using Mrs Higgson's polished floor like an ice rink he slid, on his knees, neatly between the spread legs of Harry Brisk's clumsy henchman. By the time Eugene had turned round Jim was through the open front door, had cleared the steps of the house and was bolting down the drive.

From the cab of the lorry Flynn saw the figure of Jim emerging from the fog.

'Here, Jim, in here.'

'They've got Molly!' he said running over to the Jaguar and trying to open the door.

'To me, Jim, to me, I've got her, hurry.'

Jim looked in confusion at the back seat of the Jaguar and was then persuaded to run by the sound of Eugene's heavy steps pounding the gravel of the drive.

Flynn had the lorry in gear and was rolling away down the hill as Jim ran towards it, pulling himself in through the open door.

'Molly, oh God!' he said, horrified at the sight of her bloodied head, lolling on the seat.

'She's all right, Jim, just a bang on the head,' said Flynn eyeing the two figures jumping into the Jaguar in his rear view mirror.

'Shut the door and hold on, we're not out of this yet.'

The fog was lit by an invisible sun, whose light now spread sparsely over what little could be seen in the half erased world about them.

'If only I can make half a furlong we'll be away.'

He veered the lorry suddenly into a barely perceptible side road and accelerated terrifyingly into the blank greyness. Another turn and they were hurtling down the hill that was Holland Park Avenue, Flynn navigating purely by the white lines that marked out the road.

His initial hope that they had dodged their pursuers was dashed when, after a minute, two large headlights appeared behind them.

'Maybe it's someone else,' said Jim hopefully, twisting round to look through the rear window of the cab.

'Looks like Jag headlights to me,' said Flynn eyeing the rear view mirror. The powerful car loomed quickly behind them and as the road widened to two lanes it pulled alongside.

Eugene was driving and Harry Brisk waved his gun awkwardly out of the window with his left hand.

'Pull over. You pull over or…'

He paused to bring the gun back into the car where he used the butt to club the occupant of the bag, who would not lie still but was writhing around on the rear seat.

Flynn heard a groan beside him; Molly was waking up.

'Jim, help her sit up.'

He turned towards Harry Brisk, blocking any view he may have had into the cab of the lorry.

'You can't bully me, Mr Brisk, I'm not one of your lackeys. Besides, shoot me and I'm bound to lose control, who's to say I won't kill the lot of us, you in your fancy Jag an' all?' He veered the lorry dangerously across the road causing Eugene to swerve away.

'You pull over now…' Harry Brisk shouted back grimly, 'or the girl gets it.'

Flynn checked over his shoulder and found Jim helping a very groggy Molly to sit up. She rubbed her head and looked from Jim to Flynn with some surprise.

'Where…what's…'

Flynn drew her forward so she could see the Jag driving alongside.

'Which girl is that then, Mr Brisk, wouldn't be this one would it?'

Brisk looked agog as he saw Molly's somewhat bleary face appear next to Flynn at the wheel. He turned and looked at the hostage, still thrashing around in the bag on the back seat of his car.

'Here comes the good bit!' said Flynn. Brisk had swivelled round and kneeling on his seat he reached back and pulled at the rope, which held the sack closed. Instantaneously the seven-and-a-half foot of slimy muscle, that is a conger eel, shot out of the bag and began thrashing and snapping and biting at everything in the front of the car. They heard Eugene let out a scream of surprisingly high pitch for such a large man and, as the car began to swerve wildly, a shot went off splintering one of the car windows.

Flynn took the opportunity to escape by veering into a slip road that came up and they were all treated to the sound of a very comprehensive crash as the big Jaguar disappeared from view.

'That was incredible!' whooped Jim. 'How on earth…'

Molly, who obviously thought she was still dreaming, sat there slowly shaking her head in wonder.

'The only thing in the world Eugene was afraid of…snakes.'

Flynn was still laughing.

'That wasn't a snake, that was one very large conger eel I was bringing up for London Zoo. I had it in a wet crate in the back and swapped it for you when that ape of Brisk's went back in the house.'

'But did you hear him scream?' said Molly. They all burst out laughing again and Flynn pulled the lorry over while they regained their composure.

When they had all calmed down a little, Jim looked up at the big road sign on the roundabout where they had stopped. It was getting much lighter by now and the fog seemed to have lifted a little.

'Question is though,' he said more soberly, 'where do we go now? We can't go back to Archie's.'

'What if Harry's dead?' asked Molly.

'Still can't risk it, people like Harry Brisk don't die easy,' said Flynn. 'And now he's had a good look at the lorry, the first thing I'm gonna do is get shot of it.'

The next exit off the roundabout was sign-posted 'Brighton and the South Coast'. Flynn took it.

***

It was barely lunchtime when they reached Hastings. The fog had cleared as they left town and the sky now stretched, a pristine blue, from the horizon upwards. They had stopped briefly at a petrol station for Flynn to count his haul, and for

Molly to use the lavatory sink to wash the blood from her hair. Any talk of doctors or hospital she simply waved away.

Molly and Jim took the luggage into a café while Flynn returned the lorry to his employers. Having counted the takings from Harry Brisk's safe he had no qualms about quitting his job and, since they only ever paid him cash and knew him as 'John', he felt that he would be reasonably safe from even the long tentacles of Harry Brisk.

Molly and Jim ordered a substantial lunch and settled down in the upstairs of the beach front café, the window offering a panoramic view from the cliffs to their left, across the stony foreshore, with its tall wooden net houses and fishing smacks dragged up on the beach, to the long stretch of the front, down towards the 'good' hotels.

They had barely finished their main courses when there was a loud honking and a good deal of shouting from below. Molly leaned toward the window for a better view.

'Good God! What has he gone and done?' she cried, almost spilling tea down her front, and then she was off down the stairs with Jim after her. They bowled out of the door and Jim gasped and then burst out laughing.

'What d'ya think? Better than a smelly old fish lorry eh?'

He sat at the wheel of a low cream and green open topped sports car, the chrome radiator spread in a grin almost as broad as his own. He revved the engine and the sound went from a low burble to something like an ogre clearing its throat.

Molly looked along its length and back again, her mouth agape, her eyes shining.

'Have you gone mad, Flynn? I let you out of my sight for half an hour and you come back with…with…'

'It's an Austin Healey 100, darlin', and don't worry, it's not just some spur of the moment madness. I've had me eye on this beauty for weeks! It's 'ad pride of place in the dealers down the road and they done me a good price for cash.'

He climbed out and opened the boot where Jim stashed the bags and his trumpet case while Molly settled the bill.

They got in the car and tore off down the front, Molly and Jim having to share the front passenger seat. Jim was uncomfortable with Molly sitting on top of him, her hair blowing back in his face, but it was not to be for long. Flynn pulled over outside one of the smarter hotels and stopped the car.

'Right, in you go, Jim. I've booked us a couple of rooms in the name of Slater, after me old mate Johnny I was telling you about. You go up and have a rest, Molly here is going to pay me that trip to the pictures she owes me, after…' here he revved the engine again making Molly squeal, '…we've been for a little drive.'

Jim took the trumpet case from the boot of the car and left Molly sitting in the front seat. He stood there staring at her dumbly, fighting a strange feeling similar to vertigo.

It was as if he had accidentally given away something that he didn't even realise he had, but that was surely the most precious thing in the world.

He wanted to protest but didn't know what to say, he wanted to talk to Molly but he was not sure what about. Instead he stood in the doorway of the hotel and watched Flynn spin the car expertly round, out of the car park and then, with a bark of the throttle; she dwindled away into a speck down the sunlit road to the west.

21 - Cold

Jim lay down and fell asleep before he had even the time to kick off his shoes. He dreamed of many things but mostly of Molly. After a kaleidoscope of strange adventures, he sat with her in a wood, an ornate cage on his lap. He wanted to show her what was inside, a bird of paradise with feathers redder than the heart of sunset, bluer than a clear dawn sky, but she would not look, distracted as she was by the raucous calls of crows from the branches above them, craning her head and standing, to try and glimpse them through the trees. Jim reached into the cage and drew out the bird, but as he did so a vicious wind tore through the wood, shredding the trees of their leaves. He looked up to see Molly, walking away down the path that led to the open country, following the cawing and tumbling crows against the blue-black clouds in the sky above. In his hand the bird quivered and as he watched, its feathers began to blow away in the wind, he cupped his hands, trying to protect it from the icy blast but it was no good. In seconds it was bare and, as its delicate head drooped, he felt the warmth drain from the tiny body.

He awoke slowly, struggling back to consciousness, pulling reality back from the darkness of his dream. He sat up on the edge of the bed, resting his head in his hands as torment resolved itself into mere bleakness. The sun had now disappeared and rain from the obscuring clouds rattled in gusts against the window. Jim reached for his trumpet case and took the beautiful instrument in his hands, turning it this way and that, drawing strength from its form and comfort from its provenance. Across time, this thing of beauty had been offered to him, and he at least had been able to reach out and grasp it. Now he needed to play.

The room was the wrong place, so he replaced his trumpet in its case and took the lift down to reception. A kindly looking middle-aged woman stood behind the desk and listened to his unusual request.

'I need somewhere to play my trumpet, I wonder if you could help?'

'Oh really, dear, how nice, do you have a concert to practise for?'

Jim shook his head.

'No, I just need somewhere to play,' he said, not feeling as if he wanted to lie, even a little bit. The woman hesitated a moment, looking curiously at him.

'Well, I think you may be in luck, follow me.'

She called someone from the back office to mind the desk and took a large key from one of the drawers before leading him off down a carpeted corridor which ran towards the rear of the hotel where, he expected, there was an unused storeroom or something similar. Jim was surprised as she unlocked a set of double doors and swung them open to reveal a large curtained ballroom. As she led him across the empty floor she explained:

'This should do fine, dear, it's fairly well sound-proofed you see, so as not to disturb the guests if we have a late night do.'

She drew back a curtain to show Jim the light switches, most of which operated a series of chandeliers that hung from the Rococo ceiling. She switched on one and left him alone, closing the doors behind her as she left. Jim tried a few of the other switches, eventually finding one which operated a large mirror ball, sending a sea of delicate halos swirling around the walls of the huge room. He was spellbound, having never seen a mirror ball or indeed anything like it. Jim turned out all the other lights and stood there aghast as the room disappeared into a twinkling whirlpool around him.

He drew the trumpet from its case and began to play to himself, softly at first, his eyes gradually losing focus on the galaxy circling the walls. He didn't play Dizzy this time, and he didn't play anyone else either. He just played.

***

Molly and Flynn arrived back at the hotel just as the bruised clouds lining the horizon faded from purple to black. She sent Flynn through to the restaurant to book a table for dinner, before taking the shopping they had bought up to the rooms.

'Don't forget, Flynn…' she called from the lift, '…it's a table for three.'

She was puzzled and a little concerned at failing to find Jim in either of the rooms and having dropped her bags she went back down to reception.

The young lady there had not seen Jim and did not recognise him from Molly's description so she went back upstairs, her apprehension growing. When Flynn came in and found her, she made him take their things through to the other room and then stood a while, her head against the cold glass of the window, pondering Jim's whereabouts.

She opened it, lit a cigarette and stared out into the near darkness, controlling her worry with difficulty. Surely, she thought, Harry Brisk, even assuming that he had survived the crash in the Jaguar, would not have been able to track them to here, especially in one day. There was a beat of fear when she noticed that the trumpet case was missing but Jim's rucksack was still there, sat by the end of the second bed and she felt a little reassured.

The wind had died away now and she leaned out into the air, one hand on the sill, listening to the soft sound of a gentle surf running onto the beach.

It was then that she heard it, fainter than the last glimmer of light dividing sea from sky, a long drawn out note ending in a poignant little twist at the end. It seemed to climb up from somewhere below, thread its way round Molly's heart and give it a painful little tug. She threw her cigarette into the night and headed for the lift.

She soon found the corridor leading away from reception towards the rear of the hotel and, as she went along it, she picked up the plaintive sound of Jim's trumpet. At least she assumed it was Jim; this was music such as she had not heard from him before. There was a searing sadness to it; a kind of haunted melancholy that had more in common with the blues than anything she had heard him play at The Black Cat. She paused outside the double doors to the ballroom for a moment and then opened one, as quietly as possible.

Jim stood, his back to her, near the middle of the floor in the darkened vortex with which the mirror ball engulfed the room. Music poured from the bell of the glass trumpet and seemed to swirl up and around with the ten thousand tiny lights orbiting the walls. Molly almost felt dizzy with it all as she crossed the floor towards Jim, treading softly so as not to disturb him and break the spell. She looked at his face as she came alongside; his eyes were squeezed tight shut and his cheeks were wet with tears. She stood until the last long note of the piece died away. His eyes opened and he saw

Molly with a start. She stepped into his arms and, as he folded them behind her, she felt his raw emotion enter her like a charge.

'What can I do, Jim?' she said softly. 'You're still just a boy.'

She held him as he wept, unable to stop the tears, unwilling to let him cry alone.

***

Dinner that night was predictably awkward. At first it had been virtually impossible to convince Jim to come but somehow Molly managed it. Once she had got him upstairs and asked him which of the two beds he wanted, and then spent some time complaining about Flynn's flashy ways with Harry Brisk's money, while hanging her new clothes in the wardrobe, he began to feel a little less morose, a little less sure that he had lost her.

Sitting down together in the hotel's rather fancy restaurant they all felt uncomfortable, as apart from anything else, they were unfamiliar with such finery. Many of the names of the dishes were in French and only Molly knew anything at all about wine.

The conversation was no easier; Jim was the gooseberry, Flynn wanted Molly to himself and she tried to pretend there was nothing wrong. Jim left after the main course, excusing himself by saying he was tired.

After lying, unblinking, in the darkness for some while, he heard the faint undertones of a quiet argument between Molly and Flynn from outside the door. He feigned sleep as she entered the room and sat quietly on the edge of his bed, stroking the hair from his face with the back of her fingertips. She said his name softly but when he did not respond he could feel her relief. Jim watched between his eyelashes as she stood and collected together her night things. He lay still, longing for her to cross to the bathroom, but instead she quietly opened the door and slipped away into the hall. He heard the door to Flynn's room across the corridor open and close.

Jim lay unmoving for perhaps an hour. He felt overcome, as if by a rigour mortis of wretchedness and began to wonder, after some time, if he would ever rise from the bed again.

Eventually he sat up and after looking out into the night for a few minutes, he gathered together his things and left the hotel.

***

Jim just caught the last train to London. He closed himself into an empty compartment and thought about the music he had played that afternoon in the ballroom. It was new music, music that he had never heard before and strangely for Jim, music he could not fully recall. This was unique for him; his 'photographic' or as Stanley used to jokingly call it, his 'phonographic' memory for music and sound in general, did not seem to apply. All Jim could recall of the music he had made in the ballroom was the feeling it had created, or perhaps the feeling that had created it, as it flowed from him; it was hard to say which was right, both things seemed true at the same time. Now, making music this way was all he wanted to do and all he needed was a place to do it.

It was late when the last train arrived in London and Jim considered his options. He dare not return to Archie's, as that was the one place at which Brisk could find him, and he didn't want to put Archie and the Higgsons at risk. He counted what little money he had; even in the cheapest hotel it would last no more than a few days. That left the den; he crossed Trafalgar Square and caught a 59 bus up towards West Hampstead.

He found things at the den just as they had left them the night of Archie's coughing fit. It was a fairly depressing prospect after the luxury of Holland Park but at least there was plenty of firewood, left from an old chest of drawers Archie had found in the street. Jim spent some time staring into the flames of his small fire and wondering how the losing of something that you never really had could hurt quite so much. He found a nearly full bottle of whisky that had rolled off into the shadows the night of Archie's rescue and treated himself to a quick shot to warm against the cold of the night to come. The sudden hotness of it in his throat made him gasp and he wondered that Archie could consume so much of something so volatile.

The cold woke him so early that not even the café was open. He spent nearly half an hour jumping up and down and banging his arms around to get the blood to warm his body, before the woman, who he now realised was not really Marilyn Monroe, arrived to open up. She let him in with her and made them both a cup of tea before starting to prepare the café for the breakfast rush. Jim ate a huge breakfast and bought a few provisions from the shop next door, before heading back to the den to unearth the glass trumpet from its hiding place.

He spent the whole day with it. He played slowly at first, allowing great areas of darkness to fill in the space around the notes, and then gradually faster, layering runs in different keys over one another, until a great blizzard of music banked over the rubble, rising up through the roofless wreck of number seventeen and into the darkening winter sky to perplex passers by.

He burned the rest of the drawers left in the woodpile and used the fire to cook a small supper of baked beans and tea. It was too cold to play now and Jim settled down to sleep under all the clothes he could find, as close to the fire as he dared.

This settled into a pattern over the next few days, with the exception of the time that Jim had to spend hunting for wood to burn, as the shortening days became colder and colder.

As the money ran low he had to give up the café and lived entirely on what he could cook over the fire. His main sustenance was music; it was what he lived for and increasingly, what he lived on. His trumpet became a vessel for exploring the world of resonance, dissonance, rhythm and time. He discovered structures and relationships between the various notes and keys that he had never noticed before. As he became a stronger musician, wrapped up in his own escape from everything out there in the world, he scarcely noticed his weakening body. He seemed to become used to the increasingly small portions of food that he would allow himself from the dwindling stockpile. He did not even consider busking, not so much now from fear of Harry Brisk or the police, as the desire to be left alone with music all his own, music from his own lips, with his own breath, for his ears only.

It was the cold that was the biggest enemy. It was stealthy and likely to strike in the night. It was the one word Archie uttered when he finally laid a hand upon Jim's still body, where it lay, on the floor of the shattered building many days later.

'Cold.'

22 - Revelations

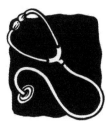

*I*t was Molly who could not forgive herself the most. She said it over and over until Archie had Doctor Savage give her a sedative and Mrs Higgson put her to bed.

She had called Archie from the south coast as soon as she had discovered Jim missing and then again every day, but he had been away from London at a sanatorium near Geneva and could not be reached. When Molly finally spoke to him on the day he returned, her alarm erupted into near panic when she heard that Jim was not staying at Holland Park.

'God, Archie, where could he be if not there? He's no money and I know he'd rather die than go back to his parents.'

Archie could think of only one place to look; he got Higgson to fetch the car and they headed over to West Hampstead.

He marvelled now, that life could endure somehow, in a body so cold, even though Doctor

Savage warned him that the rekindling of such a tiny spark was no certainty.

He left a nurse who tended Jim, even sleeping in the same room on a divan that Higgson fetched from one of the upstairs rooms. The recovery was slow and it took a while before any of them were sure it would be the same old Jim that they would get back in the end.

Archie bided his time and waited, turning over and over in his fingers the slightly crumpled photograph of a woman that had been clutched in Jim's hand when they had found him. He gazed again at her familiar face, surrounded by a hairstyle that he had never seen before. There was no doubt in his mind, it was his Elizabeth. From where Jim had got this picture, a picture of her that he had never seen before, Archie could only wonder. He opened his bureau and placed it in a drawer with the remainder of the copies he'd had made. Most of them had been given to Warnock's men yesterday, during the briefing. Archie had sat at the back of the clubroom and listened, making sure that they had all the known facts and that those facts were all correct. He had added what little he actually knew about Jim's background to Warnock's briefing notes, but would have to wait until the boy was recovered enough to tell them more.

Although he had not met Warnock before, the private detective had impressed Archie. He had worked often with Mortimer and Hume, the family's lawyers and although he had left Scotland

Yard a few years before under somewhat of a cloud, Mortimer had assured Archie that he was the very best and that, so long as money was no object, he was the most likely man to get results.

***

Molly sat by Jim's bed almost continually for the next three days and nights. He moaned a few times and once he opened his eyes, although he did not seem to focus on her. On the morning of the fourth day she awoke to find him looking quietly across the covers at her.

'Jim! Jim, can you hear me?'

He nodded infinitesimally; Molly leaned forward and took his hand. His fingers closed around hers and he gazed into her eyes, his own steady and unfathomable.

Molly looked at him in wonder.

'Where have you been, Jim?'

Jim gave an even more imperceptible shake of the head, which could have meant either 'I don't know' or 'I could never really explain'.

'We wondered if you were ever coming back.'

'I'm back, Molly,' he said quietly. 'Back to stay.'

She felt herself welling up.

'Don't cry,' Jim said before she'd even had time to shed a tear. 'I understand…about Flynn.'

'Do you?'

'Of course, Molly, more than you know.'

He thought about Molly as a small child, singing and dancing on the kitchen table while the dark, wiry figure of her father looked on, amazed that God should ever have granted him such a wonder.

'Where's Archie?'

'I don't know, downstairs probably.'

'He'll be wanting to see me, go and tell him I'm awake, Molly.'

She shut the door quietly and went down the hall, wondering at the change that Jim's visit to the threshold of death had wrought. From even so brief a conversation, she felt that he had crept across that narrow divide and stolen something of eternity to bring back with him.

Archie was out of his chair and up the stairs as soon as she let him know that Jim had come round. He sat on the edge of the bed and smiled down at him.

'Have you got my photograph?' Jim asked him.

'Yes, Jim,' he said, surprised that the subject of his obsession should come up so quickly. 'I wanted to talk to you about that.'

'She's my mother isn't she?'

Archie nodded and looked at the floor for a moment before meeting Jim's gaze.

'I think so, Jim.'

'And do you know who she is?'

'Yes, Jim, I think I do, but not where. I don't even know if she's still alive.'

'She is, I'm sure she is.'

He took Archie's hand in his own and felt the power of both their hopes in that grip. As it finally loosened, Archie looked at Jim to find him asleep once more.

He did not have long to wait before Jim's belief was confirmed; Mr Mortimer phoned early that evening, Archie took the call in the dwindling light of the clubroom.

'Well the good news is; it looks like Warnock's found her, Archie.'

'And the bad news?'

'It's where she is I'm afraid.'

Mr Mortimer read out an address, which Archie scribbled down on a pad before replacing the receiver and sitting down, heavily, on the chair nearest the phone. Jim found him there sometime later, his head in his hands.

'Did you find her, Archie?' he asked kneeling down to look up through the masking fingers.

The head nodded and Jim took the proffered piece of paper over to the one lamp that was switched on.

It had 'Virginia Water Institute for the Mentally Ill' written on it, with an address.

'You shouldn't be out of bed, Jim,' said Archie tiredly, his head still in his hands.

'I'm fine; don't worry about me. When can we see her?'

'Mr Mortimer is arranging access at the moment. He has a few strings to pull apparently. Probably tomorrow, all being well.'

In the end it took several days for the trip to be arranged. Molly watched Jim fondly but with a new respect for whatever it was that had happened to him during those long days when she wondered if she would ever see him properly again.

One afternoon Archie came to see him 'for a proper chat', as he put it. He sat stirring his tea for a long time before finally looking Jim in the face.

'You see, Jim, it turns out that it was no accident that you and I both ended up at number seventeen. You went there to find out who she was…and I just used to go there because…well, because it was the last place I ever saw Elizabeth. Long before Celia finally had enough and left me, I would get in the car, horribly drunk sometimes. I would drive down to Belsize Road and just stare up at where the house had been. Wasn't long before I found a way in and I would make a fire and just sit there drinking all night, trying to feel her presence.'

He laughed a little at the irony of it.

'Of course I never did, because she wasn't actually dead.'

Jim said nothing but sat with his hands around his knees, waiting for Archie to continue.

'Your mother and I were…we were….well we weren't 'engaged' as such but we were…in love.' He looked down at the vortex he had created in the centre of his teacup.

'We were going to marry after the war and I wanted to do the whole thing properly, you know, ask her father for her hand and all that, but she was very funny about her family. Said they were this and that, they were away, always very evasive. She was quite highly strung, I would often find her in tears after going to Church on a Sunday and I didn't want to press her too much on the subject of her family.

'It was a tremendous shock to see her photograph in your hands when we found you, Jim, you see, for all these years I had thought she was dead. She was killed by a German bomb that hit number seventeen in September 1943. That was what I found out as soon as I got back to England after the war. The damage had been so extensive that her body was never found; but that wasn't so unusual, those bloody five-hundred pounders were mostly high explosive and they didn't leave much behind.

'It was when you were at death's door I realised that Elizabeth must be your mother; the similarity is obvious once you see it. I did wonder for a moment if you...if you were mine...but the dates just don't add up. You were born nearly a year and a half after I last saw your mother, and that could only mean one thing...she couldn't have died at number seventeen, because that was bombed not long after I last saw her, which was just before I was shot down over Cologne.'

Jim considered a moment.

'But, Archie, everyone else says she died in the blast, Renee who I spoke to, everyone round there.'

'Well that's true, Jim all except...' here Archie drew a piece of paper from a file he had brought with him, '...one. This is a witness statement obtained by one of Warnock's men; it's from a woman who lived at number twenty, almost opposite number seventeen. It says that Elizabeth was taken away by an older man and a woman in a car on the night of the attack. She was put in the car and driven away after a huge row, some of it in the street. She's no idea who the people were or what the argument was about or where she was taken off to. It looks like Elizabeth was very lucky, whoever took her away saved her life, three and a half hours later the house was rubble.'

'So why was she reported dead then, if she had been seen being taken away?'

'What they call the fog of war, Jim. This lady was badly injured herself in the explosion and was in hospital for weeks. Nobody ever asked her, nobody else had witnessed the argument and nobody else had seen Elizabeth put into the car and driven off.'

Archie stood up and crossed to the window from where he could stare at the trees that ringed the garden.

'I was repatriated in 1945, I'd heard nothing from Elizabeth while I was in prisoner of war camp in Germany, but that was not so surprising as everything was totally chaotic at the end of the war. There was very little mail, very little of anything really. When I got back to England I tried to telephone the house and found it was unobtainable, so I went there.'

Jim imagined Archie coming along the road and finding the gaping sky where there was a house before, a pile of bricks and splintered timbers where he had last been with Elizabeth.

'A neighbour who had known us both found me standing there in the street, just staring at the rubble, she took me in and explained what had happened. She had a copy of the local paper, which said that there had been no survivors. She told me how she'd stopped for a chat with Elizabeth that very evening, the night of the bomb.'

Archie went quiet for a while as he stood between the curtains, still looking out into the darkening garden.

'And now…'

Archie stopped, cleared his throat and was silent for a moment.

'And now, after all these years and years…it turns out she wasn't dead after all. She's been in Surrey…just down the road.'

There was quiet now for a long time. Archie stared from the window while Jim gazed at Archie's back. The carriage clock on the mantelshelf ticked gently and the light softened and faded a little more. Downstairs the dinner gong sounded and then Molly came and tapped on the door.

'Are you two coming to dinner? It's the new cook's first night, judging by the aroma from the kitchen I think she's out to impress!'

'You two go on down,' said Archie not turning from the window. 'I'll be along shortly.'

***

The cloud had cleared the next morning and Higgson pulled the car round into the drive under a clear blue sky. Jim put the glass trumpet in the boot along with a small case and climbed in the back with Molly. Archie joined them looking rather smart in a blue suit with a dark ruby red tie and his hair neatly slicked back. Molly marvelled at the transformation from the frightening, coughing tramp she had met not so very long ago.

'We are to meet Mortimer there,' he said as they swung out onto Holland Park Avenue.

'He's pulled some strings to get us in to see Elizabeth, but he didn't sound too positive about her condition I'm afraid.'

They drove for a while before Molly, her hand reassuringly on his arm, asked:

'What are you going to say to her, Archie? After all these years?'

'I don't think I shall go in, I'm not sure really. It may not be a good idea; we shall have to talk to her doctors first. The important thing is that Jim gets to meet her, and we find out how she is.'

Jim spent the journey looking out of the window at the winter sunshine and tried not to think too hard about the meeting with his mother. He had no idea what all these nervous emotions he had fluttering inside would do when he finally came face to face with her, or even if she would understand who he was. He corralled them away in the far corner of his mind and tried to enjoy the moment, the new feeling that just being alive seemed to have.

Mortimer was waiting for them in the car park when they arrived about an hour later; he climbed in and sat on one of the fold-down seats facing them before shaking Jim's hand warmly.

'Now, from what I can gather, Elizabeth has been here a very long time, since sometime in 1943. She is classed as disturbed rather than deranged it seems, but she will talk to almost no-one except, I'm afraid, herself. On the bright side though, it looks as if she was never legally sectioned, as they call it. Technically she is a voluntary patient and in theory, in law, she is free to leave the hospital if she wishes to do so.'

He opened his case and took out some papers, handing Archie an envelope.

'Now, here is your letter detailing the appointment. Elizabeth is under a new doctor, Doctor…' Mr Mortimer studied some of his papers,'…Bennett, a nice sounding young woman and she seems very pleased that somebody is at last going to visit Elizabeth.'

He got out of the car with them and shook Archie by the hand.

'Good luck, Archie, just don't...don't expect too much will you, old man. If you need me I'll be waiting out here in the car.'

Jim turned and looked at the huge asylum building and then across at Archie, who seemed drawn and nervous.

'Come on then,' he said and headed for the entrance.

23 - Asylum

They crunched across the gravel towards the rather ominous looking tower that stood over the main entrance to the building. After a short wait a porter led them along an almost endless checkerboard corridor towards the office of Doctor Bennett.

Patients were dotted here and there along its length. Some seemed perfectly happy, like the neatly dressed man by the double doors who called: 'Tickets please, tickets please,' as they filed by. A woman by the stairwell made Molly jump by letting out a sudden loud shriek when they appeared and another swooped past with a strange bobbing motion, her gown held out like wings.

'Don't worry about these,' advised their guide in a matter-of-fact tone. 'They're all harmless really, all the dangerous ones are on the locked wing back there.' He swung his thumb up over his shoulder to indicate the other wing radiating off from the main entrance, Molly clung onto Archie's arm nonetheless.

Dr Bennett was a pleasant woman of about thirty-five. She had a neat bun of blonde hair from which protruded a spare pen, and had added to her short stature with a pair of green high heels.

'Now, I'm so glad…' she said, once she had got them all sat down in her office, '…that someone has at last come to visit Elizabeth. I've been here five years and she's not had so much as a card on her birthday in all that time. I was hoping that perhaps you could tell me a little about her, as I do think that she is one of the few patients here that might have at least some chance of release one day. I have been working with her for the last six months and reduced her medication substantially, what we really need to do is to get her talking, and with that, I'm afraid, I've been less successful.'

Archie looked up from studying his hands in his lap.

'Can you tell me who booked her into the hospital and at what date?'

'Well I shall have to check that; *technically* it is covered by patient confidentiality - but I must say that the hospital director seemed quite keen that we co-operate with you in every way possible after talking with your Mr Mortimer.'

She checked her watch.

'I have to run as I've got a staff board for an hour now but hopefully we can have more of a chat after your visit.

Dr Bennett leaned a little across the desk and her voice dropped to a more confidential tone.'

I'll arrange for Elizabeth's full records to be sent up, including her admission papers.'

She tapped a file on her desk to straighten the contents and stepped out of the door.

'If you'd like to wait here one of the nurses will take you down onto the ward and find you a visiting room.'

After a minute a nurse appeared at the door but instead of opening it, carried on a conversation, presumably with one of the other nurses in the corridor.

'No…' she said in a bored voice, '…can't, I got a visit.'

There was a pause while they could just hear the other nurse asking who with.

'Dead-Baby-Lizzie…yeah…okay.'

She opened the door, ushered them into the corridor and led them down to the ward. Jim stepped up to walk beside her.

'Why do you call her Dead-Baby-Lizzie?' he asked.

The nurse laughed and put her hand to her mouth.

'Oops sorry, you wasn't meant to hear that, it's just a nickname really. You'll soon see when you meet her.'

Archie suddenly pulled up.

'Look, Jim, I think it's better you go without me really. You and Molly go and I'll wait for you back there in the office.'

Jim realised that Archie was shaking, his hands wavered and there was a look of panic in his eyes.

He turned and headed back to the office while the nurse led Jim and Molly on down the corridor.

They entered the ward, which seemed largely empty and Jim's eye was immediately caught by a small figure in a red dressing gown, sitting on a bed at the far end. She neither looked up nor spoke as they approached but just stared into the empty air in front of her face.

'Lizzie…' said the nurse, '…there's someone here to see you.'

The woman looked up sharply as though surprised. Her face was thin and tightly framed by her almost black hair, streaked with grey. Her dark eyes bored into the nurse.

'The baby's dead,' she said.

'Yes Lizzie, I know. This young man is James; he's come to see you.'

The woman looked away, back to the same bit of space on which she was focusing before.

'Dead baby,' she said. 'Baby's dead.'

'I could go and get you a visiting room if you'd like,' said the nurse, 'but the ward's fairly empty at the moment and she's generally happier here.'

'No, that's fine,' said Jim. 'Here is fine.'

He looked at Molly who took the seat next to the bed, a slight expression of shock on her face, her hand covering her mouth, her eyes restraining tears.

'Dead baby,' said Lizzie again, as Jim sat down in front of her on the edge of the bed.

He looked into her eyes and took her hand between the two of his. He could still see the woman in the photo, the warm laughing woman, her gaunt cheekbones now merely stretchers for the battered canvas that was her face. She stared right through him.

'Baby's dead,' she said again.

As he looked straight back into her dark eyes from his own, Jim felt her focus on him.

'Baby's dead,' she said again, more softly.

Jim shook his head almost imperceptibly, as their eyes held one another.

'No…' said Jim.

'The baby's not dead.'

'Dead baby,' she said, even more quietly.

'No…' said Jim, unblinkingly. 'It's not dead, baby's alive. It's still alive.'

She said it again but this time, although her lips moved, no sound came. Jim still held her eyes in his and shook his head even more slightly.

'No,' his lips mouthed the word. There was silence for a minute or two and then he leaned forward and embraced her. 'Not dead,' he said quietly. He looked down at Molly in the chair and saw that the tears were streaming down her face.

'Still alive,' he said again, 'still alive.'

***

Jim led Lizzie slowly back to Doctor Bennett's office. She did not speak again, she did not say 'dead baby, baby's dead', or indeed anything at all. Nor would she let go of Jim's hands or the hold that her own eyes had on his. She walked slowly along gazing up at him with a slight expression of bafflement.

Archie sprang up as they entered. He looked at Lizzie in amazement, struggling to believe it really was her.

'Lizzie?' he said but she would not look at him, fixated as she was on Jim.

Jim sat her in one of the two chairs in front of the doctor's desk and held her hand.

'Molly, would you go back to the car and get my trumpet case and the small suitcase with it?' he asked.

Molly left them and Archie crouched down by Elizabeth's chair. He called her name softly but she would not turn her head towards him. They stayed like that for the few minutes it took Molly to return from the car with the two cases.

Jim had some difficulty disengaging his hands from Lizzie's but he eventually managed it and brought forth the glass trumpet.

'I want to try playing her this,' he said. 'It's the music inscribed on the bell of the trumpet.'

Almost as soon as he began playing the tune Archie tore his gaze away from Lizzie. He looked at Jim, surprised.

'That's the music on the trumpet? Jim, it's 'Someone To Watch Over Me', it was our favourite tune!'

He looked back at Lizzie, who was swaying slightly in time with the music.

'See if she'll dance, Archie,' hissed Molly quietly.

Archie rose to his feet and gently coaxed Lizzie into standing. He took her hand in his; put his arm across her back and they began to move slowly round to the music. Lizzie danced as if in a trance, her head resting on Archie's arm, eyes open but staring into space again.

Jim caught Molly's eye as he played and nodded towards the small case she had set down by the desk. She opened it and found inside an RAF officer's peaked cap. She looked up quizzically at Jim who nodded at Archie. He looked surprised but allowed Molly to place it on top of his head, as he circulated slowly with Lizzie. After a minute or so he called gently down to her.

'Lizzie... Lizzie.'

She looked up slowly into his face. For a moment there was nothing, save the soft trumpet and their swaying bodies. Then:

'Archie?' she said.

***

To her credit, Doctor Bennett had taken it all pretty well when she returned to her office and found such a strange scene being played out. She was gratified to see Elizabeth finally in contact with someone, after so many years of total isolation. When Jim finally stopped playing the tune, they found that she was still humming it to herself and would by no means stop slow dancing Archie around the office. It was as if she had found, after all these years, a happy dream and did not want to wake up. She still would not speak but she had at least stopped saying 'dead baby'.

Any attempt to detach her from Archie caused her to struggle and cry out. In the end Doctor Bennett had a nurse give Lizzie a sedative injection and she soon fell asleep in his arms. He refused to place her on the trolley that the nurses brought and instead carried her back to bed. Jim watched them go off down the long corridor, enveloped in the flaring light from a low winter sun as it blazed back off the checkerboard tiles.

The records, it turned out, could not be made available that day. Lizzie had been in the hospital so long that they had been moved to another site for storage. Archie was not keen on leaving Lizzie in the hospital either.

'I want to take her home, with us,' he said as soon as he arrived back from the ward.

The doctor tapped her papers straight and leaned across the desk.

'Mr Hargrove, Elizabeth has not been outside the hospital grounds for nearly sixteen years. As far as I know she hasn't talked to anyone in all that time. Don't get me wrong, I'm delighted that you have come and with the progress you seem to have made with her already but you can't just whisk her off, back into the real world, she needs time.'

Jim looked at Doctor Bennett and puzzled for a moment. Although he agreed with Archie in principle he could see her point.

They sent Molly back with Higgson in the car that afternoon and booked into a nearby hotel. Every morning they would walk to the hospital and spend the day with Lizzie. At first it seemed that she could only understand Archie being there as if he were part of some kind of dream. The two of them spent a lot of time dancing slowly along the corridor but gradually, day after day, the words came.

One afternoon she looked up at him and asked: 'Do you remember me, Archie?'

He nodded and smiled a small smile.

'Of course, silly, that's why I'm here, to see if you remember me.'

Lizzie smiled back up at him.

'I do, I do - I do remember you, Archie,' she sang softly. 'Always.'

She still had no idea who Jim was, but loved to hold his hand and stare into his eyes as she had done on that first day. They felt instinctively that it was too early in her recovery to tell her that Jim was her 'dead baby' but there was something profound and touching in her attachment to him. It was as if he was the first person to have levered open the door to her world, closed as it had been for so many years, and that made him precious.

Archie began taking her on small excursions, just round the grounds at first, with which she was familiar, and then gradually further afield, to a small park nearby where they could feed hungry ducks, then to a shop where they bought some sweets and more bread for the hungry ducks.

She was in turns enraptured with their past and shy about it, and while her world still appeared removed from reality and dreamy in nature, as time went on she seemed to become a little more awake to the everyday.

After a week Jim returned to Holland Park to make ready the house for Archie to bring her home.

The plan had been to bring her up for the day but she was so happy from the moment she crossed the threshold of Holland Park, that it would have been cruel to put her back in the car, and return her to Virginia Water and the wards of the swaying, the screeching and the silent sufferers.

***

Jim began to feel a strange restlessness, much as a traveller might who has stopped at an inn too long when his journey was not quite done. He took Molly aside one morning when she came to visit.

'You can drive, can't you?'

'Yes, why?'

'Could you get Flynn to lend you the car for a day or two? There's something I still have to do.'

Flynn had been lying low for the last few weeks, waiting for news of Harry Brisk, which had proved frustratingly difficult to come by. It was hard to ask around and keep your head down at the same time, and although the underworld was rife with rumour, hard fact was not on offer. The Black

Cat seemed to have closed, but nobody knew if it was for good.

Molly had little trouble getting Flynn to do most things she wanted, so the next morning she had him bring the car over. She and Jim loaded their bags into the small boot of the Austin Healey and headed for the coast, leaving Flynn to enjoy the attentions of the Higgsons and the comforts of Archie's house.

24 - The Letter

Jim was glad to leave Holland Park behind them as Molly swung south and let the little sports car pick up speed. Lizzie was his mother, of this he was now certain, despite the still missing medical records he felt an affinity with her that made official pieces of paper irrelevant. It was frustrating though, that he still could not tell her. Lizzie's recovery, although clear, was slow and he and Archie had agreed that they should wait a while before broaching the subject of Jim's identity. It was as though, when she looked at Jim, she knew who he was in her heart, but not yet in her mind, and that mind was a delicate thing. So many years of saying nothing but 'dead baby' are, Jim realised, not easily undone.

What was needed, before a revelation of such immensity, was the final piece in the puzzle. Jim needed to find out more about his father, the maker of the glass trumpet. There was, he knew, plenty more he would have discovered in The House of

Glass had he not been interrupted all those months ago, and this is where he and Molly headed now.

Once in the country she gave the car its head and after stopping for an early lunch just outside London they put the top down, despite the chilly weather, and revelled in the wind that buffeted them through the winding lanes and blurry hedges of Kent and Sussex. They intended to arrive in the early afternoon and go straight to the pier. This time there would be no sneaking across perilous roofs of glass by moonlight, for Jim had made, courtesy of Mr Mortimer, a remarkable discovery a few days before. Mortimer's searches had uncovered a copy of the letter that Jim had seen burned, as he'd perched, frightened, on the window ledge on that freezing December night; the letter that had led, via the card attached to it, to all the adventures and discoveries since then.

For the umpteenth time that week Jim drew it from his pocket and began to read.

Dear James,

It is with both the greatest sadness and the greatest regard I write to you now. I am sorry if nobody has told you this yet but I believe, James, that I am your father.

I have always known that I had a son but for many years I was unable to find you and even when I did there was no way on earth that I could have proved that you were mine. I have not long left to live now, or so the doctors tell me and it is unlikely that we will ever get to meet, so I want to set down here the truth about who you are, as I think that this is something that everyone needs to know about themselves.

Your mother and I had a brief affair during the war and you were, I believe, the result. There are some things with regard to this matter of which I am not proud but you are certainly not among them.

I first met your mother, Elizabeth Davis, in July 1943 when I had the sad task of delivering the news to her of the death of her fiancé, Archie Hargrove, the captain of the aircraft on which we both served. We were shot down on a huge raid over Cologne on the night of 30th May 1943. I managed to bail out and was lucky enough to escape back to England, but I saw our aircraft take a direct hit from the anti aircraft guns and I knew that Archie had 'bought it' as we used to say back then. He had been a good friend of mine and that is probably why I felt so guilty about what happened later on.

Elizabeth was very badly shaken by this news and I felt unable to leave her, upset as she was, so ended up staying on a few days at her place in Belsize Rd.

War is a strange time Jim and it throws people together in a way that it is hard to imagine today. Life seems to be made all the more precious by the fact that one can lose it at any moment, whether you are in the nose of a bomber over Berlin or asleep in your bed in West Hampstead. Suffice to say that we became lovers for a short while until I was posted to Canada to help train flight engineers. While there I was shocked to have my letters returned and even more so when I arrived back in England after the war and discovered that the house where she lived had been destroyed by a bomb and everyone inside killed.

Luckily, a neighbour of Elizabeth's, who lived opposite, saw me standing in the street and told me that she had seen Elizabeth leave the house the night of the bombing. It took me many months from there to track her down but I got a very strange reception when I did. Someone who could only have been Elizabeth's mother answered the door to me at a house in Crouch End, north London. When I asked after Elizabeth she seemed confused and said that she was away and wouldn't be back for a long time. Her father then came to the door and began shouting at me that she was a filthy sinner and her life had been taken by God in the war. During this exchange I heard a young child in the house begin to cry and the mother hurried off to deal with it.

As I travelled home it became obvious to me that they were lying about Elizabeth's death in the bombing and that in all probability the child was hers, or more likely; ours. At the next visit I was thoroughly abused by the father once more and told that he would go to the police if I were to turn up again. I even tried going to the police myself but they were completely uninterested. No crime had been committed and as far as they were concerned Elizabeth was dead, that's what the records said. The next time I went to the house they had moved, leaving no forwarding address.

It took many years before I could find them again and by that time you were a fully-fledged schoolboy. I trailed you home several times and even tried to get some photos, though they never came out very well. I had given up the idea of approaching you and telling you all this, as by then it seemed so remote and I thought, that for the sake of your own happiness, you were best left to grow up without the burden of the story I am telling you now. One thing I did manage to find out about you however, was that you played the trumpet and this is why I now give you this gift. I have had a fascination with glass all my life and I am glad to say that my training as an engineer has allowed me to do things with it that would not have been thought possible, even a few years ago. It has taken me some time to fashion a trumpet of glass that actually works and I am pleased to be able to leave you something of myself that I hope you may actually be able to use. Music is a wonderful gift James and from what I have learned you have much of it to share with the world, I hope the trumpet helps. Inscribed on it is your mother's favourite tune, I do hope one day that you may get to play it to her.

The property I inherited from my aunt, her grandfather built the pier at Walsham-on-Sea and another at Beckly. That sadly collapsed in a storm, I wish you better luck with this one. As the will says; all the personal property in The House of Glass I leave to you, please feel free to dispose of it as you see fit. There are some photographs of me I hope you will choose to keep and one I long treasured of your mother.

Whatever course in life you choose James, I hope with all my heart it brings you happiness. I'm only sorry that I have not had a chance to share some of it with you.

Best Regards

Your Loving Father
George Armstrong

Jim swallowed the lump in his throat that always seemed to rise, no matter how many times he read this letter. He placed it carefully back in his inside pocket and looked up to see the road curving away down towards Walsham-on-Sea and there, across the red roof tiles of the town, was the pier, his pier.

***

They collected the keys from a local estate agent in the town, drove down to the front and parked by the entrance to the pier, under the Victorian street lamps, which still decorated the fading promenade along the front. Molly tied on a headscarf and together they braved the bitter wind, which gusted over the sea and made Jim's ears roar. He had to fiddle with the keys for some time before finding the one that freed the large padlock securing the slightly rusty trestle-gate. Molly became excited.

'God, Jim, I just can't *believe* it! You, owning a whole pier! Let's go down to the end.' She took his arm and they ran the length of the old boards, past The House of Glass, past the little fairground with its mysterious rides, muffled in canvas for the winter, past numerous kiosks and a restaurant, past the big ballroom that stood at the very end. They stood next to the helter-skelter and looked down at the marble green swell that sluiced, ever and again, over the black spindles which held them up from the sea.

'It's incredible,' she said, raising her face to the rushing wind and the far shapes of ships on the horizon.

Jim turned and saw the place where he had crouched down and consumed his chocolate bar all those months ago. He looked back along the pier to The House of Glass, sadly even more shuttered up since his last visit.

'Come on,' he said.

The board over the doors came off quickly and they stepped in, away from the blistering wind. Crunching across the broken glass and standing in the dank gloom created by the tarpaulin that had been thrown over the roof to protect The House of Glass from the rain, they absorbed the strange atmosphere of abandonment and mystery.

Molly was fascinated with the cases and the intricate glass sculptures they contained. After examining a few with her, he left to properly explore upstairs and the world of George Armstrong.

He paced up the creaking spiral staircase, which seemed smaller now, in the daylight, and entered the room where he had discovered the glass trumpet. All seemed as he had left it, the curtains still drawn, the papers on the desk. He remembered the picture that had slipped down the back and brought it out. It was the whole picture from which the news cutting had been taken. Lizzie sat, still laughing at the camera, the man with his hand on her shoulder looking fondly at her was wearing an RAF uniform with a flight engineer's badge on his chest. He examined the face of George Armstrong but it was hard to see the features clearly as his head was tilted too much towards the camera as he looked round into Lizzie's laughing face. Jim looked over the room again but there were no other pictures on the walls. In the top drawer of the desk he found used notebooks and a few technical manuals, a slide rule and some books of tables. In the second drawer were a great many hand written sheets that Jim found to be drafts of the letter that he now had in his pocket. There were many starts and restarts, crossings out and underlinings. The letter, it seemed, had been made with as much thought, care and feeling as every one of the sculptures in the cases downstairs.

In another drawer he found a photograph of seven men in flying jackets and inflatable life preservers, lined up by the rear door of an aeroplane. He recognised Archie immediately, standing more or less in the centre but struggled to make out George Armstrong among the rest of the crew, despite having the other photograph for reference.

He heard Molly gasp in amazement, probably at another of the sculptures as he crouched to go through the rest of the papers in the final drawer.

She started up the stairs with, Jim thought, the tread of an elephant for one so slight. He soon saw why. She came through the door, her eyes wild with fear, her head forced back by a leather gloved hand clamped over her mouth - and with Harry Brisk's gun forced hard against her spine.

25 - Size Nine

*H*arry Brisk swung the gun at Jim and pulled Molly's head back hard against his shoulder.

'Get over there,' he gestured towards the far end of the room where the bed stood. Eugene followed Harry Brisk through the door and gave Jim a swift kick up the backside to help him on his way.

Jim lost his balance and fell, then Molly was thrown onto the floor next to him. They looked up in horror at Harry Brisk. He towered over them, rage and triumph mixed together as his usually cool expression seethed with emotion. He had acquired, as a result of the accident Jim supposed, a patch over his right eye, which added to his frightening appearance.

'Thought you'd seen the last of Harry, huh? Old Harry Brisk, the man who took you in, the man who paid your wages. Thought you'd just RIP HIM OFF AND DO A RUNNER, EH?' He kicked Jim hard in the stomach.

Jim was bent double but only for a moment; Harry Brisk seized him by the collar and jerked his face up towards his own. The voice came out as little more than a low rumble.

'Where's my money?' he shook Jim. 'And where are the papers from my safe?'

Jim looked into his face and saw the hatred sketched in every line.

'I don't know,' he said simply.

Harry Brisk threw him back down on the floor, banging his head on the bed frame in the process.

'And what about her, young Molly, does she know where all Uncle Harry's money went, mmm?'

With this he picked Molly up off the floor in a similar fashion and forced the end of his gun into her mouth. She squeaked with fear and shook her head as much as was possible.

'NO?!' roared Harry Brisk.

He turned his face to Jim's. 'But the sight of your brains all over the bedspread here might refresh young Jim's memory, eh?' He cocked the hammer of the gun with his thumb.

'Eh, Jim?'

Jim looked into Molly's terrified blue eyes.

'Flynn,' he said. Molly began squealing and shaking her head and uttering a muffled, 'No, Jim, no!'

'Ah, I see,' said Harry Brisk, dropping the panting Molly in a heap back on the floor. He turned and paced across to Eugene, who lounged against the doorframe, his own gun dangling from his fingers.

'Flynn…' He tapped his big henchman lightly on the lapel and repeated, 'Flynn, Flynn, Flynn,' as if trying to recall something.

'Flynn Mitchell, Boss!'

'Yes…' He spun round to look at Molly and Jim. 'I KNOW IT'S BLOODY FLYNN MITCHELL. You must be IMBECILES if you think I'm that stupid!' Harry Brisk began counting his fingers as he leaned over them. 'Old man's a safe cracker, he's done four years for safe cracking himself, packed in his job driving a FISH LORRY, bit of a clue there perhaps…and has been seen poncing around Bethnal Green in A NEW SPORTS CAR!' Jim was shocked and even more frightened of Harry Brisk now. He had brutalized Molly with the gun even though he already knew who Flynn was. It was as if he wanted to kill them right now and could hardly restrain himself.

'It's just…' Harry shook his head slowly and the splayed fingers folded into a grasping hand and then tightened into a fist, '…where is he…and where is my money?'

He left the fist there, in front of them and raised an eyebrow. Jim looked into his eyes and realised he had only a second to save Molly's face from being broken up.

'London, he's in London, at Holland Park. You know where that is.'

'And is that where my stuff is?'

'Well the rucksack's there but that's just got all the papers and stuff in, Flynn has the money but I don't know where he keeps it.'

Harry Brisk stood up and paced the room.

'Papers and stuff! Have you any IDEA of what you've taken? I almost…almost don't *care* about the money.'

He turned on Molly, unable to restrain himself from sharing the reason for his fury.

'You remember Mr Greco, my American guest? Well those "papers" as you call them, contain four – hundred-and-seventy-five-THOUSAND pounds worth of French government bearer bonds that I arranged for him. Now, since I can't provide them – or the cash that he gave me to buy them – it's MY head on the block. And worse, he thinks, because of that business with Katie, that I'm trying to blackmail him over the money and now he wants me dead. What - between Greco, and the coppers going on and on about that silly bitch - I can't even go back to my own club!'

Harry Brisk ransacked the desk while Eugene handcuffed Jim and Molly together, hands behind their backs. He tried the phone and dropped it in disgust on the desk when he found no connection.

'I'll have to go and find a phone, Eugene, you stay here and keep and eye on them.'

'They can't move, Boss, these are proper police cuffs.'

'All the same. Gimmie the keys to the gate and the car.'

Eugene dipped his hand in Jim's pockets, removing the keys to the pier, which he threw across the room to Harry Brisk, along with the car keys.

'So, it's just me here, to keep you company…' he leaned in close to Jim and tugged his collar aside, showing a livid wheal on his neck where Jim had applied several thousand volts a few weeks before. '…I'm looking forward to it.'

'Don't touch him, Eugene, not yet, you can have 'em when I've finished with 'em.'

Jim and Molly sat, as the failing light blended the details of the room into a deep grey and the hissing surf brushed endlessly against the pier stanchions below. Eugene slumped in the chair, feet on the desk and dozed, his hat over his eyes. He looked exhausted Jim thought, they both did, and Harry Brisk, King of the West End, seemed desperate. It was that desperation that Jim feared. For the first time he truly believed Harry Brisk was capable of almost anything.

He pondered the hopelessness of their situation. Brisk had two big problems; the money and bonds that he could only retrieve by getting hold of Flynn, and the fact that he and Molly were the sole witnesses to Katie getting into the American's car that night; which he could only solve by killing them both. Jim had told no-one where they were going that day; he had felt a little shy of discussing George Armstrong with Archie, so there would be no rescue party.

Before long they heard Harry Brisk returning. He stamped up the stairs and threw his hat angrily down on the desk.

'That bloody Warnock. I've just spoken to Charlie and he's got the Hargrove place rammed with men. All arrived in a big rush about an hour ago. There's no way Charlie can get in there and lift him now.'

'What are we gonna do, Boss?'

Harry Brisk thought for a moment. He produced a hip flask, took a long swig and then looked across the room at Molly.

'I reckon he's sweet on her, it's worth a try, undo her.'

Eugene undid the handcuffs that looped around Jim's and jerked her to her feet.

'Make sure he's secure, Eugene, I need you to come with me this time.'

Jim was dragged roughly across the room and handcuffed to a radiator, then he was left alone as the two gangsters hustled Molly off down the stairs.

***

Dusk was falling as Mrs Higgson put her head around the door of Molly's room where Flynn lay, propped up reading a magazine on her bed.

'I've got Molly on the phone for you; take it in the library down the hall, the clubroom is full of Mr Warnock and his men at the moment.'

Flynn lifted the receiver; at the other end Harry Brisk listened for the click as the extension was put down.

'Hello,' said Flynn. There was a moment of silence and then Harry Brisk, standing in the wind blown telephone box at the far end of the promenade, with Eugene outside on guard, punched Molly hard in the ribs with a knuckle. He took his gloved hand from her mouth, just long enough to let the small scream produced by the sudden shock of pain escape, and then clamped it suddenly back in place.

'Hello!' said Flynn anxiously.

Harry Brisk's voice came on the phone.

'You know me, Flynn Mitchell, and though you've never met me, I know all about you.'

'What have you done to Molly? Let me talk to her.'

'No deal, where are the papers you took from my safe?'

Flynn thought for a moment, he knew they were all in his case down the hall. He had taken a brief look in the manila envelope containing the bonds but, not speaking any French, had failed to realise their worth, assuming they were cheques of some kind.

'I've got them.'

'Are they all there?'

Let me talk to Molly or it's no deal.'

Harry Brisk held the mouthpiece up to Molly's mouth, but kept the earpiece away.

Molly sniffed back a tear.

'Flynn I just want to say...I love you very much...and... DON'T COME, DON'T COME DOWN HERE...'

'Bitch!' yelled Harry Brisk and clamped his hand quickly back over her mouth, choking off the words.

'Well it's up to you, you little pikey bastard, you either get *all* those papers down to the pier at Walsham, along with the rest of my cash, or sweet Molly bloody Malone here goes OFF THE END OF THE PIER WITH A BULLET IN HER HEAD! You got three hours.'

'What if I just call the cops?' asked Flynn.

'You're welcome to try, Mitchell, it's pot luck really, half of West End Central work for me.'

Flynn tried to think straight. 'It's a three hour drive and I need to get a car,' he said, trying to keep any panic out of his voice.

'No you don't, go out of the house, turn left up the hill and you'll see my man Charlie there in a black Jowett Javelin parked near the phone box – he'll bring you to me.'

Harry Brisk checked his watch. 'The tide goes out at half past ten, if you're not here with my money and *all* the stuff in that bag, she'll be going out with it - then I'll be coming after you.' He hung up and had Eugene drag Molly out of the phone box and back into the car while he called Charlie to brief him. Eugene shut the door of the car and checked again the length of the promenade. Off-season it was just like an empty back street facing the sea. Not a shop was open, not a person to be seen. He got into the driver's seat and waited for Harry before driving them back to the pier.

***

Flynn quelled his fear of Harry Brisk with anger. The sound of Molly in pain, each time he recalled it, jetted more adrenalin into his bloodstream.

After packing all the papers into Jim's rucksack with a few essential tools, he slipped out through the kitchen door, crossed the lawn to the Higgsons' and then went quietly through their side gate and into the mews that ran behind the big houses. This brought him out at the top of the hill and he spotted the slanting back of the black Javelin on the other side of the road as soon as he turned the corner. He approached it from an oblique angle so that the occupant, slumped low in the driver's seat, would not spot him coming in any of the mirrors. Flynn needed the guy in the car to be awake if he was to carry out successfully what he had in mind. Part of him wanted to stop and observe for a moment, but he was afraid that the fear would immobilise him. He recalled Molly's squeal of pain, surprise and fear - and felt his anger rise again. As he came closer, Flynn broke into a light trot. At the last moment he accelerated and ran straight up the sloping back of the car and onto the roof. As expected, Charlie was out of the door in a flash and spun round just in time for Pentonville's finest winger to connect neatly under his chin with a perfectly placed size nine boot. Charlie fell in the gutter and Flynn jumped down next to him, feeling around for the gun. He put this in his pocket and then dragged the unconscious man onto the back seat of the car, where he tied him hand and foot with some boot-laces, before dumping him on the floor just behind the back seats.

The keys were still in the ignition. Flynn started the car, drove down the hill and headed for the coast.

Charlie's timing was good; he started to come round just as Flynn left the outskirts of London and plunged into the unlit lanes that led down towards Walsham-on-Sea. After a few minutes listening to the moaning and groaning coming from behind him, Flynn found what he was looking for and swung the car up a narrow track that led into some woodland.

He dragged the bound man out onto the ground and shone a torch in his face.

'You're goin' to tell me exactly what the plan was and if I think you're lying, even for a moment,' Flynn produced the gun and levelled it at the man's groin, 'then I'm gonna shoot yer nuts off.'

'You've broken my bloody jaw,' said Charlie in a muffled voice.

'Well I can still understand you, Charles old man, so you'd better start talking.' He walked round to the back of the car and opened up the boot. There was a spade and a hessian sack of the type good for tying up eels in.

'Were we meant to arrive together, or were you gonna do me over on the way down?'

Charlie said nothing. Flynn could see the fear in his eyes, but it wasn't fear of him, it was fear of Harry Brisk.

He threw the sack and the spade down on the ground next to Charlie and pointed the gun down at his chest.

'Speak, Charlie, or forever hold your peace – actually…' Flynn lowered the gun still further until it was pointing at the gangster's groin, '…speak now or never hold your "piece", ever again.'

There was a moment's silence while Flynn watched fear and dread battle it out in Charlie's face, followed by a sharp bang as Flynn pulled the trigger. Charlie jumped but no blood came from the neat hole in the crutch of his trousers.

'Singe you, did I?' asked Flynn, re-cocking the gun.

'He wanted me to handcuff you in the car and then check the stuff in the bag when I could find a quiet place to pull off.'

'Like here?'

Charlie rolled his eyes around the dark clearing.

'Yeh, I 'spose.'

'And if you had all the stuff?'

Charlie gave a small shrug and looked away, anywhere but in the light or at Flynn. Flynn brought the gun back to bear.

'Kill you…bury you.'

Flynn paced the clearing for a minute or two, trying desperately to formulate a plan that had at least some chance of success. He checked his watch; just over two hours before the tide turned. He looked down at Charlie again.

'How tall are you?'

'About five nine.'

He went over to the car and pulled Charlie's hat out from the rear seat. It was quite a distinctive Homburg, with a light band and a large brim. He bent down and placed it over Charlie's face, making it difficult for him to lash out, before untying his hands and stepping back with the gun.

'Right, up you get – now strip.'

'What?'

'Strip, you heard me, everything down to the underwear.'

Within a few minutes Flynn was pulling back out onto the road wearing Charlie's clothes and the broad brimmed Homburg hat. Their owner he had left handcuffed to a tree, wearing his own.

He still felt desperate and afraid.

'But at least…' he thought, '…I've got a plan.'

26 - Bonds

$\mathcal{A}$s they sat in the near darkness waiting, Jim finally gave up wondering and asked Harry Brisk:

'How did you know where to find us?'

'Easy, your dad. His name was in the paper from when you ran away, luckily I kept a copy in the office. He wasn't hard to find. I thought I'd have to rough him up but no; he was quite forthcoming, quite willing to help. It seems, young James, that should you happen to die then he, as your nearest living relative, inherits the pier.'

Harry Brisk took another drink from his flask.

'And he has plans for the pier, your dad, oh such plans.'

Eugene sniggered.

'Apparently his little flock could live on here and never have to mix with us filthy sinners again. What was it going to be, Eugene?'

'The New Jerusalem Pier.'

'Yes that was it, showed us the plans and everything, big wall along the entrance, ballroom would be the church. I can see why you ran away.'

'So have you been waiting here all this time, for us to come?'

'Nah, just slipped the agent a few bob to call us if you ever turned up. To be honest I couldn't believe my luck when he did call and said you'd arranged to pick up the keys.'

Harry seemed more relaxed now. Perhaps it was the whisky, perhaps the prospect of Flynn returning his precious bonds, of snatching his life back from the edge of disaster. He checked his watch.

'It's getting near, Eugene, muzzle these two just in case and then you'd better start the lookout.' Eugene kneeled down and removed his tie which he used to gag Molly and then produced a large handkerchief which he tied tightly across Jim's mouth. Satisfied, he moved across the hall to the kitchen window, from where he could see the road that curved down into the town.

**

The phone on the clubroom side table jangled and made Archie jump.

He had been on edge since the intelligence had come in earlier that day about the reappearance of Harry Brisk. Archie had immediately called Warnock's and had him send some men over; he was in no mood to take risks after Harry Brisk's last visit to Holland Park. Later he sent Mrs Higgson to fetch Flynn down so they could ask him where Jim and Molly had gone on their day trip. Finding that Flynn too had disappeared ratcheted up the tension another few notches.

'Warnock,' said the ex-detective, lifting the receiver to his ear. He listened to the tiny voice a moment. 'Where on the coast?' He listened a little longer and then hung up.

'Right, Mr Hargrove, it seems that Brisk and his sidekick turned up at the club in a great rush. Our man says he thinks it was to pick up some weapons and to collect a car. He overhead some talk about the coast but that was all. Any idea what that might mean?'

Archie thought but it only took a moment.

'Oh my God; the pier, it must be the pier at Walsham, that's where they would have gone.'

'Right get your coat,' said Warnock. He went over to the service door that led to the kitchens, where six of his men sat eating around Mrs Higgson's table.

'Come on you lot, in the cars, sharpish.'

They had to wait a minute while Archie went to fetch something from upstairs. He opened a locked drawer in his bureau and stood there, gazing at the service revolver, which had lain untouched for the last dozen years or so. After a minute he let out a large sigh and put it in his coat pocket. He stopped at Lizzie's room to kiss her sleeping head and ran back down the stairs and out to the cars. Then they were rolling, out of the drive and down the hill in the direction that Flynn had gone just an hour and a half before.

Warnock, sat in the front next to his driver, opened the glove-box revealing a radio set inside. He flicked a switch making the various dials glow and picked up the microphone.

'Bugbear to control.'

'*Control,*' came the instant crackling reply.

'Call Phillips at Scotland Yard, ask him to get someone down to the pier at Walsham-on-Sea and see if there's any activity. Tell him just report - no action, repeat no action to be taken, over.'

'*Roger, sir – no action, just report – over.*'

Archie peered interestedly at the radio from the back seat.

'That's a familiar looking bit of kit,' he said.

'Probably is, Mr Hargrove, ex-RAF, got one in every car.'

Archie thought for a moment.

'Mind if I try something?' He reached over, took the microphone and began adjusting the dials and switches on the radio set. After a few modulated wows and wees he spoke into the mike.

'St Mawgan tower, calling St Mawgan tower, over.'

After a moment the radio crackled back with the familiar professional tones of an RAF controller.

'*This is St Mawgan tower, please identify your aircraft and position - over.*'

'Slightly unusual request here, St Mawgan – do you have Wing Commander Greaves on station – over?'

'I believe I saw the C/O in the officers' mess about twenty minutes ago, what is your position, over?'

'Could you send someone down to tell him Archie Hargrove, ex-commander 48 Squadron, needs to speak to him urgently, over?'

There was a short silence and then another voice, with a strong Scottish accent, came over the air.

'Archie Hargrove? It's Stuart here, sir, Aircraftsman Stuart as you'd remember from the war, I was your flight's radio technician, sir.'

'Stuart! Remember you well, how is that little Scotty dog of yours?'

'Bumpy's long gone, sir, buried in the mess garden. I'm running the tower now, and it's Group Captain Greaves is station commander. What can we do for you, sir?'

'Be a good chap and tell him I need a quick word, would you, Stuart?'

***

Flynn pulled the car over at the top of the hill leading down into Walsham-on-Sea. The road had been empty for the last few miles and nothing seemed to move in the quiet seaside town below. The pier jutted out into the dark sea, held up over the foaming breakers by its hundreds of black stanchions, and lit intermittently by a full moon through the scudding clouds.

He threw a last cigarette butt from the car and flashed the lights twice, the signal Charlie had given him. Almost immediately there was the answering blink of a torch from the top floor of the first building he could see on the pier.

He took the Homburg from the passenger seat and put it on his head, trying to remember the exact way Charlie wore it, as he checked himself in the rear view mirror. It was a little large but he hoped the broad brim would do its job and prevent Harry Brisk or Eugene recognising him until it was too late. He felt the gun in his right hand pocket, restarted the engine and headed down the hill towards whatever fate awaited him.

**

As he parked the car he saw the figure of Harry Brisk waiting behind the gates in the darkness. He opened the door and got out, fetching the rucksack from the front seat and started towards the pier. He tried to put his hand into the right jacket pocket in the most casual way possible, wondering how close he should dare try and get before pulling it out.

It was the wind that was Flynn's undoing; a sudden gust whipped up and blew Charlie's hat off his head and down the promenade. He tried to pull the gun out but it got stuck in his pocket and before he'd gone another step Eugene, who had been covering the pavement from a hiding place between two parked cars, hit him heavily from behind with the butt of his gun.

'Good work, Eugene,' said Harry Brisk as he lifted the rucksack from the pavement. Eugene carried the groggy but still conscious Flynn into The House of Glass and up the stairs, as Harry Brisk re-locked the gates to the pier behind them. He was thrown unceremoniously to the floor next to the others and then handcuffed to them, hands behind his back.

Jim felt his heart sink and Molly looked distraught. She tried to ask him if he was okay through her gag; Flynn shook his head sheepishly.

Harry Brisk angled the light properly onto the desk and began to empty out the contents of the rucksack.

'Did you kill my man Charlie?' he asked, matter of factly.

'No, he's handcuffed to a tree in the woods.'

'Where?'

'Somewhere between here and London.'

He was about to order Eugene to hit him again but was distracted by the discovery of his bonds. He drew them from the manila envelope and thumbed them like a pack of cards.

'They all here?'

'I haven't touched 'em,' said Flynn wearily.

'Better make sure,' he said, clearing a space on the desk and sitting down to count them.

After a minute or two Harry Brisk stood up, replaced the bonds in the envelope and put them back in the rucksack with the other papers.

'All there,' he said, the satisfaction and relief evident in his voice.

Eugene straightened his arm, bringing the gun a few inches from the top of Jim's head.

'Shall we…'

'No,' said Harry Brisk, checking his watch, 'not yet, still twenty minutes 'til the tide turns, Eugene; we get this right they'll never find the bodies.' He grinned down at his prisoners, taking obvious pleasure from their fear. 'Just gag him too and then…'

He stopped mid sentence and looked sharply at Eugene.

'What was that?'

'What, Boss?'

'That noise, sounded like the gates!'

They rushed through to the kitchen, the window of which offered an oblique view of the entrance to the pier. There was silence for a moment and then the figure of a large policeman appeared, still on the outside of the gates. He paused and shone a torch down the pier, looking this way and that between the bars, before pacing back the other way, leaving the small field of view afforded Harry Brisk and Eugene from the window.

'Downstairs,' hissed Harry Brisk. 'Got to see which way he goes.'

The two large gangsters tiptoed as quietly as they could down the spiral staircase in order to get a better look from the back windows, which offered a full view of the entrance to the pier.

Jim realised that Flynn was twisting his head as far round to the right as possible. He turned as far as he could and saw Flynn produce a small piece of metal from between his teeth which he then spat out, over his shoulder and down into the well produced by their three backs.

'Have you got it?' he said quietly to Jim, who shook his head.

'Damn, find it quick.'

They both scrabbled around on the floor until Jim closed his fingers around the slim pick.

'Mmm – mmm,' he said through the gag and passed it over.

Within twenty seconds Flynn's hands were free and he quickly picked the other two sets of cuffs.

'What'll we do now?' asked Jim pulling his gag down.

'Well for one thing...' Flynn quickly unbuckled the rucksack on the desk and removed the manila envelope containing the bonds, '...we'll have these, even if we do end up in the sea, Brisk'll still be knackered, and you never know...' he winked at Jim while hastily re-buckling the bag, '...we might just get away with it, good as cash these are!' He tucked them into his jacket.

Their excitement was to be short lived as the heavy steps of Harry Brisk and Eugene signalled their return through the shop.

'What shall we do?' hissed Molly, '...fight them?'

'Nah, we don't stand a chance against the guns, sit back down, quick!' Flynn got quickly back into position on the floor and the others did like-wise.

Jim was ready last, just as their captors neared the top of the stairs, when he suddenly realised to his horror that the envelope containing the bonds had slipped from under Flynn's jacket and lay on the floor between them and the desk. He lunged forward and was just able to grab it and get his hands back in position as Harry Brisk and Eugene entered the room.

They looked down at their captives and seemed satisfied.

'What now then, Boss?'

Harry Brisk waited a few more minutes, until he was sure that the policeman had gone, before picking up the rucksack. He seemed to weigh it in his hand, causing Jim and Flynn's hearts to pound even more furiously, as they were sat facing him. He eyed them for a moment or two before hoisting it onto his shoulder and leading Eugene out onto the landing, where he spoke to him in a low voice.

'I'm gonna take this to the car, make sure it's all safe and sound, then I'm gonna call Greco's man and tell him we've got the bonds, ask him to call the dogs off. When I get back here we'll finish the job we came here to do…' In that small silence Jim could imagine Harry Brisk nodding in their direction, '…and not with the gun, we'll do the old baseball bat and whisky job. That way even if they do pull 'em out of the sea there's no evidence, looks like they got pissed and fell off the pier.' He started down the stairs. 'I've got one in the car, present from Greco funnily enough.'

**

'Roger, Archie, that's no problem, perfect training scenario for them in fact. We'll have them on standby five miles out. Do you want to make a note of the aircraft frequency, that way you can talk to them directly and monitor what's happening - over?'

Archie wrote down the relevant numbers, thanked his old second in command and then allowed Warnock to retune the radio set. He found his control room calling.

'Firefly calling Bugbear...Firefly calling Bugbear.'

'Bugbear here, go ahead, Firefly.'

'Phillips just had the call from his local constable, no activity at all on the pier, sir, it's all locked up and there's no lights, no sound, nothing.'

'Roger, Firefly, standby.'

He turned and looked questioningly at Archie, who shook his head at the detective's doubtful expression.

'They have to be there, it's the only thing that adds up.'

**

Eugene walked slowly around the captive trio, occasionally stopping to point the gun at one of their heads and mime the little kick it would give were he to pull the trigger.

'Not long now eh?' he would say. 'Not long now.'

Jim could feel Flynn tense occasionally as he thought he might have an opportunity to lash out and surprise Eugene but it never seemed to come. He knew that Harry Brisk's errand would not take him long and became increasingly anxious. What little chance they had against Eugene with the gun, even allowing for the element of surprise, would virtually disappear once Harry Brisk returned with his bottle of whisky and baseball bat. Jim decided that they could not afford to wait any longer and that as Eugene came past him next time he would kick out and try to trip him. Even if one of them were shot as they jumped him, at least the others would have some chance. He heard the quiet 'Pi-yow' as Eugene pretended to execute Flynn, then the same as his slow steps took him past Molly, he tensed, ready to try and take Eugene's trailing foot as he came in front of him but instead Eugene turned, went out of the door and onto the landing. They heard him open the lavatory door and step inside.

Instantly all three were on their feet. Flynn put his finger to his lips and made a tiptoeing motion with his fingers while Jim stuffed the manila envelope into his inside pocket. As they went silently into the hall they could hear Eugene begin a long thundering piss. Flynn, last out, grabbed the sturdy wooden chair that stood by the desk and wedged it gently under the handle of the toilet door. They slipped down the stairs as quietly as possible. At the bottom Jim halted them.

'Just a minute, I've got an idea.'

He bent down and, in the near darkness, found the brass loop to the trapdoor that he had noticed on his first visit, set into the floor at the bottom of the stairs. He pulled it open and laid the door flat. Below, the white horses of spume roared as they crashed and broke against the legs of the pier.

'Quick, pass me that mat.'

Just inside the main doors was a piece of carpet into which was woven 'Welcome to The House of Glass'. Flynn dragged it over and they covered the gaping hole.

Suddenly mayhem was let loose upstairs as Eugene discovered his predicament. Thunderous banging and shouting erupted as the big gangster began kicking the toilet door to pieces.

They ran, only the short distance to the gates of the pier separated them from freedom; it was not to be. All that awaited them at the doors of The House of Glass was the muzzle of Harry Brisk's revolver. He held it at them, straight-armed, menacing as he advanced, backing them into the shop.

27 - Solar One

'Back, get back, go on! How did you get free? What have you done with Eugene?'

They retreated into the shop, hands raised. Harry Brisk lined them up against the glass cases as they heard the toilet door finally give way. Eugene came running down the stairs only to stop dead at the bottom as he saw Harry Brisk; his gun levelled at the prisoners' heads.

'Can't I trust you with ANYTHING?' roared Harry Brisk over his shoulder at his unfortunate henchman.

'I dunno how they got free, Boss, honest, all I did was go to the…'

'SHUT IT! It doesn't matter now.'

Eugene raised his gun at Jim's head and cocked the hammer.

'Let's just shoot 'em now, Boss, before they try something else.'

'No, we'll do it my way; get the bag,' he said, indicating a long holdall he had fetched from the car which now lay by the front doors.

Eugene, his revolver still levelled at them, stepped forward.

There was a scream and the gun went off, the bullet shattering the glass display case just behind Jim. Harry Brisk turned his head just in time to see his unfortunate assistant disappearing through the trapdoor, his arms flailing helplessly as the carpet engulfed him. Molly took her chance and shoved Brisk hard in the chest. He staggered back towards the now uncovered gap in the floor as Eugene's scream was ended by a mighty splash. Harry Brisk windmilled his arms frantically, struggling to avoid the drop, a shot from his gun showering glass from the roof down everywhere.

'Run!' shouted Jim and all three of them tore out of the door and down the pier. Just as he was about to join Eugene in the thundering sea below, Harry Brisk managed to swivel round and place one foot on the far side of the trap. He caught his balance and his breath, then looked down, but he saw no sign of Eugene in the churning black water.

Flynn got to the gates first and tugged at the chain in despair. Harry Brisk had taken the precaution of relocking them in case of any further interest by the police.

'Pick it!' said Jim.

'No time,' replied Flynn desperately.

They thought about trying to scale the gates but offering such an easy target put them off so they turned and ran back up the pier, looking for a place to hide or a way to escape.

***

Archie looked out of the window at the dark rushing hedges, he caught sight of a signpost whipping past and checked his watch.

'How far now?'

'Sign said eight miles, sir, ten or twelve minutes depending on the roads,' said Warnock's driver.

The radio suddenly came to life.

'Firefly calling Bugbear, Firefly calling Bugbear, over.'

'Bugbear, go ahead, Firefly.'

'Just had Phillips back on, sir, his man is reporting shots heard from the area of the pier, sir.'

'Blast,' cursed Archie.

'Tell him to get down there, quick as he can,' replied Warnock into the microphone.

'I did suggest it, sir but he sounded doubtful, think he wants to wait for the firearms unit.'

'Okay car two, you monitor Firefly and flash us up if you need us, we're going to switch frequency for a few minutes.' He turned and passed the microphone to Archie. 'Over to you I think.'

Archie dialled in the correct wavelength and pressed the button on the mouthpiece.

'Bugbear calling Solar One, Bugbear calling Solar One, over,'

'Solar One, Bugbear, receiving you loud and clear.'

'What is your position, Solar One?'

'Bit of a problem there, sir, we've lost the navigation beacon and we're on dead reckoning, we're in the right area but there's a lot of low cloud. It's broken cloud but we don't have a visual on the target at the moment, sir.'

Archie hung his head in frustration.

'Roger, Solar One, remain on station and call me the moment you have a visual, Roger?'

'Roger, Bugbear.'

He looked grimly over at Warnock.

'They're on their own,' he said.

***

Harry Brisk had some difficulty in getting himself safely off the yawning trap, as it was wide enough to force him halfway to the splits. He found he hadn't the confidence to simply push off with one leg and step away, and was reduced to bending down so as to be able to reach the floor beside the hole with his hands. He then shuffled and crawled his way back to safety, ruining his Saville Row suit trousers and cutting his hands on all the shattered glass that covered the floor in the process.

He had heard the running feet of his erstwhile captives over the roar of the surf but emerged from The House of Glass unsure of which way they had gone. He ran to the gates and found them still safely chained, then turned and stood with his back against them, looking up the pier, considering his options.

He wished now that he had taken poor Eugene's advice and simply shot the slippery trio when he had the chance. Searching the pier with one person was a far trickier proposition than with two; he had to choose one side and risk his quarry slipping back down the other. He considered simply getting back in the car and heading for London; at least he would get the Americans off his back, but for how long? Now he had Warnock on his case, he knew it was unlikely that he would be able to brush the Katie business under the carpet for much longer.

There was unfinished business there; it was no accident that Warnock had been dismissed from the service, after getting a bit too close to Harry Brisk and his inner circle at West End Central police station. Much as he would like to return to London, Harry Brisk knew he had tracks to cover.

He chose the right hand side and began to move up the pier as quickly and quietly as he could, past The House of Glass and various kiosks. Clouds scudded quickly across the silver spotlight of the moon, which would lift hidden corners from the darkness into mere gloom for a moment or two, before allowing them to sink back into blackness. He stopped and listened out over the wind and the waves for the thud of feet on the boards but all he could hear was the sound of a distant aeroplane.

When the chance arose he would swap sides, running quickly in between the buildings from one side or the other, in the hope of catching them out, but it was as if he were the only person left on the windy pier.

The three fugitives crouched behind the small carousel by the restaurant some halfway up the pier.

Flynn peered down the boards towards the shore.

'Right, you two get up the far end and try and find a hiding place. I'm going back into the shop, see if I can't find a weapon or maybe tempt him in there and do 'im in with a lump of glass.'

'No, Flynn, he'll kill you!' cried Molly, seizing him by the hands.

'You got a better idea then, darlin?' he asked and wiped away a tear from the corner of her eye.

'Thought not.'

He looked stealthily over the dark humps of the tarpaulin swathed carousel animals, just in time to see Harry Brisk dart back across to the opposite side of the pier.

'Right, you go that way, and quick,' he whispered - then kissed Molly briefly on the lips and took off landwards in a low crouching run.

'Come on,' said Jim and he and Molly set off in the opposite direction, past the ballroom, heading towards the dead end of the pier.

Flynn reached The House of Glass and crunched across the shattered remains of the display cases as quietly as possible, not wanting to alert Harry Brisk to his whereabouts before he had had a chance to prepare some kind of ambush. He edged past the open trapdoor, wondering if there was any way they could consign him to the watery wastes as they had done so successfully with Eugene. He discovered a small door, set into the bottom of the thick column that contained the spiral staircase. It was locked; Flynn reached into his pocket for his picks.

***

As Molly and Jim reached the head of the pier they had still not found a decent place to hide. They crouched down by the back wall of the ballroom in the buffeting wind.

'How about the Helter-Skelter?' she suggested. 'We could see right down the pier from up there.'

'Okay, you wait here, I'll see if it's unlocked.'

Jim peered cautiously round the corner to check there was no sign of Harry Brisk, and then scooted across the boards and disappeared into the little porch which held the ticket booth and entrance to the towering ride. He had only to unhook a chain and jump over a small turnstile to reach the stairs.

Molly watched him go nervously. If Harry Brisk was not coming up the right-hand side of the pier she thought, that could only mean that he was coming up the other side. She turned to her left and slowly, ever so carefully, put her head round the corner of the ballroom to see if she could see him. She watched for a moment but saw nothing. What she missed was the bulky but silent figure of Harry

Brisk emerge from the shadows and follow Jim through the entrance of the Helter-Skelter.

Jim reached the top a few seconds later and took in the whole view of the pier. He could see the quiet town beyond the gates, The House of Glass, the silent carousel and the restaurant; nowhere could he see Harry Brisk, so he motioned to Molly to come up and join him, but found she had already started to run quietly across the deck to the bottom. It was then the shock hit him: if that was Molly running across to the entrance, how come he could already hear footsteps on the stairs below him? It couldn't be Flynn; he was in The House of Glass. These were heavy steps, they could only belong to one person and that was Harry Brisk.

Jim began to panic, he could easily take to the slide but that would mean leaving Molly to the unlikely mercy of Harry Brisk when he realised that she was coming up the stairs behind him. He could call out to Molly but that would give her away. The steps came closer and he could now hear heavy breathing as the bulky gangster struggled towards the top. Jim realised that his hand was resting on something cold; it was a fire extinguisher hooked on the wall, he grabbed it from its mount and with no time to do anything else he swung it back behind him and brought it sharply round the curve of the spiral staircase into the darkness. There was a dull thud as it connected, not with Harry Brisk's head but with the wall just in front of him. The heavy cylinder fell from Jim's grasp and, although it had failed to brain his enemy as intended, it still served some of its purpose by rolling down the stairs with a huge clatter and taking Harry Brisk's tired legs from under him. He joined the fire extinguisher in a long, painful and very noisy descent to the bottom of the stairs.

Molly, horrified that Jim, as she thought, was falling down the stairs towards her skipped quickly to the bottom to avoid being caught up in the accident herself. She was even more appalled, moments later, to find a battered, but still conscious Harry Brisk, lying at her feet and pointing his gun up into her face.

'One move,' was all he said as he got to his feet and replaced his hat, still holding the gun at her.

He got hold of Molly by the collar, muscled her roughly through the turnstile and out onto the deck. The wind had blown a gap in the clouds and Jim looked down in dismay to see Harry Brisk march Molly out into plain view. He took her hair and held her head up, as one that has been decapitated, and stuck his gun in her ear.

'You get down here NOW, you little shit or it's brains time!' he shouted up and shook Molly like a doll by the hair.

***

Flynn, after an unaccustomed battle with the lock to the cupboard under the stairs, finally heard it click and pulled open the door. He flicked open his lighter and examined the contents by its slender flicker. At first he was disappointed but after a moment he was smiling to himself.

'You little beauty!' he said, reaching inside.

***

Jim had one card left to play; he reached into his jacket and pulled out the thick wad of bonds.

'I've got these,' he yelled down brandishing them from the top of the huge spiral slide.

'What, you've got what?' shouted back Harry Brisk.

'Your bonds, all of them.'

'Sod off, they're in the bag.'

Suddenly Harry Brisk realised that Jim was not lying, the darkness vanished, lights spiralled up around the great twisting shape of the Helter-Skelter, lights raced along the railings to the shore, lights outlined the ballroom and signs flashed into bright life from one end of the pier to the other. Flynn had found the main switch.

***

'One mile, sir,' said Warnock's driver as the two cars careened around yet another bend in the darkness. Archie held on tight and tried not to bite a hole in his lip.

'Solar One, Solar One to Bugbear, target acquired, it's just lit up like a Christmas tree, sir!'

Archie snatched up the mike.

'In you go, straight in, Solar One, what's your ETA, over?'

'About one minute, sir, turning in now.'

***

Harry Brisk could see the rich green of his bonds waving back and forth in Jim's hand, although he was at a loss to know how they had got there. The sudden appearance of the lights had frightened him badly and this added impetus to his threats to kill Molly.

'You got ten seconds, son, then her brains go!'

Jim put one of the mats from the pile onto the slide and began the long rush down the Helter-Skelter. It felt like an absurdly inappropriate thing to be doing, but he did not doubt that Harry Brisk was at the very end of his ragged tether and that he was prepared to carry out his threat.

He arrived at the bottom with a bump and got up, brandishing the bonds high over his head. Harry Brisk switched the aim of the gun to Jim, who could see that he was only dissuaded from shooting him by the thought of what the buffeting wind was likely to do with his precious bonds.

'Let her go, Harry! Let her go and you can have them.'

He advanced towards Harry Brisk, still holding the fat bundle of bonds aloft.

'Let her go, or I let go of these.'

Light seemed to halo Jim as he came closer, there was a roaring in Harry Brisk's ears, he reached for the bonds, he could nearly touch them, almost grasp them, his lifeline, his salvation. The light got brighter, Jim came closer, the roaring got louder until suddenly it was blinding, deafening; as the huge shape of an RAF Shackleton search and rescue plane rose over Jim's head and Harry could hear nothing but the bellow of the four enormous engines, see nothing in the blinding whiteness which poured from the twelve million candle power searchlight mounted in its belly. He touched the bonds but failed to grasp them before he had to close his eyes against the cyclone of sound and light, and then, when he opened them, they were gone, whirling around him in a cyclone of spinning paper.

'Run, Molly!'

She felt her hand taken in Jim's, felt herself running.

Jim looked over his shoulder as the huge plane rose into the night, banking steeply, its searing searchlight panning round to illuminate Harry Brisk in his snow storm of lost riches; he was turning round and round, reaching up as if to gather them back into his arms. Then he stopped and levelled the gun. The muzzle flashed and Jim felt the bullet pulse the air between him and Molly as they ran. Then another sang off the rail in front of them and another went past his ear so close he heard it cut into the air.

The rail was coming up; there was nothing else for it.

'Jump, Molly. Jump!'

They both vaulted the handrail but it was only as he fell through the air that Jim remembered that he had never learned to swim.

He flipped over as he hit the sea and sank like a stone, despite thrashing his arms and legs for all his worth. His last sight was of Molly, outlined in the water above him by the light of the banking aircraft, sudden spears of tiny bubbles appearing around her as Harry Brisk leaned over the rail and emptied his revolver into the sea.

***

Warnock's lead car mounted the pavement and skidded to a halt in front of the locked gates of the pier. A man with some large bolt cutters parted the padlock and in a few seconds the four men were joined by another four from the following car and they were running up either side, to where the spotlight from the circling aircraft touched down.

At the far end they found Harry Brisk flat on his back, a pool of blood spreading out across the wooden boards, his gun still in his hand, his one remaining good eye open, looking up, as if to spot the last of his bonds circling like lost birds in the beam of the searchlight. Nearby, Flynn was sunk to his knees, the crowbar he had found in the electricity cupboard lay bloodied next to him.

He had come across Harry Brisk firing madly into the sea and called him out as he came round the corner. The gangster's last bullet had found only Flynn's left shoulder and then Flynn had set about him with the crowbar, not stopping until Harry Brisk lay dead at his feet.

'The sea, they went in the sea,' he said gesturing towards the rail as he slumped to the floor.

***

The light dwindled, though whether from the plane flying away or his consciousness fading Jim could not tell. He was left with only the sense which had made his life so special to him, sound; the sound of the shingle being shifted up the beach by the endless waves, the sound of the last few bubbles of air escaping his lungs, the tiny voices of distant people still living in the air above. Then the music came to him, his music, the music he had made for himself in the shell of number seventeen, the music that only he would ever hear, swelling and rising, mournful, plangent and beautiful. If there is despair, it said, it is only because there is beauty and love, after struggle, it sang, there will, in the end, be peace. He began to feel this peace come over him now as his elbow touched gently down on the giving stones beneath the tumbling waves, and the soft touch of a frond of seaweed brushed at his cheek. Then through the music, distantly, came the voice of Molly, calling.

'Jim, Jim! Oh please, Jim!' it said. 'Please don't die, Jim, please come back!'

The music began to fade but the voice seemed to get stronger. Then he was on the stones, a large man pressing down on his chest and torrents of salty water issuing from his mouth, like great gulps in reverse. He felt the air sting his lungs and gasped, he was rolled over onto his side and the last of the water he had inhaled ran out onto the shingle. He found Molly's face in front of him wet with the sea and with tears.

'Oh God, oh God, Jim,' was all she could say, over and over again.

28 - The Glass Trumpet

*I*t was at the end of the concert that it happened.

The event was held both to celebrate the ballroom's re-opening, as a jazz club called (of course) The Glass Trumpet, and to thank all those who had helped Jim on his difficult and dangerous journey.

He stood in the wings with Molly, pulled the curtain back and looked across the large newly refurbished room, warm under its big new chandelier. It was mostly full but people were still filing in, finding seats or joining the crowd at the bar, where Danny and his assistants for the evening were attempting to keep pace with the demand for drinks. This was created in large part by the crew of the aircraft from Archie's old squadron, now transferred from bombing duties to the saving of lives for the air-sea rescue branch of Coastal Command. It was their mighty searchlight that had confounded Harry Brisk long enough for him and Molly to make their break for the cold winter sea. They all stood together, their smart uniforms adorning the end of the bar, while the young women of the town milled around them holding onto their arms and demanding champagne cocktails. A few of Warnock's men hung around vying, mostly unsuccessfully, for the attention of the girls.

Jim looked along the front two rows. He saw his mother, nervously adjusting her lipstick and new hat in a tiny mirror taken from her handbag. Archie had brought the Higgsons down from London and having settled them was now showing a somewhat bemused looking Old Tom to his seat.

There were a couple of photographers, one from the local paper and the other accompanying a music critic that Jim had been introduced to in London a few weeks before.

They saw Flynn break away from the bar to bring Lizzie a drink before taking his seat next to her. He leaned close to make himself heard over the hubbub of the room and she smiled at him, raising her glass for him to clink.

The small circle upstairs was filling up fast with a mix of the older local people and some of the more serious music lovers that Jim had already seen attending the London concerts they had given.

'Jim, it looks wonderful!' said Molly in his ear.

They heard Archie behind them, talking to the chorus girls from The Black Cat, asking if they were ready, and then he was beside them looking out across the room. He smiled at them and checked his watch.

'You two ready?'

They nodded and Archie signalled the man on the lighting desk, who threw a couple of switches. The house lights dimmed and a single spotlight illuminated Archie as he stepped up to the microphone in the centre of the stage.

'Ladies and gentlemen, welcome. As you know, many of us have been invited here tonight as a thank you from the young proprietor of this wonderful new venue, the very talented Mr Jim Davis...' He paused and indicated Jim who had joined the band in the small orchestra pit at the foot of the stage. A ripple of applause filled the room. '...But I just want to say that, in my view, it is *to* Jim that many of us should be offering thanks.

'I thank him for helping to save me from myself and for helping me find Lizzie, lost to me for so long. Likewise I'm sure Flynn and Molly would like to thank Jim as without him they would never had found one another, and we would not have had the opportunity to experience that mixture of hospitality, which could only have been extended by an Irish wedding in an East End setting.' He paused, as there was some laughter.

'I know that Barney and the boys will want to extend their heartfelt thanks, it's not very often they got to play in front of the London critics at the old Black Cat Grill.

'Also from The Black Cat, I would like to welcome our chorus line, now an independent troupe, who have just finished an engagement at

London's Windmill Theatre; to open our show tonight, ladies and gentlemen - The Ladyettes!'

The deep red plush curtains behind Archie swished open, the band kicked up with a big show tune and there were the ten girls who had teased Jim so mercilessly at the bar of The Black Cat. They entered, sequins flashing, plumed head-dresses fanning the air and stocking seams accentuating their long legs, as they traversed the stage doing an old fashioned high kicking routine. The little theatre was suddenly filled with a glamour and thrill not felt in the town for decades. The crowd roared their approval and the girls burst into song, 'Is You Is Or Is You Aint My Baby?' in the middle of which Stanley blew a classic swing sax solo.

As the applause died down, a single spot lit Molly as she took centre stage among the girls. She looked spectacular in a shimmering sapphire dress with long velvet gloves and a diamond hairpiece, which fired little sparks of spotlight back into the darkness. She sang 'At Last' with such intensity that the whole audience seemed drawn into that spotlight with her, as though there were only a single point in the whole room and they were all in it with her. Even Danny took care not to clink a single glass, such was the persuasive spell Molly threw over them all.

After the applause had finally died away she thanked them all and sang 'Lullaby of Birdland' to lighten the mood and then 'Yes My Darling Daughter', aiming it specifically at her new husband in the front row. She looked down at Flynn's face, shining up at her from behind the footlights and finally realised the source of that missing adulation all these years; she was a little girl again, performing on the kitchen table for her daddy, his uncritical gaze fixing her place in the world, holding firm that pedestal on which she felt safe and needed. When he leapt up to lead the cheering even the London music critic, cool jazz aficionado that he was, found himself on his feet and bellowing for more. Molly needed a hanky, provided by one of the girls, before she could carry on. Her final choice was, of course, 'Someone to Watch Over Me', the glass trumpet's very own tune. Archie took Lizzie from the front row for a slow dance at the back of the room and Jim put a sixteen bar solo in the middle.

After that there was an interlude, while the band moved from the pit up onto the stage. The side doors were opened so people could wander out onto the deck and enjoy the cool breeze coming in from the sea. Jim managed to avoid the photographers as they arranged The Ladyettes and Molly for a picture in front of the club, the new neon sign of The Glass Trumpet above them.

He took Archie for a walk up the far end of the pier and they stood quietly for a while, gazing together at the dark horizon.

'Molly was wonderful,' Archie said after a while. He looked across at Jim who nodded gently.

'Wonderful,' he agreed.

'Are you…' Archie struggled for a way to ask Jim how he felt.

'Yes, Archie…I'm fine, I'm very happy for her, and for Flynn too, come to that.'

Archie took the pipe - which his doctors no longer allowed him to smoke - from his pocket and sucked pensively on it for a while, as if it contained something.

'I need to talk to you about something else, Jim.' He paused and Jim could almost feel him reassessing some carefully chosen words that he now doubted.

'It's just that, well I've been talking with your mother, who as you know is very much better recently, and…'

There was another pause as Archie blew more imaginary smoke into the breeze. Jim took the opportunity to cut in and save him any further floundering.

'It's all right, Archie, I worked it out for myself. I know my grandparents took me away and told Mum I was stillborn; I know they hid me for nine months and then said that I was theirs. They could get away with it, since I only ever went to the Church school. I was hardly seen by anyone until I was five.'

Archie shook his head in disbelief at the cruelty of it all.

'It was the shame you see, they couldn't bear the shame. He was leader of the Church; it would have finished him. It's not so bad you know. I was actually relieved to discover my whole upbringing was a huge lie!'

They turned and looked at one another.

'I know George Armstrong wasn't my father, I know it was you, that it…it *is* you. I worked it out from the dates on Lizzie's hospital records, she was admitted two days after the birth, almost exactly nine months after you were shot down, it could only be you.'

There was an uncertain moment, and then they embraced, Jim felt the tears rising.

'I even felt guilty about that, after all George Armstrong did for me, making me the trumpet, leaving me the pier and that letter.'

'Well he was a fine man, Jim, and at least he knew you existed all those years. I can't say I blamed him or Lizzie for what happened. After all he had every reason to think I was dead, and so did she.'

They broke their close embrace to find Lizzie standing next to them, her eyes shining, and then there were three locked together at the end of the pier, holding on tight, after what was, for Jim at least, a lifetime of separation. Lizzie held on tightest, to the son she had been told was born dead, and the man she thought she had lost in a burning aircraft.

Eventually Molly found them. She looked on wonderingly, sensing something had happened but not knowing what. After a minute or so she broke in gently.

'They're all ready, Jim, all they need is you.'

Together they returned to the club. Jim gave his mother one last hug and shook Archie's hand before going in through the small door at the back and walking out onto the stage. The crowd offered the band generous applause before they had played a note; Jim bowed his head in acknowledgement and they fell silent as he raised the glass trumpet to his lips.

***

It was lucky that Humphrey Dill, the jazz journalist and reviewer of his generation, was there at all. As he was to point out later, he could have easily missed the Concert on the Water, as it became known, if Johnny Dankworth had not been taken ill and cancelled his gig in London.

There are no recordings of course, so the music played that night lives on only in the memories of those who were there to play it, and hear it, and yet it now has such legendary status.

Jim, it seemed, was one of those players whose genius was to raise all those around him up towards his own level. The music went in and out of him at the same time, as if hearing and playing were the two sides of a bright spinning coin.

They opened with his 'Groovin' High', as a reminder to him and Barney and the boys of how they had first met.

Lester was there of course, nodding his head appreciatively, amazed that the young man he had introduced to jazz all that time ago, was now up there on stage, blowing out his favourite tunes as easily as a man might write his name. Sat next to him was Mr Eldridge, Jim's old music teacher, for whom Bebop was more akin to hieroglyphics if he was honest, but still his eyes were wide and sometimes his mouth too.

They went on through a host of what are, these days, jazz standards; 'Crazeology', 'A Night in Tunisia' and 'Slow Boat to China'. There were some longer extemporized pieces, which dragged in everyone from Gershwin to Vivaldi before Jim stepped up to introduce something of his own.

'I wrote this,' he explained, '…in a very special place, a place where I discovered a lot about myself, a place which led me, in its way, to where I am now, a place from which I nearly never returned…it's called simply – "Number 17."'

The band finished shuffling their scores and Jim began to play. Humphrey Dill's pen stopped where it was on the page, the girls of the town stopped pestering the men from the RAF, motes of dust hung still in the beam of the spotlight and even the waves seemed to stop their ceaseless washing of the nearby shore. At the time nobody could say how long the piece went on, no-one could tell you just what was in the music Jim played, but they knew afterwards and were never again to forget, the power that music has. It was, Dill wrote later, a testament to every painful nuance of what it was to be human. As Jim swept his audience up like so many rapt acolytes to a new cause, they each forgot who they were and yet realised together how unique was the collective experience which united them.

Nowadays, as any music student will tell you; 'Number 17' finishes with the trumpet on a high C. It is a challenge to even the greatest players today, as the breath is very long and it first recedes and then returns as the backing changes from minor to major, making that strong final statement for which the piece is so deservedly famous.

As the band made the final chord change, Jim raised the trumpet slowly towards the ceiling, the high C swelling in power, the hackles on each and every neck erect, the audience straining at the slips towards the relief that applause would bring.

Before a single hand could clap another there was a loud crack, a shivering splintering and the glass trumpet shattered in Jim's hands. A thousand glittering jagged diamonds appeared in its place and fell to the floor at his feet. There was a gasp of horror from the audience and then silence.

The only glass trumpet the world had ever seen was gone.

Epilogue

Strangely, Jim was less fraught than most about the loss of his unique instrument. It seemed a fitting end, that, having brought his life together it should depart by shattering into so many pieces. He made them clear away the chairs and the band played swing so people could dance. He took the congratulations and the commiserations with equanimity and sat with a drink, away up in the circle where he could watch the people enjoy themselves, with only his parents for company.

Archie sold the big house in London and he and Lizzie bought Highgrange Farm when Old Tom died. Jim lived there happily with them until he left home.

Lizzie was reunited with her mother who spent her last years living quietly in one of the farm cottages.

Abraham, Jim's grandfather, soon went insane having been left alone and was, ironically, incarcerated in the same hospital to which he had committed his own daughter for so many years. He is mostly locked up alone as he has a tendency to round up the other patients into a congregation, which he then bewilders or terrifies.

Harry Brisk had hidden his money away so well his estate could not be found and he was buried in a pauper's grave. Nobody came. He was proved right about the tides that night on the pier and Eugene's body was never found.

Jim still visits Highgrange when he is in England. He likes to sit on the stone terrace and look out across the town to the pier and sea beyond. Millet is an old lady now but she enjoys sitting with him, even if she is too stiff to come bounding down the hill when he goes to the club. It is still run by Flynn and Molly and has had some very distinguished artists visit over the years.

Jim never picked up a trumpet again after that night but has no regrets. If anyone asks him to play he just says, 'Oh, I've lost the lip.'

After the now famous concert he went on to study composition at the London School of Music and tours the world conducting either his own music or that of his favourite composers. Despite being rather unfashionable with the modern music critics for a few years, Jim has rarely failed to fill a concert hall and now seems to be enjoying a revival.

He was asked at a recent interview how he would like to be remembered.

'I think,' he said, 'I'd like to go out on a high note.'

Acknowledgements

Don Rendell (reader/jazz), Digby Fairweather (reader/ jazz), Dave Gelly (reader/jazz), Nat Mumford (trumpet), Michael Ehr (trumpet), Bob Pilinger (safes), Robert Munster (buses), Suzie Shiers (principle proofreader), Margaret Glover (editor), Suzie Phillips (proofreader), Danielle Spelman (reader), Anne Kember (reader), Marian Leak (reader), Caitlin Evans Storrie (reader), Ruth Llewellyn (reader), Felicity Perera (reader), Jane Smith (illustrator), Tim Varlow (graphics), Claire Stevens (graphics), Neville Yildiz (graphics), Joel and Nicole Onyems (house), Giles Curtis (gittes), Guy Barrett (WebDesign),
and, most of all...Diane Leak (faith).